BIG SHOTS
and
BULLET HOLES

B. David Spicer

Big Shots and Bullet Holes

Copyright© 2020

Author
B. David Spicer

Editor
Sarah E. Glenn

Cover designed by
Brandon Spicer

Published by
Mystery and Horror, LLC
Clearwater, FL

ISBN: 978-1-949281-09-5

This is a work of fiction. Historical persons and events depicted in this book are carefully researched but the primary concern is in telling a compelling story. Any resemblance to any actual person living or dead, or to any known event or location is included only where it is relative to the setting and history.

Dedication

To Caitlin

Prologue
Big Shots and Bullet Holes

July 1935

The scam worked like a charm, for about a week. Day after day we'd stand in the train station, the big one in Queensgate, hawking subscriptions to *Look* or the *Saturday Evening Post*, whichever magazine we could find in the trashcan behind the drugstore. We'd patrol the platforms, selling an 'annual subscription' for a buck, mostly to prosperous looking women who tended to trust other women. It'd probably be months before they remembered they were supposed to be getting magazines in the mail. By then, we'd have moved on.

Today was Tuesday, but for whatever reason, the station was a ghost town. I saw Mary at the far end of the platform, leaning against a post and running her fingers through her golden hair. I made my way to her. "Any luck?"

"Not the good kind. I've made two bucks. How about you?"

I shook my head. "Nothing. I think this one's just about worn out."

"Yeah." She looked so tired. "No steak dinner tonight."

"We could try the bus station for a while. Maybe we'll find some luck there."

"Maybe."

I could see her lack of enthusiasm. "What's wrong?"

Her eyes drooped for a moment, and she took a deep breath. "Kissy, how long can we live on a bowl of turkey broth and a corned beef sandwich a day? I'm so tired."

She looked close to a swoon, so I steered her toward a

bench. "Mary, come on girl, don't give up yet. I'll figure something out."

She shot me a weak smile and patted my cheek. "Sweet Kissy. You'd better hurry. There's not much of me left."

I couldn't argue with her there. Her ratty brown dress hung off her bones and flapped like Old Glory when the wind blew. Not that I looked any better; my own bones poked through my dress like tentpoles. We both needed a few good meals, and we needed them soon. I gave her arm a pinch. "Yeah, but what's left is as tough as old shoe leather."

She chuckled. "If that was supposed to be a compliment, you should give up making compliments. You're no good at it."

That made me smile. "There's the Mary I know, all sass and smarts." I pulled her to her feet. "We need another two dollars if we expect to sleep under a roof tonight. Let's get to it."

"Right, boss." She snapped off a jaunty salute, hoisted her armload of magazines, and started down the platform. I watched her for a minute, not liking her listlessness one bit. Usually Mary was as bright and energetic as a spring morning, but now she walked under the pall of ominous storm clouds and her natural radiance seemed eclipsed, almost extinguished. I tugged at my lip as I watched her, ice-water settling in my guts.

As I was about to resume my own subscription peddling, four men, all dressed in black and wearing top hats, marched through the door carrying a well-polished coffin. My breath caught in my throat for a second, the victim of my own morbid fears, and it took several moments before my heartbeat stopped trying to outrun me. The men carefully placed the coffin on the platform. One of them consulted his pocket-watch and said something to his comrades.

Opportunity comes in every shape imaginable, and the mark of a resourceful grifter is not in pulling off the long con, but in realizing when and where to attempt the con in the first place. These four gents were spiffed up plenty, pressed trousers, shiny shoes, and the pocket-watch I'd seen had to be gold. The coffin itself glistened like a new penny. When I took in the scene as a whole, I saw money; damned if I couldn't smell it!

I strode up to the man in charge, the old one with the watch. "Excuse me."

He tipped his top hat, showing me about an acre of his bald head. "Good afternoon, madam."

"Thanks. Why are you fellas here? Has somebody died?"

The old man nodded his head slowly. "Yes, a most unfortunate situation. A passenger on the 4.50 from Pittsburgh passed away."

"You mean he died on the train?"

"Oh yes. It happens that way sometimes. We all hope to die at home, surrounded by our loved ones, but sometimes folks are not that fortunate." He clucked his tongue and looked sad.

I shoved a little sorrow of my own into my voice. "That's terrible! Just awful."

He nodded sagely. "Yes, it is. So very, very sad."

"What was the deceased's name?"

The old man's mouth drooped into a little frown, and he gave me a dose of eyeball.

"I'm sorry, sir. I just want to say a prayer for the departed." I put on my most vapid expression, the same one I used to sell fake magazine subscriptions to gullible old women. "I believe that everybody needs someone to pray for them."

He grunted and slipped his hand into a pocket and withdrew a slip of paper, which he squinted at for a long moment. "Lisbon. Frank Lisbon."

I snatched the man's hand and gave it an enthusiastic shake. "Thank you, sir. I'll put Mr. Lisbon's name on my church's prayer request list right away! Thank you very much."

The clock on the platform read 9:45, which meant that Mr. Frank Lisbon's mortal remains would arrive at Cincinnati Union Terminal in five minutes, and I had exactly that long to figure out how to profit from the man's passing. The possibilities rode through my mind like boxes on a conveyor belt that I would lift, give a shake, and throw over my shoulder. My fingers worked at my lip, a sure sign that the dynamos of my mind were spinning up.

Mary snapped her fingers in front of my eyes. I had no idea how long she'd been standing there. "Kissy! Are you awake?"

I blinked a few times before my eyes focused on her. "Mary! We have to hurry!"

"Hurry where?"

"To the telegraph window!"

"What? Why? Kissy, I don't understand."

I snatched her hand. "Follow me." We dashed toward the telegraph window. A few feet from the window stood a long table covered with little slips of paper and stubby pencils to use for composing telegram messages. I snatched a pencil and scribbled a note on it that said:

Cassandra,

I shall arrive in Cincinnati on the 4.50 from Pittsburgh on July 16th. Please meet me on the platform.

Love always,
Uncle Frank

Mary's eyebrows rose as she read what I was writing. "Kissy, what are you up to?"

"Hopefully I'm financing our steak dinner tonight!" I towed her back to the platform just as the 4.50 roared into the station. The doors opened and disgorged a riot of travelers eager to get off the train. An army of porters unloaded the baggage car while surly conductors bellowed out the next departure time. I selected one of the conductors, a portly man who looked like he'd worked on the rails for centuries and approached him wearing my best doe-eyed expression.

"Excuse me, sir."

He tapped his hat with his hand. "Yes, ma'am. Can I help you?"

"I was supposed to meet my uncle, here on the platform, but I don't see him."

The conductor looked somewhat annoyed. "Maybe he missed the train."

"No, my aunt sent me a telegram that said she just saw him board the train in Pittsburgh."

I handed the note to him. His lips moved as he read it. "What is your uncle's last name?" The look on his face told me that I'd aroused just the right suspicions.

"Lisbon, sir. His name is Frank Lisbon."

The conductor's eyes widened a little. "Oh. Oh, my." He licked his lips and wrung his hands. "Oh. I'm afraid I have bad news, miss."

I grasped Mary's hand and clutched it to my chest. I opened my mouth but didn't speak.

He stammered on. "You see, miss, your uncle, well he was just riding along in the dining car like everyone else, when he, well, he clutched his chest and fell over. I'm afraid he's passed on."

I collapsed against Mary, shuddering in a paroxysm of grief. She patted my shoulder and made soothing sounds while the conductor jammed his hands in his pockets and stared at his feet. I peeked over Mary's shoulder and saw the four men from the funeral parlor exiting one of the cars carrying the coffin between them. I'm sure there must be some rule about the pace pall bearers are allowed to move when carrying a coffin: they must maintain a dignified, unhurried stride, but just then I wished they'd sprint through the train station with my ersatz uncle's husk. I could only cry so long before I lost the conductor.

Mary played her part well, stroking my hair and patting my back. "There, there, Cassandra. It'll be all right. You'll see." She had no idea where I was going with this, but she'd worked with me long enough to know how to improvise. She shot piteous glances at the conductor, clearly making him uncomfortable, as was her intention. God bless her, Mary was one of the best!

I turned to Mary, tears still streaming down my face. "We'll have to break the news to Aunt Petunia. She'll be all broken up!"

She almost smiled, 'Aunt Petunia' being a little over the top. "Yes, we can telephone her from the drug store."

"What about the funeral? What will he wear? Where

will we get clothes for him?" I turned to the conductor, seemingly near absolute panic. "What will we do?"

I found out that day that one didn't have to be a genius to be a railroad conductor. I'd all but taken his hand and led him where I needed him to go, but his own mental train was running behind schedule. Way behind schedule. I had to make a few more wailing mentions of clothing before his mind came around to poor old Uncle Frank's luggage.

"Miss don't fret about the funeral. Your uncle had two suitcases; yes, I know it was two! Certainly, he'd have packed something, uh, something appropriate for a funeral."

My eyes lit up and I sniffed back some tears. "You think so? I'd forgotten about his luggage." This time Mary had to cover her smile with her hand when I said that, but the conductor didn't seem to notice. He waved over a young porter and sent him to fetch Uncle Frank's suitcases.

We waited, Mary's arm over my shoulders and me playing the part of the grieving niece. The porter didn't seem to be in a hurry, and after a few minutes the conductor went to find him. Mary gave me a sunshine bright smile. "Kissy, I don't know where you come up with this stuff, I really don't."

My pout looked genuine. "What do you mean? Poor old Uncle Frank, so sad that he shuffled off on a train."

"Oh, yes. Very sad."

"Very sad, for him. Very lucky for us."

"You hope it's lucky. He could be as broke as we are."

"No, someone hired the funeral parlor guys. I saw them waiting for the train, they looked expensive. Someone must have sent a wire to his family, and they hired the funeral parlor. That means money."

Mary covered her smile again. "You've got it all figured out, don't you Kissy?"

I didn't have the chance to answer because the conductor and his crony arrived just then with two suitcases of the leather-and-brass sort. The porter plopped the bags on the platform, touched the bill of his cap and tottered away. The conductor passed along his heartfelt condolences on Uncle Frank's untimely passing. By then the outbound passengers were clamoring to board the train and the conductor had to excuse himself.

"Thank you so much for your help." I gave him a hug and kissed his stubbly cheek. He blushed and wandered away with his hand covering his jawline.

"Was that necessary?" Mary picked up one of the suitcases.

"Not really." I picked up the other suitcase. "But he was a helpful fellow."

We locked ourselves in a washroom and opened our ill-gotten loot. The first suitcase only had clothes: suits of good cloth and excellent cut. The second one had a rumpled fedora, a pair of brown shoes, and four cartons of cigarettes. Mary started laughing then, sounding a little frantic.

"Well, Kissy, we've hit the motherlode this time. At last, we can indulge in a life of luxury."

"You give up too easily, Mary." I started going through the pockets of the suits. I found a box of matches in one jacket pocket and a leather wallet in another. "Well, well, well." I opened it up and my jaw swung open. "Look at all that folding green!"

"Oh, Kissy! How much is there?" Mary's eyes almost rolled out of her head.

I counted it, slowly and theatrically. "Two hundred fifty."

Mary's chest heaved, and I couldn't tell if she was gonna laugh or cry or keel over dead. "Can we get dinner tonight? I know it has to stretch, but can we get one good dinner? Please, Kissy?"

"Of course we can, doll. We're having steak tonight!" I smiled crookedly and handed her a $5 bill. "Go flag us down a cab. I'll be out in a minute."

I stared at the money in the wallet, money taken by guile from a dead man. Money he wouldn't need. Money that would put some flesh back on Mary's bones. Money that we needed, but still money that rightfully belonged to Frank Lisbon. Judging by his clothes, Lisbon had a good tailor and a small frame, and I briefly wondered what he would be buried in now that I had his suits. I looked at myself in the mirror, a skeletal woman in a tattered green dress. "Pitiful. You look pitiful." I held up Frank Lisbon's suit and liked what I saw.

A few minutes later I stepped out of the washroom wearing a dark brown suit, brown shoes and a gray fedora. I dropped the suitcases as Mary approached. I stuck a snipe between my lips and lit it with a match. "Hiya, doll."

Mary laughed. "Who are you supposed to be?"

"Name's Lisbon. Kissy Lisbon."

Chapter One

June 5th, 1942

Mrs. Marion Kendall stepped tentatively into the diner, a scared little mouse of a woman. Gray hair in a bun, ankle length dress that had seen better days, and a face wrinkled like an unwrapped mummy. I watched her from under the brim of my hat and through a cloud of cigarette smoke. She slid into a booth and ordered a cup of the sludge that Lou called coffee. She kept glancing through the window, as if she thought the police might nab her any second.

I waited long enough to watch her wring her hands raw before I dropped into the seat across from her. She looked like she might just run, so I introduced myself.

"Mornin' ma'am, Kissy Lisbon's the name." I lit another smoke and took a drag while she looked me over. "What can I do for you?"

"Miss Lisbon?"

"Missus."

"I'm sorry, Mrs. Lisbon." She bit her lower lip and peered around the room. "Will your husband be arriving soon? I have something to discuss with him. Something of a, uh, delicate nature."

I tipped my hat further back on my head and blew smoke through my nose. "Oh yeah? You'll need a seance to talk to him. Frank died at Pearl." I watched her lower her watery blue eyes. Now we were just two widows having a chat in Cincinnati's grungiest diner. "I told him joining the Navy would get him killed, but he didn't believe me. So, I've taken over the business. A girl's got to make a living."

Kendall winced as some loudmouth at the counter complained that his bacon was burned and his eggs were raw. Lou offered a knuckle sandwich in exchange, but the man declined that offer.

"I don't think you can help me, young lady." She started to scoot her way out of the booth, but I put my foot on the seat beside her and she stopped. I took another drag as she chewed her lip and stared at me.

"Lady, you don't know what I can help you with. You dragged me down here, so out of courtesy, I think you at least owe me a story." I flicked the ash of my cigarette into a heaping ashtray. "What have you got to lose?"

She scowled down at my foot, clad in a man's shoe beneath the leg of a man's trousers, and then at my face, beneath a man's hat. "When I telephoned, I assumed you were Mr. Lisbon's secretary. The advertisement in the newspaper was for 'C. J. Lisbon' and said nothing about your being a woman." She looked almost irate. "I don't believe you can help me."

I flashed her my teeth and shook my head. "Ma'am, maybe you haven't heard, but women are just as capable as men. Ever heard of Amelia Earhart?"

She frowned a little, but I could almost see her mind coming through the wilderness. "I *have* heard of her, of course I have, but ..." She didn't finish and squinted at me a little harder than before.

I savored my cigarette, sucking the life out of it. I only had two left and no money for more, but finally had to bury it in the ashtray amongst the other smoked out corpses. "Look, Mrs. Kendall, on the phone you said this was a matter of a love affair. Why not tell me about it? I'm a woman, so you know I'll understand your situation. Right? I've probably been there myself."

She mulled that over for a second, then finally spilled her story. "Very well, if you insist." She sniffed imperiously and began. "My youngest daughter, Heloise, has always been a good girl. She did well in school and took shorthand classes so she could find employment as a secretary. With the war on, and so many men being sent abroad, she found work in a law office as a clerk. She took dictation and filed papers.”

I took out my grubby little notebook and the stump of a pencil. “What is the lawyer’s name?”

“Mr. John Martingdale.”

“Is he rich?”

“I believe he does quite well, yes.”

I felt my brows furrow as I made a note. “I take it he’s much older than Heloise?”

She looked startled. “Yes, I suppose he is.”

I dropped my pencil and felt in my pocket for my smokes. I started to see any hope of eating tonight vanishing. “Look, the May-December relationship aside, if he’s got a lot of dough, well, your daughter could do worse than gettin’ hitched to a lawyer.”

Kendall surprised me then by braying in my face. “My dear Mrs. Lisbon! You’ve got it all wrong! Heloise didn’t run off with Mr. Martingdale. If she had, I’d be consulting a preacher instead of a private investigator.” She rooted through her purse and pulled out a pack of Luckies and shook one out and slid the pack toward me. I took one, gratefully.

“My mistake.” I lit her cigarette and then mine. “Go on with your story, ma’am.”

“Mr. Martingdale is a trial lawyer; what I believe they call a defense attorney.”

I grinned. “I’m familiar with them.” That much was true.

She puffed her cigarette daintily and exhaled a blue jet. “One of Mr. Martingdale’s clients was a hoodlum named Joe Shultz.”

“A kraut?”

She held out her hands and shrugged. “I don’t really know, you see, I never met the man. He does sound like a kraut though. He’d been arrested for felonious assault, but Mr. Martingdale got him off on some sort of technicality. That would have been the end of it, except that Mr. Martingdale then hired this Shultz fellow! Can you imagine!” She thumped her purse in her lap angrily.

I could imagine. There was a war on, and manpower was a scarce commodity. “So, Shultz put the moves on your girl?”

She strangled her half-smoked cigarette and mashed it

in the ashtray-graveyard. "Oh, he sounds like quite the smooth character. Heloise talked about him every night during supper. It was 'Joe said this' and 'Joe did that' all through the meal. One night she mentioned that Joe had asked her to the pictures. Well, of course I forbade her to go! The man was a criminal, or at least one step removed from one. Not the sort of man one goes out with. Not at all."

Her frown deepened with disgust. She could have charged a nickel a head to see that pruned-up face. She'd have made a mint. "I take it she didn't listen to you?" I inhaled a lungful of tobacco, savoring it as long as I could.

"She did not. She started coming home from the office later and later. She said Mr. Martingdale was a busy man and needed her to stay late. Fool that I am, I believed her for far longer than I care to admit."

"Until?"

"Until Mrs. Anderson, a neighbor of mine, saw Heloise and Shultz at the cinema. Mrs. Anderson is an inveterate film-watcher who has an unfortunate interest in Mr. James Cagney. She saw Heloise and Shultz at a screening of *Captains of the Clouds*. Of course I could hardly believe that Heloise would deliberately disobey me, and then lie about it, but Mrs. Anderson was adamant. She firmly maintained that she saw Heloise with a young gentleman at the cinema."

"Did you ask her about it?"

Kendall favored me with a look that could sour milk still in the cow. "Of course I did! She flew into a rage and spoke most disrespectfully! She said that I had to understand that she was a grown woman and that I couldn't rule her life anymore. She said that, as an adult, she could date any man that she pleased, and it pleased her to date Joe Shultz! I'm sure her father turned over in his grave at that moment!"

The loudmouth at the counter was on about the coffee being cold, and demanded the waitress bring him another cup. He grumbled loudly until she did.

Kendall watched the man for a minute before continuing. "I again prohibited her from seeing him, but she just laughed. She said I was wrong about Shultz, that he was a good man and I'd see that if I gave him a chance. Give a criminal a chance! Clearly the man had deranged her mind by then!"

I nodded and tried not to grin. I lit another of her cigarettes and tucked one behind my ear. She didn't seem to notice. "What happened then?"

"One afternoon I came home from the bakery, and Heloise was simply gone."

"Gone?"

"Yes, she'd taken her clothes and left."

"When was this?"

"Two weeks ago."

I scribbled that in my notebook. "Well, two weeks is a long time, Mrs. Kendall. They could be at Niagara Falls by now."

She smiled and waggled a finger at me. "Ah, you're wrong, Mrs. Lisbon. You see, my dressmaker telephoned to congratulate me on my daughter's upcoming nuptials, and that her wedding dress would be ready by next Tuesday. I cannot imagine what sort of rat's nest they're holed up in, but it's certain that they haven't left town."

I noted the dressmaker's name. "So, you want me to find your daughter before she gets hitched to this Shultz fella?"

She eyed me for more than a minute before she spoke again. "Mrs. Lisbon, I appreciate your situation, and I do wish you well in your career, but perhaps you didn't hear what I said about Shultz."

I knew this moment would inevitably come. "What about him?"

Kendall sighed expansively. "He was, as you might recall, arrested for felonious assault. He is clearly a man with violent tendencies, and not one that a female private detective should tangle with."

The loudmouth at the counter spun around on his stool. "A what? A girly detective?" He laughed loudly, pounding his fist on his thigh. "Oh, that's a good one!"

I pulled my hat lower and frowned at him. "Hey buddy, why don't you just button up? This is a private conversation."

He roared again, his mouth opening like a grouper. "So, that's you? A dame playin' P.I.? That's a riot, girly, a real riot!" He guffawed again.

Kendall sat motionless. She held her purse in a death-grip.

I stood up and looked the loudmouth right in the eye. "Look pal, take a hike before I lose my temper."

He stopped laughing and stuck his face in mine. "Hit me with your best shot, girly."

So, I did. I gave him a jab in the gut, which caught him off guard and doubled him over. I brought my knee up into his nose, which spouted blood. With both hands I hauled him upright and shoved him toward the door. He stumbled backwards and fell flat on his back. I straightened my suit jacket and reseated my hat as he looked up at me from the floor.

"Well, well, well. Looks like this 'girly detective' just beat the tar out of you, right, buddy? Pick your sorry carcass up and get out of here." I put my hands on my hips and glared at him until he managed to stand up. He wiped his bloody nose and scowled at me.

"This ain't over, girly. You'll see me again. You'll see me soon." He jabbed his finger at me. Lou, bless his heart, came from behind the counter and shoved the loudmouth out the door.

"Sorry, Lou. He had it coming."

Lou, who never smiled, didn't smile now. "I don't like fights in my place, Kissy. This is your only warning."

"You're all heart, Lou." I sat back down, pulled the cigarette from behind my ear and lit it. I took a long, sweet drag, and exhaled slowly before I looked at Mrs. Kendall. "Sorry about that, ma'am."

After a long pause, she smiled. "When can you start, Mrs. Lisbon?"

We stepped through the glass door and stood on the street. I waved down a taxi, and Mrs. Kendall slid inside. She rolled down the window. "Thank you, Mrs. Lisbon, for helping me with this, ah, situation."

"No problem ma'am. Please call me Kissy."

"Kissy? An odd sort of name."

I chuckled. "It's short for Cassandra."

She nodded and waved as the cab pulled away from the curb. I watched it disappear around the corner. I heard footsteps and knew who it was without turning.

"Hey. Girly. I said I'd see you soon."

I turned to face the loudmouth. "So you did."

He grinned. "What did you get from the old lady?"

"Check for seventy-five dollars."

He whistled. "Not a bad haul. That bit about losing a husband at Pearl was a nice touch, though. Brought a tear to my eye. Really, it did."

"It could have happened."

"You'd have to have been married for that to happen, and who'd marry you?"

I tilted my head back and laughed. "Come on, Norman, she was going to walk out of the place! I had to think fast. I got us seventy-five bucks, didn't I?"

He shrugged. "You did, I don't know how, but you did."

"I told you that dime we spent on a newspaper ad would work, but you didn't believe me. Nobody ever believes me."

"This P.I. scam was pretty smart, I'll admit." He gingerly felt the end of his nose. "Did you have to bloody my nose though?"

"Norman, your nose bleeds if a fly land on it. Quit complaining."

He rubbed his hands together with gusto. "Let's cash that check and drink beer until we forget how to walk! It's time to celebrate!"

"Sorry Norman, but we have to stretch this cash until it squeaks. You know that."

He shoved his hands in his pockets. "You're a real killjoy, Kissy."

I favored him with a glare. "Shut up, Norman." I looked down the street where Kendall's cab had turned the corner. I had to admit, I felt bad for the old woman. Her daughter probably was making a huge mistake with that Shultz fella. I turned to Norman. "Have you forgotten that we have rent to pay?"

He grinned, and I felt another of his advances coming on. "Rent would be cheaper if we shared a room." He held out his hands imploringly. "Right?"

I waved that away. "Pssht. That's never gonna happen,

Norman. I've told you that about a million times."

"I'll wear you down, Kissy, one day you'll be mine."

"That'll be the day, Norman. Not gonna happen. I know you don't believe me when I say that, but that's just because you're stupid."

He grinned. "We'll see, Kissy, we'll see. So, what do we do now?"

I looked down the street again, pulled out my last snipe, lit it and blew smoke in Norman's face. "I think we're gonna find Mrs. Kendall's lost lamb." Of course, he didn't believe me. Nobody ever does.

Chapter Two

"I don't get it, Kissy. Why are we gonna waste our time findin' that broad's chickadee?" Norman spoke to me through the door to my room as I changed clothes. His voice carried through the transom loudly. "What's she to you? Nobody, that's who. So tell me why. That's all I want to know. Why?"

"Because that's what she paid me to do. Now shut your mouth." I rooted through the trunk that held my worldly possessions in search of a dress. I supposed I must own one, but it took such a long time to find it that I began to wonder if I really did. When I found it, I decided it was a sorry looking thing, more gray rag than blue dress. "Perfect." I slipped it over my head and burrowed into the trunk again.

"Norman, are my shoes in your trunk?"

"What? Your shoes? Weren't you just wearing them?"

"Not those shoes. The other ones."

"You have other shoes? Since when?" I heard the doorknob rattle.

"Oh, here they are. We'll need to stop by a drug store while we're out."

"Are we going out?"

"Yes, Norman. Try to keep up. We're going out. I told you that an hour ago."

"Yeah, but I didn't believe you."

"Of course not." I snatched open the door and watched his jaw tumble to the floor.

"Kissy! You're wearing a dress! You almost look like a woman!"

"I am a woman, you dolt." I had to smile though.

"I know, but you never usually look like one." He eyed

me up and down.

"Put your eyes back in your head before I decide to take offense." I locked the door and started downstairs. He had to trot to catch up. "Come on, Norman."

"Where are we going, Kissy?"

"I told you, to the drug store. I need a smoke in a bad way."

Norman shuffled along a step behind me, his hands crammed into his pockets. "So, are you hoping to hit the old lady up for more cash? Is that it? You know, act like you're looking for her brat and ask her for another check to cover expenses? Is that the game?"

"Nope. I'm gonna find the girl."

"How? Kissy, you're not a detective! Not a real one, anyway! What do you know about detecting? You don't even know where to start!"

"Just because *you* don't know where to start, Norman, doesn't mean that I don't. Don't confuse what you know with what I know. It's insulting."

We walked a block or two in silence until we got to the drug store. "Wait here."

He pouted at the ground. "Sure, Kissy. Sure."

I went in and bought two packs of Camels and a bright red lipstick, and at the last second, I bought Norman a fat cigar. He grinned when I came outside and handed it to him.

"Thanks, Kissy!"

"You're welcome. Hold this." I shoved my handbag at him while I painted my lips with the lipstick. It'd been a while, but I managed it by looking at my reflection in the drug store window. I smacked my lips and smiled at Norman. "What do ya think?"

"You're beautiful." His blue eyes were so painfully earnest that I had to laugh. I savored a smoke and snatched my handbag out of his limp fingers.

"Thanks." I ran my fingers through the unruly brown mass of my hair, wishing I'd bought a comb. "Come on, we have a long walk ahead of us." I started down the street and Norman followed me.

"So, where are we going?"

"Well, the way I see it, we really only have two places where we could begin looking for leads. We know two people who have been in contact with Heloise and Shultz since she left her mother's house, right?" Norman shuffled along in silence, so I continued. "The lawyer and the dressmaker. While it's possible that the dressmaker has the girl's new address, it's more likely that Heloise just let her think she was still living at home with her mother. Since the dressmaker telephoned Mrs. Kendall's house to tell Heloise when the dress would be ready, I think it's safe to assume that's the case. No, the dressmaker probably doesn't know anything that will help us."

"Of course."

I flipped my cigarette butt at Norman's head. "We're left with the lawyer. I think we'll find out something there."

"That's where we're going now?"

"Yeah. I didn't put on this damned dress to go dancing with you."

"How are you gonna get the lawyer to talk? You want me to get tough with him? Rough him up a little?"

I'll never know how I didn't die laughing right then, but I managed it. "Uh, no thanks, Norman. I have a different idea."

"Oh." He liked playing the tough guy.

I patted him on the cheek. "Tell ya what, if I don't find out what I want to know, I'll let you rough him up for me. All right?"

Norman grinned. "All right!"

We hoofed our way toward Martingdale's office, and I began to swear revenge on the sadist who invented women's shoes. We rode the streetcar until we got within walking distance of West Seventh, but when we finally got to the office building, I had to take the torture devices off my feet and rub them for a minute before I could go inside. I looked squarely at Norman. "I need you to stay out here. Keep an eye out for Shultz."

"How do I know Shultz from Adam? I've never seen him."

"Neither have I. Kendall gave me a snapshot of Heloise, but she's never even seen Shultz." I took the snapshot out of my bag and showed it to him. "If you see this girl with a man, especially if they're arm-in-arm or holding hands, then you'll know you've found Shultz."

"What do I do if I find him? Want me to wrestle him to the ground?"

"No, that won't be necessary, Norman. Just watch him. If he has a car, note the make and model and any other noticeable features. Got it?"

"Sure. I got it." He pulled his cap low and stood near the entrance, as inconspicuous as a tap-dancing elephant. At least he'd be out of my way.

I hiked up the stairs, cursing my shoes with every step. Martingdale's office occupied space on the third floor, where an orchestra of typewriters ticked out a percussive symphony, accentuated by sonorous little bells. I found two accounting firms and a correspondence school before I saw a door with 'Martingdale & Associates' painted on the glass. I pulled an envelope out of my bag and stepped inside.

Behind a large desk, a blonde woman of forty-odd years hammered away on an old Remington typewriter. Her thick glasses magnified her eyes into two enormous blue pools that exactly matched the color of her blouse. She turned and threw a practiced smile at me.

"Good afternoon. How can I help you?"

I shot her a vapid grin of my own. "Hello there. I have a telegram for a Mr. Joe Shultz. I was told I could find him here." I held the envelope aloft.

The blonde clicked her tongue and shook her head. "I'm sorry but Mr. Shultz doesn't work here anymore."

"Oh dear! What am I to do now?" I twisted my face into an agony of dejection. "My boss told me if I couldn't deliver this telegram, I shouldn't even bother to come back!" I sniffled and dug a handkerchief out of my bag to wipe my eyes. A single tear trundled down my cheek. "I'll lose my job for sure!" My chest heaved as my breathing stuttered.

The blonde rushed over, took my arm and guided me to a chair. "Oh my! It's not as bad as all of that!" She patted my shoulder kindly, but she'd clearly had onions with her lunch. "It's really not as bad as all that."

I flashed my wet eyes at her. "What will I do? Oh, what

will I do?" I piled it on thick, but she finally got the idea.

"Well, look here miss, I have Mr. Shultz's home address over there in my desk. How about I just write it down for you? That way you can deliver the telegram to his house. I'm sure your boss would find that acceptable." She patted my shoulder again.

"Oh! Thank you so much!"

"Of course, my dear, of course." She returned to her seat behind the desk, opened a black leather address book, and copied out the address for me. She handed me the note and smiled. "Here you are, miss. I'm sure you won't have any trouble finding it."

I held my breath as I took the note from her but thanked her kindly when I got a few feet of fresh air between us. I left the room and pulled the door closed. I heard a man's voice rumble inside. I pressed my ear to the door frame, hoping desperately that they couldn't see me through the frosted glass.

"Who was that?"

The blonde answered. "Just a telegram-girl. Said she had a telegram for Shultz."

"Now that's interesting. Don't you think?"

"I suppose it is."

"Did she say who sent the telegram?"

"No, she didn't."

"You should have asked her. It could be important."

"I'm sorry, Mr. Martingdale. I wasn't thinking. She was just a scared wisp of a girl, afraid she'd lose her job. I gave her Shultz's address."

"I see. I think I'd better get in touch with Colonel Greene. He'll want to know who's sending Shultz telegrams and why."

"Yes, sir. I'll get him on the telephone for you."

"Thank you, Agnes."

I couldn't hear any more, so I hurried back down to the street. Norman slouched against the wall and I waved him into motion. "Come on. We have to go!" I kept walking while that sunk through the thick bone of his skull.

"Huh?" He jogged to my side. "Kissy? What's wrong? What did you find out?"

"Keep moving, Norman."

He did, but not silently. "What's wrong?"

"I'm not sure."

"Then why are we running away?"

I turned back toward the building and saw a gray-templed man watching us from a third story window, Martingdale presumably. He had a telephone pressed against his ear. "Because I think we should." We walked another block and I sketched out for Norman what I'd overheard Martingdale say.

"Guy must be in some sort of trouble if the lawyer called the cops." He scratched his head thoughtfully.

"I don't think it was the cops he called."

"Then who was it?"

"The Army. He mentioned a colonel; that sounds like Army to me."

"Oh, jeez, Kissy. This is starting to sound like a bad deal. If the Army is after Shultz, he must be dangerous. Think he's a spy? I mean, he *is* a kraut after all."

I frowned. "Norman, you're a kraut too. Or did you forget that 'Osterhagen' was a German name?"

"Hey, just because I was born in Germany doesn't make me a kraut, Kissy! I've lived here since I was a kid and I'm one-hundred-percent American!" He thumped his chest proudly.

"Don't have a stroke. I'm just pointing out that Shultz isn't necessarily a spy."

"He could be though. Why would the Army be interested in his telegrams if he wasn't?"

I shrugged and lit a cigarette. "I don't know."

"Kissy, this is too big for us. I mean, come on! We could get arrested. Or killed."

"There's no denying that. We've stepped into something way bigger than a wayward daughter."

"What if she's in it with him?"

"In what?"

"The spy racket."

I exhaled smoke thoughtfully. "We don't know there is a spy racket, not for sure. If there is, well, all the more reason to find her." We walked in silence for a while until I stopped to take off my shoes. "My feet hurt. Let's get a cab, then some supper. How does that sound?”

"Sounds fine, but then what? What do we do next?”

I took a long drag on my cigarette. “I think I need to pay Mr. Shultz a visit.”

Chapter Three

I sat on my bed staring at the gun in my hand until the sun went down. Billie Holiday's voice sang out of the radio and across the hall from Norman's room and I knew that meant he'd finished his bottle of rye whiskey. He'd be asleep before long, so I slipped the gun into my jacket pocket, put on my hat and made my escape as quietly as I could.

Shultz's house sat along a squalid little street just off Beachmont, and I had the cabbie drop me two blocks away. The houses along either side of the street looked shabby and forlorn, several had "For Sale" signs in the yard, and one had recently burned down. Despite the drizzling rain, I strolled down the sidewalk slowly with my hands in my trouser pockets, taking in the sights, not that the view had much to offer. I saw two galoots sitting in a car smoking cigars and trying to be unobtrusive. Of course, the house across the street from their car was Shultz's.

I walked past the car without looking at the mugs in it, crossed the street at the end of the block and continued until I was out of sight. I stood and thought, huffing tobacco beneath a burned-out streetlight. Who were the men in the car? Police? Feds? Army? Could be any of them. Someone besides Mrs. Kendall wanted to find Shultz, that much was certain. I took a final drag of my smoke and threw it into the wet street.

A filthy rut too narrow to be called an alley ran behind the row of houses. I stepped around garbage, dead rats, and worse before I found the rear of Shultz's house. The gate stood ajar, so I let myself into the yard. The sodden grass hadn't been mowed in a long while and I was drenched from the calves down before I managed to get to the back door. I peered through the dirty glass and saw that the lights in the kitchen were on. The icebox, an old model, stood in one corner. A smallish table had been set with cracked white dishes. Not a soul in sight though.

I turned the doorknob and, somewhat surprisingly, the door creaked open. I bit my lip in indecision, but only for a moment. Dew falling from my trousers irrigated the brown tile of the floor, making little rivers. The ceiling hung low, barely a foot over my head; it lent a feeling of suffocation to the room. Robins, blue jays, and whole flocks of printed birds peeled off the walls in curling strips. "Hello? Is anybody home?" I waited for a reply, none came. "Hello, Shultz?" Silence. The door latch clicked loudly when I closed it, making me jump. My ears strained but registered only the deafening roar of nothing. A whole lot of nothing.

The room sweltered at about one degree above Hellfire and Perdition, and I found out why. A gas oven smoldered in the corner opposite the refrigerator. I snatched a towel off the cluttered counter and opened it. Whatever dinner had been, a beef roast or meatloaf, had been reduced to charcoal. I shut off the gas and opened the window above the sink. A tin bowl of half-peeled potatoes sat in the sink itself.

I stepped through the door that led to the front of the house. The living room swaddled itself in darkness, but that was fine with me. There wasn't much to see anyway, just a threadbare davenport and a little table with a decrepit radio on it. The curtains, however, looked new, clean with gay embroidered flowers on the edges. I stepped to the window and edged the flowers back enough to let me see out the gritty window. The two men still lurked in the car across the street.

When I turned around, the radio caught my eye. The dial glowed like a miniature sunset, which meant that the power was on. I twisted the volume dial and, sure enough, music spilled into the darkened room. Classical music. Wagner. *Das Rheingold*. I shushed Wagner and moved toward a hallway that burrowed further into the heap.

I found the bathroom first. A string hit me in the face when I took a step into the room. I gave it a yank, and a sickly yellow lightbulb reluctantly woke up. The usual amenities, none too clean. A brassiere and linen slip hung from the shower-curtain rod. They both felt damp. Damp, but not truly wet. "Hmmm."

Directly across the hall from the bathroom, a black doorway gaped. I groped for and found the string to the lightbulb. This room, unlike the rest of the house, was neat as a pin. The walls looked recently painted, a bright shade of sunflower. The carpet on the floor wasn't exactly new, but it still had some life left in it. The bed waited, neatly made, and was topped with a handmade quilt: not the utilitarian kind of quilt that poor folks make out of old clothes, but rather the kind of quilt rich old women made in quilting circles.

Opposite the door stood a dresser that might have been expensive at one time, but now held itself together with spit and hope, and hope was running out. On top of it I found a framed photograph of a young blonde woman and a man with short-cropped blond hair of his own. He had his lips puckered up as he kissed the girl's laughing face. I took the snapshot of Heloise Kendall out of my jacket pocket and compared it to the laughing face on the dresser. The same girl, without a doubt. The puckered man would be Shultz then. I took it out of the frame and slipped both photos into my pocket.

I opened the top drawer of the dresser and found neatly folded undergarments of the feminine sort. They felt expensive as I pawed through them. At the bottom of the drawer, I found a rumpled paper pamphlet titled *How Can You Serve the Reich?* My stomach churned as I flipped through the pages and saw illustrations of young boys and girls giving the Hitler salute with one hand and holding little American flags with the other. Blazoned on the back page was "Printed by The Friends of Teutonia, New York Chapter, 1933. Rolf Weber, editor" followed by a downtown address. I copied the address into my notebook. I could have just taken the whole pamphlet, but it made my skin crawl. I carefully wiped my fingerprints off of it and the picture frame with Heloise's underpants. Suddenly I didn't want to be associated with Kendall or Shultz in any way, fingerprints included.

The closet door hung ajar, and I opened it with the toe of my shoe. A couple of dresses dangled off wire hangers: one linen, one silk, both expensive. I took the silk one out of the closet and pressed it against myself. Heloise must've been shorter than I am, or maybe she just liked short dresses, because the green stopped above my knees. I chuckled and put it back in the closet. I straightened my jacket and tugged the light off.

The last bedroom began where the hall ended. I stepped into the room, but my foot got tangled up in something and I went sprawling. I scrambled to my feet; I had an idea what I'd stumbled over. I found the pull and the light sputtered to life. The body on the floor wore a navy blue suit and lay face down with one arm stretched forward. He'd been shot once in the temple and twice in the back. A river of blood had trickled out and soaked into the floorboards, dried, and was rather tacky now. Lucky for me, I'd tripped over his feet and fell away from the blood; otherwise I'd look like I'd just butchered a hog.

My stomach gave a lurch, but I forced my gorge down. Who was this guy? Short blond hair, blue eyes. Seemed familiar. I took the photo I'd found in the other bedroom out of my pocket and held it next to the dead guy's face. Looked like I'd found Joe Shultz. I sighed and slipped the photo back into my pocket. Then I went through his.

I found an unopened pack of Camels in the first pocket I tried. The second pocket had a piece of paper with an Over-the-Rhine address written in pencil. After the address, tomorrow's date, Saturday June 6th, had been scrawled in ink along with the time, 12:00 P.M. I rolled him over and found him stiff as a straight shot of whiskey. His shirt ran red and oozing and I had to be careful to stay out of it. His inside jacket pocket had a roll of fifty-dollar bills, $200 worth of them. I whistled and tucked them in my own pocket. "Where did you get the dough, Shultz?" The rest of his pockets were as empty as a politician's promises, so I rolled him back on his belly.

I stood over him, tugging my lip as I do when I'm thinking hard. Dead, but with cash in his pocket, so not a robbery. Shot twice in the ribs, fell to the floor and then shot in the head. An execution? A chill ran down my spine. "Who wanted you dead, Shultz? What did you do to deserve this?"

I took a look at his outstretched arm. It seemed like he'd been reaching for something at the moment he'd been shot in the head. Kneeling, I searched under the bed. He'd been reaching for a gun, a big Colt revolver. Beside the revolver lay a slip of paper, which wasn't nearly as dusty as the gun. It said, *"When presented to the cashier of the Bremen Street Club, Pay to the bearer $1000.00."* My jaw swung open and I had to read it several times before I could believe it. A marker for a thousand bucks!

That went into my pocket along with the Camels and the other slip of paper. Just then, I heard the front door creak open. I snapped off the light and darted to the other bedroom, where I hid in the closet. My pistol, a .22 Colt Ace automatic, felt heavy and unwieldy in my suddenly sweaty fist. Footsteps thudded through the house like a herd of bison. Voices then, deep and harsh. "I'm telling you I saw a light in here!"

The second voice had an accent. "Vell, vhere is it then?"

"I dunno." The bathroom light flickered on. "Someone was in this house." The light snapped off again.

"Perhaps Herr Shultz turned on ze light?" A chuckle.

"Not funny, Gottlieb." The bedroom light sputtered on. The floorboards squeaked as the men entered the room and my grip on the pistol tightened. "Check the closet." My guts felt like ice-water just then.

Gottlieb sighed. "Herr Braun, there is nobody here except Herr Shultz, and he is dead."

"Fine, I'll check the closet myself." I heard a sound like a razor being stropped and then a cannon blasted into the wall beside my head, spitting splinters into my face. I yelped, how could I not? Through the new hole in the door I saw a man's face. He scowled at me.

"Come on out of there! Drop your heat first!"

My pistol plunked onto the floor. "All right! I'm coming out! I'm not armed!" My heart ran a marathon in my chest as I struggled to stand.

"A dame? What the hell?" Braun tore the door open and jabbed his Mauser into my face. "I'll be damned! It *is* a dame!"

Braun had dark hair and a face that not even his mother would spit on. Gottlieb's bald head glistened with sweat, but his icy blue eyes twinkled from behind his round spectacles. *"Guten abend, fräulein."* He sketched a little bow. "Vhat are you doing here?"

Braun picked up my pistol and slipped it into his pocket, then he grasped my arm with all the gentleness of a hyena. "Move to the kitchen. Try to run, and I'll drop ya like a moose. Got it?"

Gottlieb chuckled through his thick mustache. "Herr Braun, you are a man of infinite politeness. Ja?"

"Yeah, that's me." He shoved me toward a chair at the kitchen table. "Now, you're gonna tell me who you are and what you're doing here. If I don't like what I hear, I'll put you back in that closet. Permanently. Got it, sister?"

Chapter Four

"Start talking, lady." The Mauser bobbled up and down as he spoke. I figured I had one way to get out of this mess with my skin unperforated.

"Nothin' doin', buddy."

Braun blinked a few times and looked over at Gottlieb. "You ain't got a choice, sister." He tickled my ribs with the pistol's barrel. "I'm losin' patience with you."

Very slowly, I pulled a cigarette out of my breast pocket and lit it with a match. Braun watched me, rage and incredulity blurring together on his bulldog puss. I took a long drag and spouted the smoke at him. "Here's the problem, Jack, I come to visit my good friend Heloise Kendall and what do I find? Her fiancé pickling in his own juices on the bedroom floor. Next thing ya know, you two chumps come busting in waving iron around like it was nothing. I note, gentlemen, that you weren't at all surprised to find Shultz dead, seemed to know all about it." I sucked in another lungful of tobacco. "So, until I get an earful of who *you* are, I ain't got a name to tell ya. Got it?" I held Braun's eye until he looked away. My heart thumped so hard I thought it'd jump out between my ribs and run off down the street.

Gottlieb guffawed and slapped Braun on the back. "She's not afraid of you, Braun!"

"Dames these days, I tell ya, it ain't right." He crammed the Mauser in his shoulder holster. "You run your mouth awful free, so you must be somebody. Or think you are. My name's Braun. The bald one is Gottlieb."

The bald one clicked his heels together and stood erect. "Charmed, fräulein!"

They both got a dose of my eyeball. "Not cops. Not Feds either. Why'd you kill Shultz?"

Gottlieb fielded that one. "Oh no, fräulein, you misunderstand. Ve did not shoot the unfortunate Herr Shultz. Ve came here to pick him up for the meeting ..."

"That's enough, Gottlieb! Now that we've introduced ourselves, would you do us the courtesy of telling us who *you* are?" Braun's frown went all the way to the bone.

These guys were krauts of some sort, that much was clear, and Gottlieb mentioned a meeting. I rolled the dice, wagering my life on a hunch. "My name's Weber, Eva Weber. From New York."

Gottlieb's brow worked. "Weber?"

"Yeah, Weber. Heloise Kendall is a pal of mine from way back, and I'm in town for her wedding. Guess I won't need to buy her a gift now." I grinned as I mashed my cigarette out on the tabletop and lit another one. "Seems the wedding is off, though a funeral is on, I suppose."

Braun rubbed the stubble on his lantern jaw. "Why are you wearing a man's suit?"

"Same reason you are."

He didn't have an answer for that and shot a glance at Gottlieb. "What do you think?"

"Hmmm. Tell me, Fräulein Weber, vhat is your father's name? I haff been to New York, and I know several Webers there."

Damn the man, he wasn't as dim as Braun. It took a moment to recall the name from the pamphlet. "Rolf. His name is Rolf Weber."

A smile oozed across Gottlieb's face. "Rolf Weber! Indeed, I know a Rolf Weber, but by reputation only! Ve haff *friends* in common, I believe."

The emphasis he put on 'friends' confirmed my suspicion. "Yeah, daddy has all kinds of *friends* in both New York and Cincinnati."

"Gottlieb?" Braun hadn't kept up at all. "You know this crazy broad?"

"Herr Braun! Her father is *Bundesführer* of the New York chapter of the Bund!"

"No kiddin'?" Braun looked me up and down. "Why didn't you say so?" He visibly relaxed.

"Why didn't you?" I took a drag on my cigarette. "So, where is Heloise? I need to break it to her that her fiancé got himself a severe case of lead poisoning."

Gottlieb spread his hands. "Ve don't know, Fräulein Weber. Ve vere supposed to pick Herr Shultz up in the car for tonight's Bund meeting. Ve found him as you did, dead. Ve vere vaiting for Fräulein Kendall, vhen ve found you."

"How long has Shultz been dead? He's all stiff."

"Ja. Rigor mortis. Dead men take a few hours to get stiff. Three, maybe four hours."

Braun handed my pistol to me. "He telephoned me this afternoon, to arrange a ride."

"When was that?"

"Around two. We found him at seven-thirty, and he was stiff then." Braun looked distinctly uncomfortable discussing the corpse.

I nodded slowly. "So, somebody waltzed in here and plugged him between three and four-thirty in the afternoon? In the daytime, under the shining sun?"

Gottlieb nodded. "Ja, a brave man."

"Or a brave woman."

"Huh?" Braun frowned again.

"It could have been a woman, Braun. Heloise is missing, after all." I tugged at my lip. "Did you kill your fiancé, Heloise? If so, why?"

"You think that broad shot Shultz?" Braun shook his head. "I tell ya, dames used to make sense. Not anymore." He laughed.

I showed him my best scowl. "It'd make sense if Shultz beat her, wouldn't it? How well did you know him?"

"Not well at all. He never said much at the meetings."

"But you knew him well enough to give him a ride?"

Braun shrugged. "We want the boys to come to the meetings, sometimes we give them rides. It's no big deal. I didn't drill him, if that's what you're getting at."

I took a long, slow drag on my smoke. "Well, somebody wanted him dead. If it wasn't you gents, who else would shoot him?”

“Besides the dame?”

I gusted smoke at Braun. “Yeah. Besides the dame.”

“Got me, sister. I don’t even care. Chump got himself shot, no big loss. I ain’t gonna cry for him.”

Gottlieb chuckled, eliciting a scowl from Braun. “Herr Braun has a morbid fear of corpses.”

“Shut your damned mouth, Gottlieb, before I turn you into one. I ain’t afraid of nothing!”

“He vouldn’t even enter the room vith Herr Shultz’s body.”

Braun punched Gottlieb’s bicep. “I said for you to shut up!”

Gottlieb shut up, but his smirk stuck around for a while.

I shook my head. “I need to find Heloise. You boys know where she might be?”

Braun waved away the question. “How would we know that? She was Shultz’s old lady, not mine, not Gottlieb’s. Who the hell knows where a woman goes? She’s probably out getting her hair done or something stupid like that.” He laughed, a huge fan of his own humor.

Gottlieb cleared his throat. “I am sorry, fräulein, but ve vere not acquainted vith Shultz’s fiancée.” He shot an annoyed glance at Braun. “Perhaps she returned to her family home?”

“Could be. Her family’s from Columbus. I’ll give her old mother a ring.” I crumpled my smoke on the table. “So, what are you gonna do with the body?”

“Nothing. It’s not our problem.” Braun licked his lips nervously.

“You’re just gonna leave him rot right there on the floor?” I raised my eyebrows.

“It is the best thing to do, Fräulein Weber.” Gottlieb crammed his hands in his pockets and stared at the floor.

“Okay. Whatever you say.” I stood and glanced at my wristwatch. “Well, boys. This has been great fun, but I have to go. I’ve got things to do. Will one of you call me a cab?”

Gottlieb demurred. “*Nein, nein, nein*! We shall drive you vhere you vant to go!”

I yawned as I waved that away. “That works too. You can

drop me off at the train station.”

Braun frowned. “Train station? Are you leavin’ town?”

“Not necessarily, but I have business at the train station.”

“What kind of business?”

I stood up and gestured vaguely at Braun. “My own business.”

“Of course, of course! Come Fräulein Weber, ve vill drive you to the station!” Gottleib gestured to the front door. His obsequious grin made me a little queasy.

“Right. Come on then.” I strode out the front door with both krauts hard on my heels. Gottlieb opened the car door and I sat in the back seat. Both men sat in front of me, and I had my pistol. I could have popped them both before Braun choked the engine to life. I found out in that moment that I wasn’t a cold-blooded killer. News to me, disappointing news even. Instead of killing them, I sat in a swirling cloud of blue smoke, blasting gusts of tobacco at the back of their heads instead of lead.

I watched the darkened houses slide by the car as we drove toward Queensgate. I had to smile. A half-hour ago these men had me at gunpoint, now they were chauffeuring me around town. I chose Union Terminal because I could lose myself in the crowd and I’d be able to get a cab no matter how late I got there. “Drop me off in front.”

Braun slowed the car and I got out. Gottlieb rolled his window down. “Fräulein Weber, I hope that you vill haff good things to tell your father about your trip to Cincinnati.”

“Good things to say about you? That’s what you mean isn’t it, Gottlieb? I might forget to mention that you goons had me at gunpoint.” His face fell. “It was just a misunderstanding after all. Right?” I didn’t wait for an answer but spun around and stalked into the station. I watched them pull away before I felt safe enough to breathe. I bought a cup of coffee and toppled, boneless, into the nearest chair.

I sipped my coffee and tried to sort out just what the hell was going on. Who were the Friends of Teutonia? What did ‘*Bund*’ mean? Who murdered Joe Shultz? Most importantly, where was Heloise Kendall? I had all kinds of questions, but precious few answers.

I pulled out the marker and read it again. Another

question: What was the Bremen Street Club? Bremen Street. I'd never heard of it. The newsstand sold maps of the town for a nickel. I bought one and spread it out on a bench. I looked it all over and found a fat load of zilch. No Bremen Street in Cincinnati. I cursed in an unladylike way.

Map tucked under my arm, I went outside and hailed a cab and we set off toward my place. As we careened through the darkened streets, I leaned forward to speak to the cabbie.

"Hey Jack, I got a question for you. Where the heck is Bremen Street?"

"Bremen Street?" He sounded confused, not a hopeful sign. "Bremen Street?"

"Yeah, Bremen Street. Ever heard of it?"

"No, can't say that I have. Is it across the river in Newport?"

I hadn't considered that. "I was told it was in Cincinnati."

He shook his head. "You were told wrong. I've been drivin' here for twelve years and I ain't never heard of Bremen Street. Sorry."

I sighed. "That's all right. I'll check the address, maybe I got it wrong." I tipped him a buck and he drove away happy. I climbed the steps and stopped outside my room. I could hear Norman's breath buzz sawing from his room. At least one of us had had a good night. I unlocked my door and stepped inside my own room. I leaned against the cool, stout wood of the door, happy as a pig with a new mud puddle that I'd made it back to this room without having been blown apart by a .45 shot to the ribs.

I hung my suit in the closet and pulled out the bottle of Old Granddad that I kept tucked away for emergencies. I poured out a double and tossed it back, and immediately followed it with another. The hooch lit a fire in my guts; it always did, but I felt better for it. Burning guts meant I was alive, and I still wanted to be alive. I slid under the covers and tried to stop shaking. I clutched my pistol to my chest, and it still took an eternity to fall asleep.

Chapter Five

I dreamed about Mary. She and I walked along the river, chewing the fat and laughing like loons. She carried a picnic basket in one hand and lit my cigarette with the other.

"Isn't it a lovely day?" She smiled her smile, so painfully alive.

I looked at the sky, crowded with roiling clouds, and at the madly rushing water of the river, as it splashed out of its banks and over our feet. "It's a day, anyway."

Mary laughed her laugh, sweet as honeyed sugar. "You're always so negative!"

Thunder pounded rhythmically above us, and we both looked up. When I looked at Mary again, she had her face turned away from me. "Mary?" Suddenly I felt worried about her, manically worried about her, but I couldn't remember why. "Mary? Are you all right?"

She turned to face me, and what I saw made me stagger back. Mary's eyes stared, glazed and unblinking, the cold, sightless eyes of a dead woman. Blood trickled down her chin and onto her gore-spattered blouse. Her stiff fingers clutched at me. "Kissy ..." Her voice scraped like rusty steel and the thunder pounded away at my eardrums. "Kissy. Find him, Kissy. Kill him ..."

Mary faded away, but the thunder rumbled on. "Kissy! Kissy Lisbon, Ah know yore in dere, so you just better open this here door raht now!" Unmistakably, Mama Jose.

I sat up in bed, holding my head until the world decided to stop skittering around the room. "All right, Mama! Stop using the door for a punching bag; I'm awake!"

The thunder, mercifully, stopped, but the powerful

instrument of her voice boomed on. "Open up, Kissy! We needs to talk about de rent, girl. I done let y'all slide as long as Ah ken, but Ah got to eat too, girl!"

I shrugged my way into a shirt, buttoned one button and opened the door. Mama Jose sweated in the hallway, wringing her ham-hock hands. "Lord Almighty, Kissy! Put some clothes on, girl!"

I winced as her voice tried to chisel my head in two. "Mama Jose, I had a rough night. Can this wait a while?"

Mama Jose put her hands on her voluminous hips. "Kissy child, I done tole you, I let you go as long as Ah ken ..."

I held up my hand and stopped her. "All right, all right, Mama. You win. How much do we owe you?"

She wrung her hands as she thought. "Bes' I figure it, you and him," she jerked a thumb at Norman's door, "each owe thirty dollars. I can settle for fifteen each, but I need somethun' *today*. I'm sorry girl, I really am, but I got to eat too." She really didn't look very sorry, and I'd bet a buck she hadn't missed many meals in her life. Probably had more than a few extra.

"Fine, Mama, fine. I got the money."

"All of it?"

"Yeah, all of it." I went to the closet and rummaged in my jacket pocket. I peeled a fifty-dollar bill off the roll I'd found in Shultz's pocket, added a ten and handed it to Mama. Her eyes bugged when she saw it.

"Girl, where you find a fifty? I ain't seen one o' them in a dog's age!" She squinted at the bill and rubbed it between her fingers.

"I have a job, Mama. I got paid last night."

"What kind of job? Yore awful hung-over to have worked much last night. You ain't turning tricks, are ya? I ain't having none of that in my buildin', Kissy!"

I closed my eyes and rubbed my forehead. "No, Mama, nothing like that. A woman paid me to find her daughter, that's all."

Mama eyed me for a minute, frowning. "If I fahnd out yore a-lyin' to me, yore out. Both of ya." She tucked the money away in her pocket and chugged down the hall like an angry locomotive with a full head of steam.

"Thanks for having so much faith in me, Mama." She didn't even slow down.

I gathered up some clothes and staggered down the hall for a long, hot shower. My headache had receded into the innermost cavern of my brainpan by the time I made it to Lou's and slid into the booth across from Norman.

"Morning, Kissy." His runny eggs, gasping for air in a puddle of ketchup, made my stomach churn. "You look like you're ready for a coffin. Are you sick?"

I ordered a coffee and lit a cigarette. "No. I'm not sick, but you're closer to the truth than you might think, about the coffin."

He stopped chewing and his brow beetled. "Huh?"

"I got a question for you, Norman." I leaned closer to him; we weren't the only people in Lou's. "What does 'Bund' mean? It's a German word, right?"

"My German is really, really rusty ..."

"Just tell me what it means, Norman." I huffed out a cloud of smoke in his face.

"I think it means 'alliance.' Where did that question come from?"

"Ever hear of the 'Friends of Teutonia'?"

His fork stopped halfway to his mouth and slowly sank back to his plate. He quickly glanced around the room, and then at me. "No. Why would I?" He shoveled eggs and toast into his maw, but kept his eyes busily watching me with those little glances that I knew so well.

"You're lying." I sat back and took a long drag on my cigarette before tossing it into his breakfast. "I hate when you do that. You're too stupid to do it right." I gave him a long disapproving stare and watched his jaw work while his brain tried to catch up.

"Kissy, I ..."

I held up my hand. "No. Stop." I gnawed my way through a mouthful of Lou's coffee. "I can see you're not ready to tell the truth yet, so don't say anything. I'll wait." I did wait. It took Norman almost five minutes to think his way through to the truth.

His voice suddenly crackled with enthusiasm,

uncharacteristically upbeat, and a little too loud. "It's such a nice day, Kissy, maybe we should go for a walk?" He waved Lou up for the bill. He grinned as he slid it toward me to pay. I stacked three quarters on the table, and we stepped outside. The sun shone brightly, but the spring wind still carried a chill.

"Ready to talk, Norman?"

He glanced up and down the street before nodding. "What's this all about, Kissy? Why are you asking about the Bund?"

"The Bund? Is there only one?"

"Only one that matters, The German-American Bund, or in German, *Amerikadeutscher Bund.*"

I felt for my cigarettes, but the pack was empty. "What is it?"

His voice dropped to a low whisper. "A group for American Nazis."

"That's what I was afraid of."

"Kissy, why are you asking me these things? How do you know about the Bund?"

"I found Shultz last night. He's dead, shot in the head. Back too. Someone didn't like him and I'm guessing it was the Bund." I briefly filled Norman in on my trip to Mount Washington. "So, Shultz is dead, and Heloise Kendall has vanished down a rabbit hole."

Norman's hands rasped as he rubbed them together. "So, I guess it's all over, right, Kissy? If Shultz is dead, the Kendall girl will just go home, so we're all done being detectives."

"I don't think so, not yet. Tell me what you know about the Friends of Teutonia."

Norman took a deep breath before he began. "They were a group of German immigrants, here in Cincinnati who supported Hitler. Around the time of the '36 Olympics, the Friends were merged into the larger Bund. That was before the whole thing fell apart when the war started. The Feds broke up the group and arrested most of the leaders. Including my uncle."

My eyebrows raised. "Your uncle was a Nazi?"

Norman shushed me and spun himself in a circle looking for eavesdroppers, Feds or, maybe, Nazis. "Not so loud, Kissy!

Yes, he was, a kraut from head to toe. He tried to talk my old man into joining, but Papa wouldn't have any of it. Like me, Papa is one-hundred-percent American." He stood a little taller and puffed out his chest.

"What did they do?"

"The Bund? They held parades, great big parades with hundreds of guys dressed like Nazi stormtroopers. They gave speeches and generally tried to make people believe Hitler and his thugs weren't *so* bad. They tried to keep America out of the war. Didn't work very well, did it?" He smiled a little.

"So, the Feds broke up the Bund?"

"Yeah."

"But they didn't arrest every member?"

"I suppose not. They might not have known everyone who was in it."

I tugged my lip as we walked. "If you were a dedicated Nazi, and the Feds missed you during their roundup of Bund members, what would you do? Would you stop supporting Hitler? Or would you just take what was left of your group underground?"

"Underground? Like a basement?"

"No, Norman, not like a basement. I mean would you do whatever you could do to support the Nazis, in secret? Last night Gottlieb mentioned a meeting, the one that he was supposed to pick Shultz up for. He and Braun are krauts, I know that because they thought I was the daughter of the leader of the New York Chapter of the Bund. They seemed a little starstruck at the notion."

Norman scratched behind his ear. "So, the Bund is still around?"

"Yeah, I think it is, and I think Shultz was a member. He was supposed to go to a Bund meeting last night."

"Then why did they shoot him?"

"That's one of the things we need to find out." I pointed into a drug store. "I'll be right back." I went inside and bought two packs of cigarettes and two fat Cuban cigars. I handed the cigars to Norman when I came back out with my cigarette already lit.

"Thanks, Kissy. So, what do we do next?"

"We catch a streetcar."

"A streetcar? Where are we going?"

"Over-the Rhine."

"Why? Nothing to see there but poor people."

"Shultz had a note in his pocket with an Over-the Rhine address on it. Pleasant Street to be specific."

"So?"

"So, we're going to see who he was planning to meet today."

"Kissy, that's crazy!" He threw up his hands. "You hear me? Crazy!"

"I hear you, Norman. The whole street can hear you."

He lowered his voice. "We're in over our heads! We could get killed, Kissy, just like Shultz."

I patted his cheek. "We sure could. I'll go alone if you're scared." I trotted to catch the streetcar that would take us up Vine Street. When I turned around, Norman stood in the center of the sidewalk half a block away. I shrugged and waved at him. I could see his lips moving. Funny thing, curse words are easy to lipread.

My destination, an address on Pleasant Street, turned out to be, of all things, an auction house. The warehouse building bustled with potential buyers and strewn with furniture, cookware, and a grand piano. The stuff looked high quality and expensive. I stopped an important looking man with a bald head and no hat.

"Hey, Jack. When does this show get started?"

He looked me up and down before hurling a frown in my direction. "Noon."

"Thanks." One question answered. Now, what did Shultz want to buy? I wandered through the aisles of merchandise, toward the piano, a gorgeous Steinway. The wood glistened with polish; the ivory keys shone in unspoiled grandeur.

A young man wearing a thick mustache approached me. "Good morning, uh, ma'am." He smiled through his whiskers. "Are you interested in this piece?"

I trailed my fingers over the keys. "Perhaps. What can you tell me about it?"

The young man's smiled faltered. "Well, it's a Steinway, uh, model ..."

"It's a Model D."

"Yes, I believe it is. Do you play?"

"I used to." I tapped a few keys.

"Would you like to give it a try? Maybe bang out a rendition of 'Chopsticks'." He chuckled, amused at the quality of his rapier wit.

I sat on the bench and placed my hands on the keys. "It's been a while, so don't laugh."

He smiled and shook his head. "No, of course not."

I started with something simple, Mozart's Piano Sonata #11, better known as *Rondo Alla Turca*. Halfway through the song I looked up at Mr. Whiskers. His mouth hung open, which made me laugh, though not so hard that I missed a key. I barely paused before shifting into Chopin's Waltz #6, a personal favorite of mine. I hadn't played in five years, but my fingers remembered what they were supposed to do. They danced up and down the keyboard without any direction from me. It felt good, but I stopped at the end of the song and pried my reluctant fingers from the ivory. About then, I noticed that a crowd had formed around me. They heartily applauded my performance.

I stood up. "Thanks, but the show's over, folks

Mr. Whiskers shook my hand. "Thank you, miss. That was amazing. I think you just doubled the price this piano will bring."

"If you'd had it properly tuned, the price would have tripled. An instrument of this quality should never be allowed to go out of tune, and it should certainly never end up in a grubby auction house like this. Where did it come from?"

Mr. Whiskers licked his lips. "This is an estate sale. A Mr. Hirsch, I believe."

"Hirsch? He didn't live in Over-the-Rhine, did he?"

"I can't say for sure, but it seems unlikely given the quality of his furniture. And the piano, of course. Excuse me." He tottered off into the crowd.

"A fine performance, Fräulein Weber, wonderful."

I turned and found Gottlieb and Braun smiling at me.

Chapter Six

I tipped my hat back and looked them over. Two lousy krauts, in cheap off-the-rack suits. "Well, good morning, boys. Fancy meeting you here."

Braun looked as happy a drowning cat. "Why are you here?"

"I'm thinking about buying the piano. Why are you here?"

Braun frowned. "To buy a safe. No harm in you knowin' that."

I smiled as sweetly as I could. "I know what I know, and I know enough to keep what I know to myself."

Gottlieb spoke up while Braun's brain tried to untangle what I'd just said. "Fräulein Weber, I must compliment you on your extraordinary ability with the piano."

"Thanks."

"You are quite skilled. You haff been playing for many years?"

"Something like that." I yawned and stretched my arms above my head.

"I also took the liberty of sending a vire to your father, apologizing most strongly for the misunderstanding last night."

I shook out a cigarette for myself but didn't offer one to either of them. "Oh yeah? What did dear old Dad have to say?" Nothing, or I'd have been on my way to the morgue already.

"He hass not responded yet. I understand, of course, that he is a busy man. I hope, most sincerely to hear from him soon. I vass in an agony all the night. I slept only very little."

"That's a shame. All right boys, why don't you show me

this safe?" Now that I knew what they were after, I wanted to see it. "Lead on, Macduff."

Braun frowned. "Huh?"

"It's a misquote that means, 'Show me where it's at, Jack.'" I puffed smoke at him. "Sometime before they sell it would be preferable, gentlemen."

They finally started moving. We crossed most of the cavernous brewery before we found it. "That's it?"

"Ja, Fräulein Weber, that is it."

"Well now, it's not exactly much to look at, is it?" It really wasn't. Just a tall a black box made of steel, with a combination lock. "A lot of trouble for such a dumpy thing."

Gottlieb chortled. "It is much like Herr Hirsch himself, squat and ugly."

Braun crammed his meathooks into his pockets. "We don't even know for sure what's inside the damned thing."

"Truly so, but it is vhat could be inside that is important. That is vhy ve buy it, yes?"

"Yeah, I guess so." Braun shook his head. "Probably just a waste of money."

"Or what's in there could save your life, Braun." I flicked my cigarette at his feet. "How much is your life worth to you?"

"Not so much that I'm gonna take much more lip from you, sister. I don't care who your father is."

I smiled at him and took a step closer. "Anytime you're ready, Jack. I got your number." I slid my hand into my jacket, even though my gun slept peacefully, at home, in my trunk.

Gottlieb put a hand on Braun's shoulder. "Forgive my friend, Fräulein Weber. He is not yet fully domesticated."

Braun tore his shoulder from Gottlieb's grasp. "Don't ever put your hands on me, Gottlieb."

I lit another cigarette. "Take a hike. Me and your boss have grown-up things to talk about." I jerked my thumb over my shoulder.

Braun took a step toward me, but Gottlieb stepped between us. "Herr Braun, I think you are in need of some fresh air. Perhaps a cup of coffee, yes? I think you need to step away, now."

Braun's eyes never left mine, but he finally backed away

from me. He stood a few feet off, his face a mottled purple. Finally, he jabbed a finger at me. "Make your peace with the Almighty, lady." He turned toward Gottlieb. "I'm going to try to find Richter again." He aimed his finger at me again. "Your time is coming."

"Whenever you're ready, Braun." I leaned back against the safe. "I'll be waiting for you to drum up the nerve. I guess that'll take you a while, but I got nothing better to do." I smiled sweetly. "Have a nice day, pumpkin."

Braun stomped out the nearest door. I had to smile as we watched him go. Gottlieb wiped his lenses with a handkerchief. "Fräulein Weber, vith respect, I do not understand vhy you treat Herr Braun vith such contempt."

I laughed. "He's a chump, too stupid to do anything but what he's told to do, but also too stupid to be trusted to do what he's told to do. We don't need his kind. We have too many like him already." I took a drag and watched Gottlieb seat his spectacles on his nose. "Do you disagree?"

"Not in principle, but ve must make use of vhat we haff available to us. No?"

"He'll get over it. Now, back to business." I looked around us, but nobody stood within earshot of a whisper. "This safe. What do you think is inside of it?"

"Ah, you mean specifically. Vell, financial records, meeting notes, membership lists and, ah, notes regarding other special activities." He winked at me, which chilled my blood a little.

I nodded. "So, every one of the things that we wouldn't want to lose track of. Sloppy, very sloppy."

"I do not disagree. Herr Hirsch's death hass proven most inconvenient for us all. Hiss daughter did not approve of, ah, her father's friends. So, she did not allow us to open the safe. She put the brewery, the house and everything into the auction, so ve must buy vhat is rightfully ours already." After a pause he cleared his throat meaningfully. "Ve are also hoping to find out the identity of the Wulf." He stared intently at me.

Wulf? Suddenly it felt like I was dancing with Gottlieb, dancing to his tune and I didn't know any of the steps. So, I stared back at him long enough to take a few drags on my cigarette. "Really?" I tapped the top of the safe. "In here? Hirsch knew who the Wulf was?"

Gottlieb smiled broadly. "Ve hope so, yes?"

I sucked the last bit of life from my Camel and mashed it out on top of the safe. I looked at him but didn't say anything. He was a slippery one, this guy. Everything he said meant at least two things. The problem was, I couldn't ever figure out either of them.

He took a long breath and exhaled slowly. "Vell, Fräulein Weber, I must register at the desk for a number so that I may bid on the safe." He took my hand, squeezed it lightly, and gave me a long gander at his eyes. Something passed between us, but damned if I knew what it meant. "*Auf Wiedersehen, Fräulein ... Weber.*" As he walked away, I contemplated the emphasis he'd put on my ersatz surname.

I strolled back across the room, toward the Steinway, and saw Norman from behind. He craned his neck and swiveled his head back and forth. I tapped him on the shoulder. "Your empty head is gonna fall off your neck if you don't stop twisting is around like that.

He turned and a grimace split his face. "Kissy! I found you! Thank God!"

"I found you, so thank Kissy. God took the day off ..."

Norman didn't smile or laugh. Instead, he grabbed my shoulders and, in typical Norman style, said what he needed to say to me in a voice that allowed for no secrets or discretion. "Kissy! The cops are looking for you!"

The general buzz of conversation that had filled the brewery suddenly died and dropped to the floor in a paroxysm of silence. I looked at the faces of the men who stood behind Norman, and they looked at me, curious, and no doubt making mental notes of my shifty appearance and nefarious demeanor in case they had the chance to be interviewed by the papers.

"Well, that's what happens when you have nineteen parking tickets." I chuckled and patted Norman's cheek. Some of our audience members grinned and resumed their perusal of items in the auction, more than a few, however, kept right on watching us. One nondescript fellow dressed in a nondescript gray suit, wearing a nondescript hat, leveled his nondescript blue eyes in our direction. The very nondescriptness of the man screamed "Fed!" in the most nondescript way, of course.

"I'm serious, Kissy!"

"I can see that, Norman. As serious as a gunshot wound." I leaned forward and whispered in his ear. "I'm beginning to wish you'd gotten one this morning, so I'd be rid of your stupidity."   His ratlike face crumpled into a pout and he shoved his hands into his trouser pockets. "Jeez Kissy, I was just trying to warn you." He kicked the ground with the toe of his shoe.

I snatched his wrist and dragged him out of the building like a disobedient child. Once we were half a block from the auction I turned and gave him a shove. "How dumb are you? I'm really curious, I need to know." I waited, but he didn't answer. His eyes found a crack in the sidewalk and he held onto that crack for dear life.

I fired up a cigarette and watched him staring down the ground. The soothing burn of the smoke filled my lungs and I exhaled slowly. After a few more drags I almost didn't want to beat Norman to death with a crowbar. Almost.

"Now, Norman, what do you have to tell me?"

His eyes met mine for a single second before tumbling back to the sidewalk. "Uh, I'm sorry?"

I gave him a swat on the shoulder. "No, dolt! What about the police?"

"Oh yeah!" His eyes brightened. "After you left on the streetcar, I went into that little bar that happened to be there ..."

"Of course you did." I twirled a finger to hurry his story along.

"Well, I sat at the bar and ordered a beer ..."

More twirling. "Yeah, go on."

"They have a radio on the end of the bar. The newscast said there'd been a murder in Mt. Washington! They said an 'unidentified' man had been found shot to death!"

I took one last drag on my smoke and flicked the butt at Norman. "I'm waiting to hear what that has to do with the police being after me."

"But Kissy! It was Shultz! They found him! You were there last night!"

"Sure I was, but that doesn't mean anything."

His jaw worked slowly, and I could almost hear the rusty gears between his ears grinding together. "But ..."

"But nothing. You humiliated me in front of all those people for this?" I threw my hands up and started down the block. "Someday I might put you out of your misery. Unfortunately, your body would be dead a week before your brain decided something was wrong." A streetcar clanged its way toward us.

"Kissy! Where are you going?" He scrambled to catch the streetcar as I climbed aboard.

He took a seat next to me. The streetcar was mostly empty. "Mount Washington."

"What?"

I spoke slowly, deliberately. "I said I'm going to Mount Washington."

He watched me press my eyes to the window as we passed the brewery building where the auction was being held. "Why are we going there?"

"To find out what we can about the murder." I wiped at the window glass with the sleeve of my jacket and peered through the smudge.

"Kissy, that's crazy!" He watched me for a few seconds. "What are you trying to see?" He squinted up his eyes and tried to see through the grime and dead bugs that plastered the window. "Is somebody out there?"

"Yeah." The nondescript fellow in the nondescript gray suit stood on the sidewalk. He glanced at his pocket-watch for a second, snapped it shut and watched the streetcar trundle past. His eyes met mine; they wrestled one another until the streetcar finally carried me out of sight.

Norman tapped me on the shoulder. "Who are you looking for? Who's out of the fray?"

I turned away from the window, tugging my lip. "I'm not sure." I dropped my voice to a tiny whisper. "It's either a Fed, a cop, or another kraut." I jabbed a thumb toward the window. "It's almost certainly one of the three, but I can't say one way or another which it is."

He smiled weakly. "Maybe he just thinks you're pretty.

Lots of guys think you are.”

I harrumphed that one away. “Not this time. He’s watching me.”

“How do you know that? Maybe he’s watching me!” Norman thumped his chest.

That made me smile, just a little. “You could be right, maybe he’s a swish. Maybe he thinks you’re pretty.”

Norman’s face melted into a scowl. “I meant maybe he’s a fed.”

“If he is, I hope he arrests you before I get around to killing you.”

He held his scowl in place until we reached the end of the streetcar line.

Chapter Seven

Shultz's house crawled with vermin in blue uniforms and long tan trench coats. The neighborhood looked, if possible, even worse in daylight. The afternoon sunshine, so cheery a few blocks away, here seemed sickly and pale, almost gasping for life. I lit a cigarette as we stood in a clot of gawkers behind a wooden barrier on the sidewalk at the end of the block. I nudged Norman. "Look at that. Isn't that an awful lot of blue for one dead nobody?"

He shrugged. "Guy was murdered."

"So he was." For a while I watched the blue do what they do, then I saw an old woman sitting on a milk can on her ramshackle porch. I snatched Norman by the collar and started in her direction. "Come on, Norman."

A rookie cop stopped us at the barricade on the sidewalk. "Sorry folks, you can't go any further."

I pointed to the old woman. "See that lady? She's my mother! She telephoned to tell me she was terrified, who can blame her what with a killer on the loose! Such a nice, quiet neighborhood too. I'm terribly worried about her, officer."

The kid gave the old woman a glance. "She's your mother?"

"Oh, yes, sir."

"Sure she is."

"I have proof!" I pulled a ten dollar bill out of my pocket. "See?"

The cop looked around, took the bill and slipped it into his pocket. "All right, you can go on in. Just to her house, though. Got it?"

"Yeah, I got it." I started around the barricade with

Norman in tow, but the cop slapped his hand on Norman's chest.

"Hey! Where do you think you're going, buddy?"

Norman's eyes bulged. "With her."

He looked Norman up and down. "Oh yeah? Who are you?"

I took Norman by the hand. "He's my husband."

Norman stood a little taller and a grin split his face. "Yeah, I'm her husband."

The cop rolled his eyes. "Of course, you are." He jerked his thumb over his shoulder. "Just get out of here."

"Sure thing." I tugged Norman into motion, and we marched up the street. My 'mother' lived in a house across the street from Shultz's, and two houses closer to Beachmont. I tried to shake off Norman's sweaty grip, but he held on for all he was worth. He just kept grinning at me.

When we got to the old woman's house I strode straight up to her porch. "Good afternoon, ma'am. I was hoping to ask you a few questions."

She studied me up and down with a cloudy squint. "You with the paper?"

"Yes, ma'am."

"*Post* or *Enquirer*?"

"*Columbus Dispatch.*"

The old woman's eyebrows creased her forehead. "No foolin'?"

I chuckled and finally disentangled my hand from Norman's death grip. "No foolin'." I took my grimy notebook from my pocket. "May I have your name?"

"Mrs. McKnight."

"How well did you know the deceased?"

"The who?"

"The dead guy across the street."

"Oh! Well, he'd lived there since wintertime. I 'member there was snow on the ground when he moved in. He weren't none too friendly, never spoke or waved or nothin'."

I scribbled that down. "Did he have many visitors?"

She coughed and something rattled itself loose, which she spat over the railing into the weeds. "He was always acomin' and a-going with someone. Sometimes in a big black car, sometimes in a big white car. They weren't his cars, yuh see, someone was always a-coming to pick him up."

"Pick him up for what?"

She shrugged. "How should I know? 'Bout April or May though, he got himself a girl that moved in there. Old Georgia, she talked to him, and found out that the girl an' him weren't married yet, but they was a-plannin' to get hitched sooner or later." She coughed and spat again. "It's a sin, that is. A sin for a man and a woman to live in the same house afore they're proper wedded. It's a sin." She shook her head sadly. "Nuthin' but sin left in this worn out world."

I took the photograph of Heloise Kendall out of my pocket. "This the girl?"

Mrs. McKnight took it in her talon and held a few miles away from her eyeballs. "Could be. Looks like her. I didn't see her as close as Georgia did." She handed me the picture with a shrug.

"Where does Georgia live? I might need to speak to her too."

A strange, toothless grin brightened Mrs. McKnight's face. "Can't speak to her."

"Why not?"

She pointed to the burned down house I'd seen last night. "She's burned to ashes."

Norman looked right at me. "Just like your husband at Pearl Harbor, eh?"

I shot him a frown then turned back to Mrs. McKnight. "Do you know why anybody would want to kill Shultz?"

"Shultz? Was that his name?" She scratched at something that crawled around in her hair. "Nah, I can't say why anyone would want to kill him, unless it was his girl."

"Why do you say that?"

She leaned closer and spoke in a low, excited whisper. "They been a-fightin' sumthin' fierce, him and her."

"Oh my." I jotted that down. "Did you hear what they were fighting about?"

"Oh yes!" She rocked back and forth on the milk can. "I sure did, whole neighborhood heard 'em at it. Weren't a secret they was a-fightin'."

"What was it about?"

"She was a-wantin' to leave town! They was a-fightin' about leavin' town. I 'spect her people didn't like him none, and they was a-tryin' to stop her from marryin' him. She was a-sayin' that she wanted to leave right then, but he wasn't ready to go just yet."

"I heard he was a kraut." I watched Mrs. McKnight closely, but she only shrugged.

"He was German, you could hear that when he talked. Does that make him a kraut?"

Norman spoke up, using his loud voice again. "No! He's only a kraut if he supports Hitler!"

"Oh, well then, I wouldn't know about that. Maybe he was a kraut, maybe he wasn't." Something rumbled in her chest and it was a minute before she could breathe again.

"Who found Shultz's body?"

"I reckon it was the girl. I seen her this morning, early like, before the sun was up proper. She went in and come out a few minutes later with her suitcase. 'Bout an hour later the law come screaming up the street in an awful hurry."

A voice boomed behind us. A voice I knew. "Hey! Who are you? Are you with the press?" I closed my eyes, but didn't turn around. The voice thundered again. "You two, I'm talking to you!"

I heard his footfall on the sidewalk behind me, but I still didn't turn around.

"You'd better not be with the press. I mean it." I knew he stood right behind me, only a matter of inches away, but I still didn't turn around.

He grasped my elbow and spun me around. I kept my eyes closed and forgot how to breathe.

I heard a sharp intake of breath, then he spoke. "Cassy? My God, Cassandra? Is it really you?" I finally opened my eyes, and for a moment time folded over itself, and I saw him as he was five years ago, and also as he was now, two images superimposed one over the other. Something tore loose inside my chest, in my brain, and the world wobbled for a second.

Only for a second. A cigarette leapt to my lips, and I

breathed again, a deep blast of tobacco. "Hello Paolo. Been a while."

He didn't say anything for a century or two. He just watched me with those bottomless blue pools, unchanged in all the years apart. I felt a pulse in my arm, the one he still held. I couldn't tell if it was his or my own.

"You arresting me?" I drew a deep breath through my cigarette. When he didn't move, I gestured to his hand. "If not, stop handling the goods." He still didn't make a move. "Am I gonna have to scream?"

He blinked and that smile of his crept across his face as he released my arm. The thing in my chest gave another lurch and I suddenly felt like I might collapse. Instead, I took another drag and took a step away from him.

Norman swung his head toward Paolo, and then back toward me. "You know this guy, Kissy?"

"Oh yeah. Paolo and I go way back."

Paolo didn't even look at Norman. "Kissy? You don't go by Cassy anymore?"

"Guess not. You must have missed the memo."

"I must have. Why Kissy?"

"Why not?"

His smile broadened. "Cassy or Kissy, other than your taste in clothes, you haven't changed at all."

"Haven't I? Well, that's a damned shame." I flung my used smoke at his feet. "If we're not under arrest, my friend and I have things to do."

He hitched out a long sigh. "Cassandra. It's been five years."

"Has it been that long? My, how time flies when you hate someone's guts."

He winced. "So, I guess you're still upset."

I moved closer to him, close enough that I could smell his aftershave. He still used the same brand. "Upset? Is that what I am Paolo? Am I upset?"

He held his hands up. "All right, I'm sorry."

I turned toward Norman and Mrs. McKnight and jerked a thumb at Paolo. "Hear that? He's sorry." My voice began to rise in pitch and volume. "Guess everything's fine now. No more worries, nothing to fret about at all!"

"Cassy ..."

I stabbed a finger toward his face, and I let contempt ice up my voice. "That's not my name. 'Cassy' is dead. She died the same day Mary did. She died with Mary's blood on her face. Don't ever call me Cassy again."

He watched me light another cigarette but said nothing. I spat a jet of smoke in his direction. Our mutual silence clearly made Norman uncomfortable; he fidgeted like a toddler in a candy store, but he didn't break the silence either.

Behind me a telephone bell clanged away, and Mrs. McKnight excused herself to answer it. Paolo watched the old woman enter the house, then looked at me again. "Why are you here, Kissy?"

"Why shouldn't I be here? Maybe I'm visiting Mrs. McKnight."

His face disapproved of my answer. "No. Why are you really here?" He aimed his glare at Norman. "How about you? Care to tell me what you're doing thirty yards from a murder scene?"

I answered for Norman. "Not really."

Paolo's brow knit. "You don't have anything to do with the business across the street, do you?"

"Absolutely. We butchered the whole gang over there. With dull knives." I stared into the azure depths of Paolo's eyes. "What gave us away?"

He sighed. "Fine. I can't help you if you won't let me."

"I asked for your help once, Paolo, remember?"

He waited a long time to answer, and when he did his voice was low and husky. "I remember."

"You told me to go to hell."

"I never said that!"

I dropped my cigarette to the ground and mashed it with my foot. "Didn't you? Funny, that's how I remember it."

"I couldn't do what you asked me to do. I'm a cop, for God's sake!" He ran his fingers through the blond curls on his head. "There are ways to do things, Cassandra, procedures that must be followed. I can't take the law into my own hands, and neither can you!"

"Watch me."

I started to walk past him, but he grasped my arm again. "Look, it's been five years. Haven't I done my penance?"

I shook my head. "If you believe you have, we have nothing more to say to each other."

His head drooped. "How long will you hate me?"

"How long will Mary be dead?"

"That's not fair. I didn't kill her!"

"Nope, you didn't. But you didn't kill the man who did. You're good at not killing people, aren't you? Mary bled out on the filthy street, Paolo, so don't talk to me about what's not fair. Go do your cop things and leave me alone." I stepped close to him again and looked up at his face. "Leave me alone."

I gave Norman a shove, and we stalked away from Paolo. My heartbeat finally slowed down an hour or two later.

Chapter Eight

"Where are we going, Kissy?" Norman whined in that nasally petulant voice that always put me in my worst mood. Unfortunately for him, I'd already slipped into my worst mood.

"Shut up, Norman."

"But where are we going?"

I spun around and gave him a savage shove in the chest. "Shut up means shut up. I don't want to listen to your ignorance right now!" I steamed forward, no destination in mind, but a powerful need to move. Anyone who saw me would think I had to be somewhere in a desperate hurry. Honestly, I simply wanted to get away from Mount Washington. To get myself far away from Paolo.

I stepped on the first streetcar I found, not even caring where it went. Norman sat next to me, thankfully silent. I yanked him to his feet, and we disembarked at a random stop downtown, and I resumed my frenetic footrace to nowhere. Finally, a diner caught my eye and I aimed for it. I sat down and ordered coffee for myself and Norman.

I smoked three cigarettes and drank two mugs of coffee before I felt numb enough to live again. I noticed the window was clean enough to look through, so I did, and realized I didn't know where I was. I chuckled through my cigarette. "Where are we, Norman?"

He shrugged but didn't say anything.

"Come on, you really don't know?"

He shook his head and tipped back the last of his coffee.

"Not talking to me?"

He shrugged.

"Aw, did I hurt your little feelings, Normie?"

His brows fell toward his prominent nose. "Sometimes I wonder why I stick around, you know that? You're really hard to put up with, Kissy. Or is it Cassy?"

"Don't call me Cassy."

"Fine." He leaned back and stared out the window, shaking his head.

"What do you want? An apology? Is that it?"

He didn't look at me. "I don't want anything."

I picked up the menu. "Well, I do. I want something to eat. It feels like it's high time for some meal or other. Care to join me?"

He stared out the window for another minute before he opened his menu. He ordered the steak and potatoes, and I had the vegetable soup. The waitress, a pretty young thing of blonde curls and coltish legs, freshened up our coffee. Watching her walk away reminded me of Heloise Kendall.

I watched Norman ignoring me until our food came. He salted his meal with such vigor that it looked like a blizzard above his plate. "How's your salt? Get any meat in it by accident?"

He dropped the salt shaker onto the table with a thump. He glared at me in a way I'd never seen him glare at anybody, and looked for a moment as if he might say something. Instead, he snatched up his silverware and started sawing at the snow-coved beef. He chewed slowly, deliberately, and kept up his glaring.

My mouth quirked into a crooked smile. I fell to my soup, not really tasting it, but wincing when it started up the burning in the pit of my stomach. I only ate half of it before giving it up as a bad job. Instead of eating, I fired up a cigarette.

Norman frowned at my soup bowl. "Is that all you're going to eat?"

I nodded and exhaled a blast of smoke toward the window.

"Kissy, you need to eat more than that."

I sucked in another lungful of tobacco. "Nah, I'm done. It's not all that good."

"Then order something else. You have to eat."

I chuckled. "Says who? And aren't you supposed to be giving me the silent treatment?"

"I'm not giving you the silent treatment; it's just that you really treat me bad. I'm getting kind of tired of it." He carved off another chunk of his steak.

"Are you?" I smirked again.

"Yeah. I'm especially tired of never knowing what's going on."

"Norman, I could write it all down for you, and you'd still not know what's going on. That's not my fault." I dropped my smoke into the ashtray to wither. "What do you want to know?"

"Who is Paolo?"

"A cop."

"I know that. Who is he to you?"

I spat out a long expressive sigh. "His name is Paolo Constantin Belvedere, and he once asked me to be Mrs. Belvedere."

His mouth hung open. "What did you say?"

"That, Norman, is a long story, and not one I'm going to tell you right now." I watched his brows knit. "That all happened a long time ago."

"Okay, who's Mary?"

My jaw clenched and my coffee cup froze mid-flight, and I plopped it onto the table, almost spilling it. "Look Norman, I don't want to talk about her. Got it? She's dead. That's all you need to know, and that's all I'm going to tell you."

He spread his hands and scowled. "See, that's what I mean! You keep me shut out! We're supposed to be friends, for Christ's sake!"

I pawed through my jacket looking for another cigarette but found none. He didn't miss that I remained silent.

"Right? We are friends, aren't we? Kissy?"

By now every eye in the diner had turned to our table, waiting for my answer. I just sat there, watching his stupid moon-face as he watched mine. "We're partners, Norman, and we have a job to do."

"What job?"

"Finding the girl."

He waved that away with a dismissive hiss. "Come on,

Kissy. We're done with all that."

"Are we? I don't remember deciding that."

He leaned forward and, for once, lowered his voice. "We're not detectives, neither of us. The Kendall girl got herself tangled up with a bunch of krauts. Her kraut boyfriend got himself shot, and she's probably dead in a ditch somewhere. Or maybe she's floating in the river. It doesn't matter because it's not our problem! We're in this mess deep enough, it's time to get out while our hides are still in one piece."

"Impressive." I put two-dollar bills on the table. "That's the most coherent thing I've ever heard you say." I put on my hat and we left the diner. Heads turned to watch us through the window as we scuttled up the street. "However coherent it is, though, I disagree. Mrs. Kendall paid us in good faith to find her daughter, and that's what we're gonna do."

"Will you listen to yourself? Kissy, you're not making any sense! Are you really talking about 'good faith'? How much 'good faith' were you showing that guy who owned the deli last winter? You weaseled fifty bucks out of him! Is that what you mean by 'good faith'?"

I shook my head. "I don't want to do that sort of thing anymore. I think those days are over."

"Like the days with Mary and Paolo?"

I slapped him then, hard across the chops, and handed him a handkerchief when his nose inevitably started to bleed.

"Why'd you hit me for?" He pinched his nostrils together with my handkerchief.

I shoved him into the brick façade of a bank. "I told you I didn't want to talk about Mary. Do you understand me now, or do I have to repeat myself?"

"You didn't have to hit me!"

My voice dropped to a harsh whisper. "I'm going to find Heloise Kendall, alone if you don't want to help me, but I am going to find her. I'm also going to find out what all these krauts are up to if I can." I snatched his collar and slammed his back into the wall again. "So, now you have to decide if you're going to stick around for the fun, or if you're gonna run and hide." I thumped him again. "I don't really care one way or the other. Stay or go, but decide now." I let him go and started up the street. I needed to find a drugstore in a bad way, and fortunately I found one on the next corner.

While the pimply clerk fetched my cigarettes for me, I saw Norman standing outside the window, on the street. He wiped his nose intermittently, but it looked to have stopped bleeding. I couldn't hold back a smile. I bought two Cubans and a nickel's worth of black licorice for him, though the smell of licorice always made me gag. Pimples managed to package up the licorice even though he eyed me up and down a mile a minute. He noticed me noticing and his pockmarked cheeks flushed a deep red. I gave him a knowing grin and stepped through the door. Norman shuffled his feet with his hands in his pockets.

I set fire to a smoke and took a deep drag. "Decided to stay?"

He studied his shuffling toes intently. "Yeah, I guess so."

"Good." I handed him the cigars and licorice. "Enjoy."

He showed all his teeth when he smiled. "Thanks. So, what do we do next?"

"Good question." I tugged at my lip. "Mrs. McKnight said Shultz and Kendall were arguing about when to leave. Why did Kendall want to get away so badly?"

"Because somebody scared her. One of the krauts maybe."

"You're probably right, since her boyfriend got himself killed a day later."

"He should have gone with her when she wanted to go. I can't imagine what would have kept him here with all those damned krauts running around and waving guns. Had to have been money."

"Money! Einstein! Yes! It had to be money!"

"Huh? What about money?"

I rummaged around in my jacket until I found the marker that I'd found under Shultz's bed. "He didn't leave because he needed to redeem this!" I unfolded the paper and handed it to Norman.

His lips moved as he read it. "Holy moly! A thousand bucks! No wonder he stuck around."

I wore out a six-foot long path on the sidewalk, pacing

back and forth. "So, Shultz and Kendall got tangled up with the krauts in the Friends of Teutonia or the German-American Bund, or whatever they're calling themselves this week. Kendall got scared by something or someone and wanted to bolt, but Shultz wanted to wait until he could redeem the marker before they ran. So, they stayed."

"Yeah, and Shultz got shot dead."

I nodded and put the folded marker back into my pocket. "Right, but whoever killed him wasn't interested in money. Shultz had two hundred dollars in his pocket when I found him, and the marker wasn't exactly hidden. Anyone who wanted to find it wouldn't have had to look very hard. If they shot him over a matter of money, they'd have at least taken the cash out of his pockets."

"Makes sense." He gnawed a sprig of licorice. "All right, why kill him then?"

"That's what we need to find out." I stomped the fire out of my cigarette.

The licorice turned Norman's teeth a nasty shade of gray. "Maybe the girl shot him."

"Kendall? It's possible, but I think she'd have taken the cash and probably the marker as well. I'm willing to rule her out, at least for now."

He grinned a gray grin. "Why? Don't you think a woman can kill a man?"

I watched him finish the licorice sprig before I answered him. "I absolutely know a woman can kill a man. I just think, in this case, the evidence points to someone else. Someone well-heeled, someone who didn't need Shultz's thousand-dollar marker. Someone who needed to bump off Shultz for some other reason."

"Why else kill somebody?" He lit one of the Cubans and fell to coughing.

"Could be one of any number of reasons, really, but to keep him quiet seems the most likely." I plodded my way through the possibilities. "Yeah, seems likely he knew too much, so they had to shut him up."

"What do you figure he knew?"

I threw up my hands. "That's just what I can't figure. I

know how to find out, but I can't find Bremen Street. It doesn't exist." I spat out my exasperation.

"Well, not anymore, anyway." He shook his head sadly and puffed at his cigar.

"Norman, what do you mean?"

"Bremen Street. It's not called that anymore. They changed it during the War, the first one I mean." He shook his head again. "Some people just don't like Germans. Or German names."

I had to dig my fingernails into my palms to keep from hitting him again. "So, what's it called now?"

"Republic Street, it's in Over-the-Rhine."

"Where the auction was this morning?"

He nodded enthusiastically. "Only a block or two away from it."

"We need to find a streetcar." I looked around but didn't see one. "Forget the streetcar, let's take a cab."

"Are we going there now?"

"Nope. We're going home."

"Home? Why are we going home?"

"I need to change into my other suit. And I want to get my gun."

He coughed so hard he dropped his cigar.

Chapter Nine

Norman owned exactly one suit, a threadbare brown number that he'd bought for a dollar. The trousers dangled above his knobby ankles, and the jacket sleeves petered out two inches above his wrists. Slap a floppy hat on him and he'd look like an underfed scarecrow, but in his own mind he looked more than a little like Clark Gable. He mis-knotted his ragged yellow tie and tried on a suave smile. "Why, hello there, Miss Lisbon."

I gave him a quick once-over. "I'd fire your tailor if I were you." I went back to pinning up my brown tangle of hair. "Close the door before Mama Jose sees you in here. I don't need her dying of apoplexy today." My hair put up a more strenuous fight than usual, causing me to frown at my reflection in the mirror. I spoke through a mouthful of hairpins. "I'm gonna get it all cut off, every single strand, I swear."

Norman leaned against the wall, watching my struggle with no small amount of amusement. "I feel like we're going out on a date."

"We're not."

"I know, but it feels like it. I think you should wear that dress you had on the other day."

I made a face at his reflection in the mirror. "Is that what you think? I'm so relieved you told me that. Now when I call you a ninny, I won't feel bad about it at all." I gave up the war, spat out my hairpins and slipped into my black suit jacket. I put the marker in one pocket, and my pistol in another. "Guess I'm ready. Hand me my hat." I perched it on my head at a rakish angle. "Let's go."

Norman stood behind me as I locked my room door.

"How will we find this 'Bremen Street Club'? We know which street it's on, but not what building its in. There must be a hundred buildings, maybe more, on that street."

I started down the stairs. "It'll be the only building with lots of people going in and out. It's Saturday night, so this unless this 'club' is extremely different from other social clubs, it'll be busy. We'll just look for the long line of krauts waiting to get inside." I opened the exterior door and stepped into the chill evening air. "Since they issued a marker to Shultz, there must be gambling of some sort. Do krauts gamble?"

He shrugged. "I guess they must."

I flagged down a cab, and we slid into the back seat. The cabbie couldn't have been much younger than seventy-five, so I decided to try something. "Bremen Street."

The cabbie's bushy eyebrows rose to his hairline. "You sure?"

I nodded. "You know the place I mean?"

His eyes narrowed. "It's called Republic Street now."

"Yeah, but I want to go to a specific place on Bremen Street, but I'm not sure where it is." I held up a ten-dollar bill. "I know you know the place I'm talking about."

"Yeah. I do." He snatched the bill with his gnarled fingers. "You'll still pay the fare."

"Of course." I smiled and patted Norman's knee. "See, we're on our way."

The cab careened through downtown Cincinnati at a speed just short of suicide, crossed into Over-the-Rhine, finally stopping outside an attractive, five-story Colonial building. A tobacconist shop, a haberdasher, and a store selling watches and clocks occupied the storefronts on the ground floor, but not a soul was in sight. The cabbie turned around and gave us an award-winning frown. "There's the place, go through that door there." He jabbed one stubby finger to a door between the clock shop and the haberdasher.

I handed him a dollar. "This cover the fare?"

"Yeah." He yanked the dollar out of my fingers. "Now, get out of my cab."

Norman flipped the cabbie's cap up with a finger. "You be polite to the lady, old-timer."

"Lady? All I see are a couple of lousy krauts. Get out of my cab."

I had to laugh. "Jack, we're not krauts. We're just here to collect some money we're owed by a kraut."

He eyed us for a minute or two. "No foolin'?"

"No foolin'."

He started the cab and pulled away from the curb. "In that case, I'll take you to the real place."

Norman and I looked at one another and then at the laughing cabbie. "I hate krauts, so I just took you there to make it harder on you!" He tore his way further up the street until he stopped in front of a rather shabby four-story building of crumbling Italianate architecture. The single storefront had the windows soaped over and a large sign proclaimed it to be for rent. An enclosed wooden staircase clung to the side of the building. A dozen men and half as many women meandered about on the sidewalk, smoking, talking, and kissing.

Norman craned his neck to get a better view of the place. "Doesn't look like much, does it?"

"Not really, but this is the place."

"Thanks for the ride." I offered him another buck, but he shooed us out of the car and tore the cab away from the curb.

"That old man is gonna kill himself."

I lit a cigarette. "Come on, let's go up." I led Norman up the stairs. We could hear voices before we got to the top. "Sounds like the right place."

An elderly doorman stopped us at the landing. "*Wer da?*"

Norman surprised me by speaking up. "*Ich heisse Bauer. Das ist Fräulein Weber.*" He started forward, but the doorman stopped him with an upraised hand.

"*Warten Sie einen Augenblick.*" He turned and picked up a telephone. After a few seconds pause, he spoke rapidly in German.

I nudged Norman. "What's going on?"

"I'm not sure. He says to wait. At least I think that's what he said." He tilted his head and aimed an ear toward the conversation. "He's speaking too fast now, I can't understand what he's saying."

A few seconds later the doorman hung up the receiver

and opened the door. "*Voran!*"

We passed through a short hallway before stepping into a smoky casino. Fat German men lost their money playing blackjack, craps and at least a dozen other games. Lean German women tittered over martinis and clung to their men as they lost their money. A group of musicians played music of a decidedly American sort. The singer was a young, sultry, well-built Negro woman who obviously had no idea who she was performing for. Conversation and laughter twisted gaily through the air, giving the place a lively sense of joviality.

Norman pointed across the room. "There's the bar!" He swam through the crowd without waiting for me. He had a stein of beer in his hand before I caught up with him. "*Willst du ein bier? Ja, ich werde!*" He laughed at his own joke, then tipped his head back and poured the dark brew down his neck.

"Slow down, Norman. We're not here to get drunk."

He displayed his teeth. "Come on, fräulein, it's a party."

I leaned close to his ear. "If you're drunk, I'll leave you here when the shooting starts." His smile died a quick, painful death. "Remember that, Herr Bauer." His Adam's apple bobbed below his ratty tie.

Someone tapped me on the shoulder, and I turned to find Braun's scowl. "What are you doing here, Weber?"

"Enjoying the party. You should try it, Braun."

"Well, if that's the case, let me buy you a drink!" He leaned against the bar. "I don't care for beer though, how about something a little stronger?"

I sensed the challenge in his grin. "Sure, make it a double."

"Very good! Two double bourbons." He held onto his smug smirk as he handed me the glass. "What shall we drink to? The Reich? The *Führer*?"

"To Victory, may it be swift and brutal."

"Oh, it will be. Count on it." He tapped the rim of his glass to my own. "Count on it."

I raised my glass in a jaunty salute, then swallowed the whiskey in a single gulp. I plopped the glass on the bar. "That was refreshing. Another?"

Braun looked at his own glass uncertainly, then chugged

it down. He tried not to cough but didn't quite make it.

I turned to the bartender. "Two more." I clapped Braun on the back. "Don't worry, Herr Braun, this round's on me." I shoved the glass into his hand. "To the strong, may they forever conquer the weak." I tossed back the second drink without blinking, then watched Braun force the second round down his gullet and splutter his way through the act of breathing.

"I didn't realize how thirsty I was. How about one more?"

Norman, who stood behind me, leaned forward to whisper in my ear. "What happened to being sober when the shooting starts?"

I mumbled my reply. "The shooting's already started."

Braun stared at the fresh bourbon on the bar, then at the one in my hand, and finally at my unwavering gaze. "Of course, Weber. It is a party, after all."

I raised my glass. "To the defeated enemy, may they all get what they deserve." I poured the third whiskey into myself and watched Braun struggle to swallow. It took him two tries to get it all down.

"Shall we have another, Herr Braun?" I trotted out my sweetest smile, but the inferno in my guts promised to incinerate me if I had any more alcohol.

Braun rubbed his forehead spastically. "Later, maybe. I have important things to do."

"Of course, you do, of course." I clapped him on the shoulder as he staggered away from the bar. "Enjoy the party, Braun."

I fished the marker out of my pocket and waved over the bartender. "Hey Jack, I need to cash this in, but I forget where I need to go. Too much bourbon, maybe." My words slurred a little, and I added some inane giggling into the mix. The bartender directed us to one of the side-rooms and to look for a fat man with a mustache, name of Dewitt Wexler. I tipped him a buck and tore Norman away from his second, but half-finished beer.

The room only rolled a little as I crossed it. I'm not sure what I expected Wexler to look like, one of those thickly built men with whiskers like a scrub brush maybe. Instead I found a rotund Texan with a broad smile and a long handlebar mustache. He looked me over as I approached. "My goodness! What have we here?" He raised one eyebrow and looked confused. "It's a woman!" He brayed like only a Texan can. "Look a' here boys! It's a woman in a suit!"

Several men stopped their conversations to take a peek. I offered them an unsteady little curtsy. "Thanks for noticing. You Wexler?"

He nodded. "What can ah do for you, little lady?" They all had a chuckle at that.

I held up the marker for him to see. "I just want to cash this in. They said you'd take care of that for me."

He read the paper and then held his gut as he laughed. "That's a lot of money."

"Yeah. Is that a problem?"

He tossed off the last of his whiskey. "Of course not, but you'll have to come with me to my office. I don't keep that kind of cash in my back pocket!" He jiggled his belly again. "Follow me."

The three of us went through a door and up a short flight of stairs. He took a key out of his pocket and unlocked a heavy mahogany door. "Right this way, little lady." He chuckled as he opened the door.

The room smelled musty but was well stocked with heavy Victorian furniture. He waved toward the chairs that faced a massive desk. "Have a seat." He plunked his heavy frame into a creaking swivel chair behind the desk, huffing as if he was out of breath. "I'm getting too old to be climbing those damned stairs."

I lit a cigarette and blew a double jet of smoke out of my nose. "That's a shame."

He stared at the desk for a moment, as if he forgot why he'd come here. He frowned for a moment, then brightened. "Ah! Yes, may I please have the marker?"

I handed it to him.

"We don't issue many notes of this size." He smiled as he waved it at me.

"Is that so?"

"Oh yes. As a matter of fact, this is the only one we've ever issued."

I took a long drag. "That a fact?"

He opened a drawer and rummaged around for a moment. He casually tossed a random assortment of bills on the table, twenties, fifties, hundreds. "So, that places me in a most awkward position." He continued burrowing in the drawer.

"Does it?"

"Yes, because this note was issued to a specific person." He raised his hand from the drawer and stabbed the barrel of a revolver in my direction. "And you, little lady, are not that person."

Chapter Ten

I've stared down the barrel of a gun when I hadn't had a drink in days, so now, with a snootful of fine Kentucky bourbon, I found the whole idea of being threatened ludicrous. I laughed, a fine, rich, honest-to-goodness belly laugh, and after a moment Wexler joined in, though he kept the gun in my face.

"Does that little piece of paper scare you that much, Herr Wexler?" I belted out another gale. "Careful, paper-cuts are the worst!"

Finally, he dropped the gun on his desk, within easy reach. He smiled broadly. "I like you, little lady, you got spunk. Hell, ain't many men could laugh down the barrel of a .45. Most men wet their britches when someone points a gun at 'em. You got spunk and I like it."

"Thanks." I mashed my cigarette out on the arm of the chair. "You wouldn't shoot us in here. You'd ruin the furniture."

"A fair point. Well, who the hell are you two lunatics anyway?"

"I'm Weber, he's Bauer." I lit another smoke.

Norman smiled. "*Ich heiße Bauer.*"

"Don't waste your breath. I don't speak German." He gave Norman a dubious eye before turning back to me. "You're Weber? Eva Weber? Gottlieb told me you were in town, though his description of you fell short of the reality. I know your father by reputation. I'm so glad we're all *friends* here." He smiled but watched me closely.

I threw him a crooked smile. "We're from out of town, but we're *friends* just the same." I put the same emphasis on the word he had.

Wexler relaxed a little. "Good. Pleased to make your acquaintance, but we're still left with the same problem. This isn't yours." He waved the marker at me. "Where did you get it?"

"From Shultz."

Wexler blinked. "From who?"

"Joe Shultz. He's one of our *friends* too."

A little crease formed on Wexler's brow as his mind worked. "I don't know that name." He leaned forward with his elbows on his desk. "Why did he give it to you?"

"I'm looking for his girlfriend."

"Why?"

"She's a friend of mine."

He rubbed his bulbous nose. "No, I meant is she missing? Did she leave him or something?"

I shrugged and took a drag on my smoke. "I'll ask her when I find her."

"What's her name?"

"Heloise Kendall. Heard of her?" I watched him closely for any flicker of recognition but saw none.

"Can't say that it's any too familiar. How long has she been gone?"

"I'm not sure. Does that matter?"

He hissed out a long, exasperated sigh. "It might. Your Heloise Kendall isn't the only missing person around here."

"Oh? Do tell."

He rubbed his nose again, more vigorously this time. "One of our guys is missing too. Name's Heinrich Richter; do you know the name?"

"I've heard it."

"I thought you might have. He's been missing a couple of days. We've looked for him in all the usual places, no luck. He's a good-looking young fella, fillies like his blue eyes, and believe me, he likes the fillies."

I chuffed a dual gust of smoke out of my nose. "So, you think Kendall ran off with Richter?"

A crooked grin surfaced on his face. "The thought crossed my mind. You don't think it could have happened?"

"Maybe." I tugged at my lip as I ran the possibility

through my brain. "Would you say Richter was the temperamental sort? Would he have killed Shultz for the girl?"

Wexler's eyebrows crawled up his forehead. "Shultz is dead?"

I nodded. "Shot twice in the back, and once in the head just for fun. Sound like Richter's style?"

He opened a drawer and pulled out a bottle of bourbon and a glass. "Drink?"

"No thanks. None for Bauer either." Norman shot me an annoyed glance. "He has a delicate stomach."

"Fortunately, I do not." Wexler filled the glass, then swallowed half of it. "Since we're all *friends*, I won't mince any words here. Richter was *active*. Now, that's not my end of the stick, I'm just an accountant. I don't know what he was up to, and I don't think it'd do me much good to find out. He got into some trouble a while back, in Washington I believe, so he came here to wait for things to calm down a bit. From what I hear, he wasn't any stranger to a gun. He could have killed your boy all right. That doesn't mean he popped Shultz, just that he could've if he'd wanted to."

"Best suspect I've found so far."

He squinted at me and sipped at his bourbon. "Did Shultz give you the marker before or after he got shot?"

I took one last drag and snuffed out my Camel. "After. He gave me some cigarettes too."

Wexler laughed and pounded the desktop with his beefy fist. "Shultz sounds like a generous fella. Did he happen to mention how he got the marker?"

"Nah. The holes in his lungs impaired our otherwise scintillating conversation."

He suddenly stood up and paced behind his desk. "Dammit! How did a little nobody end up with the marker? It doesn't make any sense!"

Norman cleared his throat. "Uh, who was supposed to have the marker?"

Wexler stared at a spot on the far wall for a minute, then collapsed back in his chair. "Nobody. I planted it to catch a thief."

That made me chuckle. "Are you serious?"

He rubbed his eyes and looked very tired. "It's an internal problem, and I really wish someone of your stature amongst our friends hadn't found out about it. Certain thefts have occurred lately, so I planted the marker to flush out the thief."

"I take it someone like Shultz couldn't have stolen it?"

He shook his jowls. "Shultz would have just been rank-and-file. Our thief ranks much higher."

"How high?"

"One of maybe half a dozen men."

I whistled. "So, it'd be someone prominent. A leader."

He nodded and poured himself another bourbon. "Yeah. It'd have to be."

"Who are they? The six men that you mentioned."

Wexler wriggled in his chair, making it squeal. "I don't want to engage in idle speculation. Their names aren't important. Like I said, it's an internal problem." He held up his hands placatingly. "Now, I don't mean to be rude and I don't want to offend you. I just think it's best to keep things in the family, if you know what I mean."

I shook out a cigarette and took my time lighting it. "Okay. I'm fine leaving that nonsense to you. I'm still gonna look for Kendall, but from what you tell me, there's a chance I'll find Richter with her. If I do find him, what do you want me to do with him?"

He snatched up a pen and scribbled a number on a little piece of paper which he sat on the desk nearest me. "Just leave a message at this number and we'll take care of it." He sat back in his chair, licking his lips as he poured himself another shot. His hands trembled, not bad enough to spill the bourbon, but enough to notice.

I stood up, took a step closer to him and sat on the edge of the desk. I poked a finger into the bundles of cash he'd so casually thrown there. "You've got a problem, Wexler. Right now it's your problem, not mine. I assume you want to keep it that way." His head bobbled like he forgot he had a neck. I picked up two bundles of bills and slipped them into my pocket. "Good. I'm glad we agree." I folded the telephone number he'd written in half and handed it to Norman. "We'll be in touch,

Wexler." He watched us leave and I heard glass clanking behind the closed door.

In the casino, the party droned on, louder and wilder than before. The sultry canary chirped out a lively rendition of "Jingle Jangle Jingle" as the chaos of dissipation and revelry roared to drown her out. I spied Gottlieb watching us through the miasma of smoke that hung in the room. He took off his spectacles and wiped the lenses with a handkerchief, then stuck them back on his nose.

As I started to approach him, he gave me a quick shake of the head and aimed his eyes toward a nearby poker game. There, two men stood along the wall as if they had a distinct interest of the outcome of the game, but they had their eyes aimed toward Norman and me. They stood stiffly erect, hands held together in front of them. I slipped into a winning smile and gave them a little wave as we continued toward the door. Neither of them smiled.

I snatched Norman's hand and dragged him down the stairs.

"Kissy? Why are we running?"

"Shut up and move." When we finally reached the bottom of the stairs, we found a whole platoon of half-drunk krauts smoking cigars and chewing the fat on the street. We shouldered our way through them and just as we made it into the clear a youngish blond man dressed in a pristine black suit with a cap stopped us with a bow.

"Fräulein Weber? I have instructions to drive you wherever you want to go." He gestured to a gleaming automobile parked on the street.

Norman and I exchanged a quick glance. "No thanks." I gave Norman a tug and started down the sidewalk again.

The young chauffeur stepped in front of us again. "Please, with Herr Gottlieb's compliments."

"Herr Gottlieb?" I looked over my shoulder and saw the two torpedoes Gottlieb had indicated just emerging from the enclosed staircase. They scanned the crowd but hadn't latched onto us yet.

The chauffeur bowed again. "Yes, ma'am, Herr Gottlieb sends his regards and offers you the use of his car this evening."

"Great!" I leapt for the car with Norman's scarecrow frame moving too slowly behind me. I pulled the door closed behind him and shouted at the driver. "Go!" The young chauffeur fired up the engine and the machine surged away from the Bremen Street Club, leaving the predator krauts behind us. But not far enough behind.

I watched another car tear away from the curb and pull out behind us. "Hey, Jack! We're being followed! Get this tin can moving'!"

He squinted into the rearview mirror and scowled. "They won't catch us! You'd better hold onto something!"
He stomped on the accelerator and the massive car charged forward. With an almost reckless abandon, he weaved the car in and out of traffic, dodged streetcars and ignored traffic lights, but still the pursuers hung on.

With a sudden crack, the rear windshield shattered. Norman seemed confused and turned around to look at it. "Huh?"

"Dammit, Norman! Get down! They're shooting at us!" He hunkered down on the floor, but I pulled out my own pistol. The car bumped and swerved as I tried to aim at the car behind us. I squeezed the trigger and hit the pavement behind their car. My second shot hit the driver's mirror but didn't slow him down. Another bullet punched into our fender. "They're getting closer!"

Our driver swore in both English and German, then swung over the wheel in a turn so tight the tires screeched, and the rear end of the car seemed to leave the ground and fly around the corner. I peeked out the shattered rear window and saw the other car came squalling around the corner, pursued by a black-and-white.

"Cops! Now we've got cops!" The driver manhandled the steering wheel and spun onto Gilbert Avenue, heading toward Eden Park. The car's engine protested as we raced uphill. Gunshots crackled around us, one shattering the front windshield. I popped up and fired off a couple of shots, not hitting much of anything, but slowing down their pursuit.

I decided to take my time and aim at the driver behind us. For a moment, time seemed to slow down, and I had him.

My gunsights lined up with his heart and I started squeezing the trigger. Our driver swerved suddenly, and I was thrown against the side of the car. My gun dropped on the floor of the car and skittered away from me.

Our pursuers missed the turn and sped away from us, followed by not just one, but two, black-and-whites. Our driver parked the car on a quiet side street. He turned around in his seat to see us. "Did you both survive?"

Norman patted his chest, looking for bullet holes. Finding none, he turned to me. "I'm fine, how are you?"

"Yeah." I leaned toward the driver. "Who were those men? Why were they shooting at us?"

The driver turned around. "I don't know." He pulled the car into the street and drove as calmly as if we were Okie sightseers on a Sunday drive.

"Fine. Drop us off at Union Terminal."

He shook his head. "I'm afraid not, especially not now. Gottlieb wants to talk to you, and if you want to keep breath in your lungs, you'll want to talk to him too."

I grabbed my pistol off the floor and pressed it into the back of his neck. "Union Terminal. Now."

"No." He drove on a placidly as before.

I blasted out a long, exasperated sigh and put my pistol in my pocket. "Well, hurry up. I need a cigarette."

Chapter Eleven

The driver parked outside the Aristocrat Hotel. He introduced himself as Johannes Ruger, personal driver to Karl Gottlieb. He opened the door for us but bypassed the desk, heading instead for the elevator. The spacious lobby held several benches, some rather overripe lounge chairs, and exactly one person; an older man with a white hair and mustache reading a newspaper with apparently little interest.

The elevator operator turned out to be a dwarf standing on a crate. "Where to?"

Ruger clapped him on the shoulder. "Four, please, Mikey."

The operator slammed the cage shut and gave a pull on the knob that started the lift in motion. It clanked and banged its way up the shaft, but the operator didn't seem disturbed by the noise. In fact, he smiled and chatted Ruger up. "Have a pleasant day, Mr. Ruger?"

"Not really."

"That's too bad. Did you lose the auction?"

"No, no. That went fine. Somebody broke the windshield of my uncle's car, that's all." He shook his head sadly. "What is this town coming to?"

The operator clicked his tongue. "That's a shame. That's a swell car he has. Wish I had one like it."

Norman squeezed my upper arm, and then laughed as if the dwarf had made the Joke of the Year. The little man shot an unconcerned glance up at him and continued. "Yessir, I'd like one of those great big Chevrolet sedans." Norman nearly collapsed with mirth, which he didn't even try to hold in. The operator's glacial calm never wavered. "I think it'd be a fine thing to take a drive out of town where you could really open her up. You know?" The elevator lurched to a stop. "Fourth floor." He opened the cage and we stepped out. I tipped him a half dollar and dragged Norman's laughing carcass out behind me.

Ruger led us down the hall, pulled a key out of his pocket, and unlocked the door to room 408. The room turned out to be a suite with adequate, if less than opulent, furnishings. Norman plopped down on a sofa and leaned his head back, focusing his eyes intently on the ceiling.

I sat in a chair across from him. "Are you all right, Norman?"

"I don't know. People don't usually shoot at me."

I pulled out my cigarettes and searched through my pockets for matches. "You're not perforated, so call it a good first time."

He raised his head to look at me. "First time? It'd better be the last time!"

I struck a match and set fire to my snipe. "No guarantees, partner."

He leaned his head back again, closing his eyes this time.

Ruger came from another room and sat in the other chair. "I've ordered a pot of coffee; it'll be up shortly."

I watched him as he lit a stubby cigar. "Where have we met, Ruger?"

He shrugged. "Have we met?" He looked me up and down. "I'd think I'd remember. You stand out a little."

I spat smoke at him. "Do I? When will Gottlieb get here?"

"When he can. I don't know exactly when."

"Fine. Now tell me, what's going on? Who were those men?"

He shrugged again. "How would I know? I'm just a chauffeur."

"You've got some fancy moves behind the wheel."

He grinned a grin that shaved a decade off his age. "That's why I'm a chauffeur."

The coffee came, and we waited. Norman nodded off within a half-hour, but the coffee and whiskey fire in my guts conspired to keep me awake. Ruger flipped through a ragged copy of *Black Mask* and, other than an occasional chuckle, kept quiet.

At just after five in the morning, a knock sounded at the door. Ruger opened it and Gottlieb entered the room. His bald head glistened. "Ah! Fräulein Weber, it is nice to see you again!"

"Gottlieb." I gave him a nod. "So how about you tell me what the hell is going on?"

He removed his overcoat and took a seat on the sofa beside the snoring Norman. "An interesting way to begin a conversation, I think, since you are definitely *not* Eva Weber. I know this because there is no Eva Weber. Herr Weber has only sons." He adjusted his spectacles. "So, who are you?"

I chuckled around my smoke. "How long have you known that?"

"From the moment you said it." He smiled, amused.

"Then why keep up the act?"

"It served my purposes. It has been an effective diversion."

I gave him a blast of smoke. "Glad I could help."

"Yes, vell now. Who are you really?"

I leaned toward him. "You first. Who were those hatchet men that chased us, and drilled holes in the car? Friends of yours?" I buried my cigarette in the ashtray and lit another one. "I got a problem with being shot at."

He watched me for a minute or two before he spoke. "You are an obstinate voman, fräulein. Very vell. Those men who shot at you and my car vork for Richter."

"Richter again."

Gottlieb's eyebrows rose. "You know Herr Richter?"

"Not exactly, his name just keeps coming up. Braun mentioned him, so did Wexler. I hear he's active."

"Ja, he is. Gestapo. Or perhaps *Schutzstaffel*. It matters little, he is a spy, that's all that really matters."

"I also heard he's missing."

"You hear much. Ja, he is missing. Wexler told you this?"

I nodded.

"Why were you there tonight? Going there vass very dangerous." When I didn't answer, he cocked his head and watched smoke rise from my cigarette. He cleared his throat and started again. "Now, fräulein, I ask you again, who are you?"

I sighed and mashed my cigarette out in the ashtray. "All right, I'll sign my own death warrant. My name's Lisbon, Kissy Lisbon."

Ruger looked up from his magazine. "Kissy?"

"Yeah, Kissy."

"What kind of name is Kissy?"

"What kind of name is Johannes? It's a name."

He snorted and went back to reading. A little furrow dented Gottlieb's forehead, just above the bridge of his nose. "That name means nothing to me. Vhy vere you in Shultz's house?"

"I'm looking for his fiancée."

"Vhy? Who is she to you? Vhy do you vant to find her?"

"I have my reasons."

"Vhich are?"

"My own."

He sighed. "Alvays you answer questions with answers that are not answers!"

"Yeah, it's a nasty habit I have. Do you know Kendall?"

"I haff met her, yes."

My fingers clenched into fists. "Oh, good. Where is she?"

He quirked his mouth into a little smile. "I like you, Fräulein Lisbon, and I vould like you to stay alive so that ve may avoid answering each other's questions in the future."

"Awfully nice of you."

"I need your help to keep you alive. Can that be arranged?"

"Sure, pal."

"Good. Vhy did you go to see Wexler?"

I rolled my eyes and sighed deeply. "Look, I didn't go to see Wexler specifically, I just wanted to cash in a marker that I found by Shultz's body. Folding green is hard to come by, so I take what I can get, where I can get it. I figured Shultz didn't need it anymore."

Gottlieb leaned forward, pulled off his spectacles and rubbed his eyes. "Mein Gott! That marker vass a forgery, a plant!"

"So Wexler told me. I bled him for the cash anyway." I smiled as I patted my jacket pocket.

He placed his lenses back on his face. "That is vhy they followed you. That is vhy they shot at you."

I frowned. "Huh? For the marker?"

"Richter's men vere in the room. They had orders to grab the person who tried to cash that marker. They obviously saw you giving the marker to Wexler."

The expression on Gottlieb's face would've been right at home at a funeral, except that along with sorrow, it showed just a little panic. It made me chuckle. "This thief Wexler mentioned, he must have made off with the mint. How much did he take?"

Gottlieb's eyeballs slid toward Ruger, who looked up from *Black Mask* with a jerk. Gottlieb licked his lips slowly, methodically. "Wexler mentioned the thief? What exactly did he say?"

"Only that a thief had been stealing from the Bund. How much did they get away with?" I leaned forward and gave the ashtray a shake, settling the butts and making room for more. My eyes moved from there to Gottlieb. "Well? How much?"

He swallowed hard and licked his lips again. "It's hard to say for sure, but the damage done vill almost certainly topple the Bund in Cincinnati. Maybe even nationally."

"Wow." I stood up and walked around the room, poking here and there amongst the bric-a-brac that passed for decor. "So, how do you boys fit in? Are you the thieves? Was the cash stowed in Hirsch's safe?"

Gottlieb mashed his cigar in the ashtray. "No. There vass no cash in the safe, only papers."

"Too bad." I sat in the chair again and stared right at Gottlieb. "I want to talk to Heloise Kendall. Take me to her."

"I cannot."

"Why?"

"Herr Shultz is no more. It is her desire to go away and start over."

"I want to talk to her before she goes. Will you let me do that?"

He stroked his mustache. "I vill pass your request to her. If she vants to speak to you, she vill. If not, she von't. Is that fair?"

"Looks like it'll have to do. How will I get in touch with you?"

He looked toward Ruger for a moment. "You may telephone this room. I vill either be here, or Herr Ruger vill haff a message for you."

I clapped my hands and rubbed them together. "Well, boys. It looks like it's time to go!" I gave Norman's foot a kick and he snorted himself awake. "Come on, Norman. Time to go."

He rubbed his eyes. "Can we order breakfast first?"

"No."

Ruger stood. "Give me a moment, and I'll drive you home."

I shook my head. "No thanks, Ruger. I've had enough of your driving tonight. We'll take a cab." He looked offended and sat down to scowl at his magazine again.

Gottlieb rose and escorted us to the door. "Fräulein Lisbon, I hope we are parting as friends?"

"Of course." I threw him a smile that said otherwise.

"I haff some advice for you Fräulein. Take a vacation, perhaps a long trip to the mountains. That sounds lovely, yes?"

I stuck a cigarette between my lips. "I might take you up on that offer."

A wide grin spread beneath his lip-whiskers. "I am pleased to hear that. Very pleased indeed."

"I'll start packing right after I find Heloise Kendall." I stuck a match and held it to the tip of the cigarette.

He leaned forward until his face almost touched the cigarette. "I told you I vould try. I haff told you that you are not safe in the city. If you ignore my advice and get yourself killed, it vill not be on my conscience." We stepped through the door and he locked it behind us.

The operator took us to the ground floor without saying anything, and we left the Aristocrat. It was almost six in the morning, but not a single cab could be found, so we walked.

Norman yawned. "What did you find out?"

"Quite a bit."

"Good. When are we having breakfast?"

I flipped my cigarette butt at him. "Is that all you think about?"

He rubbed his belly and made a pitiable face. "I'm a just a poor starving boy. Feed me, Kissy."

That made me laugh, so we stopped at the first open diner we found. I looked over my shoulder for a second as we were going through the door, then pushed Norman through. We took a seat in a secluded corner where there were no windows and we could talk without being overheard.

Norman looked around the room and shook his head. "Why did we sit all the way back here? The waitress'll never bring us fresh coffee."

"We have a lot to talk about. And somebody is following us."

Chapter Twelve

Norman scarfed down his ham and eggs like a man possessed. I watched him with a mixture of awe and disgust. "Ever try chewing?"

"Nope. I heard it's bad for the digestion."

"Your stomach must be solid iron."

"Yeah, it's great." He shot a glance around the room. "How much did you lift from that kraut's desk?"

"Wexler?"

"Yeah." He shoveled the last of his scrambled eggs into his mouth and swallowed them whole. "You just picked it up and put it in your pocket like it was your own money. He didn't say a word to stop you."

"You noticed that too?"

"Yeah." He slurped his coffee.

"It doesn't make sense, does it?" I nibbled at my toast.

"None of this mess makes sense to me."

"Gottlieb said that the thief Wexler mentioned had stolen enough money to bankrupt the Bund in Cincinnati, possibly every chapter in America."

"So?"

"So if they were hurting for money that badly, why didn't Wexler stop me from pocketing his cash?"

"Probably because he's afraid of you."

"He's not afraid of me." I puffed out smoke and considered that. "But Wexler is afraid, that much is true. You could see it on his fat face, but *why* is he afraid?"

"Well, you pretended to be Weber's daughter and Weber is a big shot in the Bund, right?"

"Yeah, but Weber's daughter isn't Weber himself. And Weber's in New York. Could Weber be so powerful that he could have Wexler bumped off so far from New York?" I shook my head. "Seems unlikely."

"Let me see the money you got. I want to count it."

I took it out of my pocket and tossed both bundles to him. "Have at it." I crushed my cigarette out in the graveyard. "I think Wexler is afraid of Richter. Especially since he doesn't know where Richter is. Richter is squatting right here in Cincy, not so far away as Weber. I think Gottlieb is afraid of Richter too."

Norman looked up from the cash in his lap. "Do you have any idea how much money is here?"

I shrugged. "A couple of hundred bucks?"

"A thousand!" His voice, as usual carried through the room.

My hand fell from my mouth to the table, almost dropping my smoke. "A grand?"

His grin couldn't have been broader without the top of his head falling off. "Yep!"

I scooped the cash of the table and secreted it in my pocket. I took a drag and frowned at the tabletop.

"What's the matter Kissy? Aren't you happy? That's a lot of money!"

"Yeah, it's a bundle, and Wexler didn't blink when I took it."

"So?"

"So, it makes me think they aren't hurting for cash at all. That party looked pretty swanky too, they paid for a band and that tomato singer."

He nodded. "Yeah, all that couldn't have been cheap."

"So, Gottlieb lied to me. The Bund isn't bankrupt."

Norman laughed. "So, he lied. Does that surprise you?"

"A little. At the party he warned me about Richter's men. He's playing a deep game, and I can't decide which side he's on."

"Which side are we on?"

I peered at him over the rim of my coffee cup. "Our side."

"That's what he'd say too."

That startled me, and I almost remembered why I kept Norman around. "Every now and then you surprise me by saying something intelligent."

If he'd had a tail, it'd have wagged itself right off. "Thanks, Kissy!"

"You're right, Gottlieb's playing his own game, just like we are. He also lied about Kendall."

"Kendall?"

"I think she's in it with him. Some of the cigarette butts in the ashtray had lipstick on them."

"So what? Maybe Gottlieb's got himself a girlfriend."

I wrinkled my nose. "Gottlieb doesn't live there. He didn't have the keys. He had to knock on the door so Ruger could let him in. I looked around; a woman lives in that room, not a man. I also noticed that he didn't seem surprised when I brought up Kendall's name. He knows her well enough to know she's leaving town. I don't know how, but he does, and for some reason he doesn't want her talking to me."

"Ruger had the keys, so maybe he lives there with a woman. After all, lipstick doesn't prove that Kendall lives there."

"True, but Gottlieb knows too much about her intentions. No, he knows her. I'm willing to bet that was her lipstick in the ashtray. She might have even been in the bedroom while we were there."

"Maybe she's dating the midget." He laughed at his own joke.

That made me frown. "Maybe you are." I snapped my fingers. "Gives me an idea though."

"Huh?"

"That guy was talking about getting a car. I think *we* need a car. I want to go see Nicky today." I glanced at the clock on the wall. "He'll be open in a few minutes."

Norman plunked down his mug. "No. Kissy, no."

I laughed at his obvious discomfort. "Why not? He's open on Sundays, and we need a car; Nicky can get us one."

"I don't care. We can get a car someplace else. Besides, he said he wouldn't lend us a car anymore, after you crashed up the last one."

"I didn't crash it. It only had a few scratches on it."

"And a bashed in fender."

"Yeah, and that."

"And two flat tires."

"Shut up, Norman. Besides, I don't want to borrow a car. I want to buy one." I patted the pocket where Wexler's money slept.

He made a face. "Fine, just not Nicky. Please?"

"Why not?"

"You know why. He ... he likes me."

I fought to keep my laughter bottled up. "That's why we're going to him. We might get a better deal if you flirt a little."

His voice rose. "I'm not flirting with him!" The few people in the diner leaned to see us and Norman's face took on a cheery crimson that finally broke my control and I belted out a belly laugh, loudly and without restraint. Good to let Norman know what it feels like to be on the receiving end of a big mouth.

I stood up and shrugged into my jacket and seated my hat. "It's settled. We'll go there now, before I fall over."

When we got outside I scanned the street for our tail, but I didn't see him. The bustle on the street had increased as folks made their way to breakfast or church, which I figured made him hard to spot. It would make us hard to follow as well. I hailed a cab and we took off.

Norman pouted in sulky silence during the ride to 'Nicholas Orlando Automobile Sales and Service' not far from the river. We barely stepped out of the cab before Nicky's slicked back black hair and enormous toothy grin came lilting out to meet us. "Kissy! So sweet to see you!" He pulled me into a hug and planted a kiss on my cheek. "And Norman, all dressed up and so handsome!" Norman moved just a heartbeat too slow, and Nicky caught him in an embrace and gave him a kiss on the cheek as well. "You're both looking well!"

I made a show of looking him up and down. "Still using motor oil in your hair, I see."

"Still buying your suits off the rack, I see." He pursed his lips together and gave me a sly, sideways glance, and we both burst into laughter. "Come in, come in! We need to catch up!"

He ushered us across the lot and into the brick building that served as his office. He sat in a swivel chair behind a cluttered desk, Norman and I sat in stout wooden chairs opposite him. He slid a French cigarette into a long ebony holder and lit it. "Now, darlings, what can I do for you?" He puffed out a blue jet of smoke and winked at Norman.

"I need a car, Nicky."

His smile fell onto his desk. "I was afraid of that. Look, Kissy, I love you like a sister, but ..."

I interrupted him. "I want to *buy* a car, Nicky. Buy."

He leaned back and crossed his legs. "Oh. I see."

"I have cash."

He brightened. "Indeed?" His teeth reappeared. "My, my, my, my, my. We have been prospering."

I leaned forward and picked a lighter off the desk. "I have money, but I want a deal." I lit my smoke and inhaled tobacco.

"Of course, sweetness, would I do less for you?" He sucked on his cigarette and shot me an oily grin.

"Nicky, you know what I mean. I want a good deal."

"How good of a deal?" His lips fell over his teeth again.

"Behind the garage good."

He puffed in silence for a moment, then suddenly stood up. "Oh, what the hell. Let's go see what we have." He led us through the back door and around the garage where his attendants changed oil and greased axles. Four cars sat in a row, all gleaming with fresh paint.

I walked around them slowly. "Where did they come from?"

"Indianapolis, I think. They've all been repainted. Untraceable, I assure you."

Norman frowned and pointed to a little white convertible. "Isn't that a Crosley?"

Nicky put his arm over Norman's shoulders and led him toward the car. "Absolutely! You have an eye for cars, Normie!"

He looked at me with trapped, pleading eyes. I puckered my lips and jabbed my head toward Nicky. Norman's eyes bulged, but then Nicky opened the Crosley's door and shoved Norman into the driver's seat. "Built right here in Cincinnati, so nobody will think it strange to see one here." He plunked down in the passenger seat and sat smiling at Norman.

A green Chrysler sedan caught my eye. "This one run okay?"

"Like eggs in coffee, sweetness." He grinned and patted Norman's knee. Norman gave a jerk and scrambled to get out of the Crosley. Nicky, still grinning like a loon, came to stand next to me. He fished a ring of keys out of his pocket and handed one to me. "Fire it up."

I slid behind the wheel and started the engine. It roared to life and idled smoothly. Nicky leaned in and brought his teeth with him. "What do you think, darling?"

"How much?"

He started to rub his chin.

"I mean how much did you pay for it, Nicky?"

He stood up and heaved a great, exasperated sigh in my direction. "$250."

"Fine. I'll give you $300."

He closed his eyes and rubbed little circles into his temples. "That's a '41 Chrysler Royal, Kissy. I can get a grand outta her."

"Yeah, but you paid $250 for her, and I'm gonna pay you $300 for her."

He jerked his thumb toward the Crosley. "I'll sell you that one for $300."

"Nah, I want this one." I shut off the engine and pulled they key out of the ignition. "I like the color. Do we have a deal, Nicky?"

I could see the 'no' lurking behind his lips, but he suddenly laughed and slapped his hand on top of the car. "You'll be the death of me, Kissy Lisbon!" He started for the office again. "Come inside and we'll fill out the paperwork. Coming, Normie?"

Norman crammed his hands into his pockets. "No, uh, I'll wait out here."

Nicky blew him a kiss and we went inside. He sat at his desk and lit another cigarette. He took a puff and shook his head. "I see Norman still thinks I'm making woo at him."

"He's terrified of you."

Nicky laughed through smoke. "Oh, sweet Norman. Haven't you told him he's not my type?"

"I didn't want to break his heart."

We laughed together.

He dug through a file cabinet and brought out a sheaf of paper. "Okay, who are you this week? Or do you just want me to put 'Kissy Lisbon' on the paperwork?"

"Put Eva Weber on it."

"Eva Weber? Who's that?"

"Just a name."

He chuckled. "Never tell the truth when you have a lie handy, is that it?"

"Something like that."

"You never change do you, sweetness?" He chuckled and scribbled on some of the papers.

I dug three hundred dollar bills out of my pocket and tossed them on his desk. "There you go, payment in full."

He stared at the money for a second, then looked up at me. "What are you into, Kissy?"

"Wish I knew."

He leaned back in his chair. "Bad?"

"Could be."

"How bad?"

"Some goons tried to fill me full of daylight a few hours ago." I suddenly felt like I'd drank a full glass of exhaustion. "I'll be lucky to keep breathing another day or two."

He whistled. "When are you gonna learn to play it safe?"

"One day too late."

Chapter Thirteen

At around 6:00 that afternoon I woke up with a skull-cracker of a headache. The too-bright room forced me to squeeze my eyes shut. I sat up without opening my eyes and felt my stomach roll. I stripped off my clothes and struggled into my ratty bathrobe. It took a few minutes before I had enough ambition to stumble to the bathroom, and when I got there I had to hold on to the sink until the sick feeling in my guts gave up the fight.

I stood in the shower under the scalding geyser until I felt something close to human again. I combed my hair out of my face and trudged back toward my room. Norman's radio sang through the transom and I smelled cigar smoke. I knocked on his door and heard his bedsprings creak as he climbed off them.

He opened the door dressed in trousers and his undershirt. "Hey, Kissy." He eyed me up and down. "Feeling refreshed?"

"Not really. Have you had dinner?"

"Nope."

"Get dressed and we'll eat. I need food. And a cigarette."

He held up his Cuban. "You should try one of these."

"No thanks." I crossed the hall and closed the door behind me. I rested my head against the smooth wood of the doorframe for a minute or two before I rustled up enough energy to dress myself. I chose my maroon suit and a violet tie. I put on a crisp white shirt, a new collar, and my usual suspenders to hold up my pants. I regarded my shoes critically. I'd need some new ones soon.

I washed down a couple of aspirin with a shot of rye

whiskey. After I lit a cigarette, I felt much better. I slipped on my jacket, pocketed my Colt, and opened the door. Norman slouched in the hall with his cap pulled low.

I directed my feet to the stairs. "Let's go."

"Where are we going?"

"Lou's."

"Oh." He sounded disappointed.

"I need to make some telephone calls." We trooped down the stairs, out the door and across the street to Lou's. Norman sat in the booth just inside the door, but I went to the public telephone. I asked for the Aristocrat, room 408, and waited while the bell rang. Finally, somebody picked it up.

"Ruger?"

"Speaking. Who is this?"

"It's Kissy Lisbon. Do you have a message for me?"

I heard a pause on the line, the hint of a feminine voice, then Ruger again. "I do. Kendall says she doesn't know you, and she doesn't want to talk to you. Sorry."

"Is she there now? Let me ..." The line went dead. "Dammit." I turned around and started for the table where Norman sat. Then I heard a voice.

"Mrs. Lisbon?"

I jumped, then recognized Mrs. Kendall sitting in the booth next to the phone. "Mrs. Kendall. What a surprise." I sat in the booth across from her. "What are you doing here? I know it's not for the food."

"I came here hoping to find you." She smiled weakly. "I have the rest of your money." She slid an envelope across the table. "I hope cash is acceptable."

I frowned. "I don't understand."

"Heloise telephoned me this morning. She's coming home."

"Is that a fact?"

"It is. So I wanted to discharge you, and, uh, settle the bill." She smiled beatifically.

I picked up the envelope and flipped through its contents. "Five hundred dollars? That's not what we agreed."

Her smile never faltered. "Yes, I know. Consider the rest a bonus. I'm very pleased with your work. I intend to refer all my friends to you.”

I started to smell a rat right about then. “When is Heloise coming home?”

Her lips twitched. “Why, tonight. She’ll be home tonight.”

“Oh really. How about I come over to meet her, just to make sure everything’s square?”

“That won’t be necessary, Mrs. Lisbon. We’ll be quite busy tonight.”

“That’s not a problem, I can come over tomorrow. How about noon?”

“Unfortunately, we’ll be busy then as well.”

I watched her for a minute, then lit a cigarette. “Who put you up to this?”

“I’m sure I don’t know what you mean.” She kept on smiling, made me shiver the way she held onto those teeth.

I slid the envelope back across the table. “Yes, you do. Heloise didn’t call you. She’s not coming home. Somebody told you to tell me that, and I think it was Gottlieb.”

She didn’t bat an eyelash at the name. “Who’s Gottlieb?”

“Don’t know him?” I exhaled tobacco. “Was it the Feds? Did they get to you?”

She stubbed out her smoke in the ashtray. “I don’t know what you’re talking about.” She slid the envelope toward me again and started to rise. “It’s been a pleasure doing business with you, Mrs. Lisbon.” She took my hand in her claw and shook it. “Thank you, again.” The artificial smile clung to her chin as she fled the diner.

I shook my head as I flopped into the seat across from Norman. I didn’t say anything but put the envelope in my pocket.

He looked up from his steak. “I ordered you the lamb and potatoes. Hope that’s okay.”

I watched him eat for a minute. “Have you ever felt like you were adrift in the sea, all alone and far from shore?”

He tilted his head. “Huh?”

“Never mind.”

“That old lady was Kendall, right?”

“Yeah.” I poked at my lamb chop.

"What did she want?"

"She said Heloise is coming home. Then she gave me $500."

Norman spluttered, then fell to coughing. "What?" He went on wheezing.

"Yeah, she gave me $500. Said I'd done good work. She even thanked me." I tugged at my lip. "Thing is, I know she was lying to me."

"I don't know how you do it, Kissy. People just hand you money these days." He grinned and shoveled potatoes into his maw. "This is the best gig we've ever had."

"People who lie to me give me money, or let me take it without protest. Somebody put old Kendall up to this. I called the Aristocrat."

"Oh yeah?"

"Got Ruger. He said Kendall didn't want to talk to me."

He shrugged. "Who cares? She's coming home and we got paid. I'm just glad it's over."

I hissed out smoke. "It's not over, Norman. Somebody's playing me for a fool, and I don't like it."

He stopped feeding long enough to scowl at me. "Come on, Kissy. Let it go. We got paid; who cares if the girl comes home or not?"

"I care." My lamb chop was cold.

"Why? You got the money."

"It's not about money."

He tossed his silverware on the table. "What's it about, then?"

"Pride."

His eyes took on a shade of bovine confusion. "What?"

"It's about knowing that I can be more than a grifter. All those con jobs, you think they made me proud?" My voice cracked as it rose an octave. "I've wallowed in shame until it covers me like slime. I'll never feel clean, Norman, until I can stand to look at myself in the mirror. Until I have something, some act that lets me reclaim an ounce of dignity, I'll feel dirty, ashamed. That's what this is about. I need to see it through to the end, so I can scrub away enough sin to find my soul again." I rattled some smoke into my chest, blinking the sting out of my eyes.

He sat staring at the table for a few minutes before he spoke. "I've never seen you cry before."

"I don't cry." I shoveled cold potatoes into my mouth.

"Oh. I'm sorry." We finished our meal in amicable silence.

Rain fell in sheets as we stepped through the door. We stood under the awning of the shoe store next to Lou's diner, watching the water splatter on the world. Norman fished the last remnants of the licorice I'd bought him out of his pocket and chewed it thoughtfully. "So, what now?"

I tossed my cigarette into the gutter. "Let's go for a drive."

He shot me a gray-toothed smile. "Okay!"

I'd left my car parked around the corner, so we splashed through the monsoon to get to her. We giggled like children when we got inside. I fired up the engine but didn't turn on the lights. A white Packard careened past us and turned the corner at the end of the block.

Norman hooted. "Look at them go! They're in some kind of hurry!"

"I am too." I pulled into the street and we sailed like a clipper ship through downtown.

"So, where're we going?" He sounded like an excited child.

"The Aristocrat."

I saw him slump in the seat. "Oh. Okay."

"I heard a woman's voice in the background on the telephone when I called Ruger's room. I need to know if it was Heloise Kendall or not."

He slid me a quick glance. "All right, let's go find out."

I found his willingness to go oddly touching. I grasped his hand. "Thanks, Norman. This means a lot to me."

His smile lit up the whole car. "Sure. It's fine, Kissy."

I parked as close to the hotel as I could, which wasn't really very close. We dashed toward the hotel, but still got well soaked. I don't know what it is about getting rained on, but it forces you to grin like a lunatic. We grinned our way to the elevator, where we found the dwarf waiting.

I gave him a smile. "Hello, Mikey."

"Hello. What floor?"

"Four."

He looked at me uncertainly as he jerked the lift into motion. "Here to see Mr. Ruger?"

"Yeah, is he home?"

Mikey shook his head. "No ma'am, I'm afraid Mr. Ruger has checked out."

I shot a glance at Norman, then looked down at Mikey again. "Do you know when?"

"The day operator said that Mr. Ruger checked out before lunch."

I gave my lip a tug. "That can't be right. I just telephoned him an hour ago."

"Perhaps I misheard." Mikey retreated into his superhuman calm.

"We'll check. You're probably right."

"Yes, ma'am."

He rattled open the cage door, and we stepped down the hall. I stopped in front of room 408 and knocked. We stood there, straining to hear the sound of approaching footfalls. Nothing.

Norman shrugged. "Looks like nobody's home."

I tried the handle, which turned easily. I gave it a little shove and the door creaked open, showing a swath of opaque murk. I stepped into the room and tried the light switch. Nothing. I took another step. Still nothing.

Norman threw me a harsh whisper. "Kissy! Come out of there!"

As I turned toward him, a ton of bricks wearing a cheap suit slammed me into the wall. My receding headache cracked open again and showed me the stars up close. I heard voices, grunts and the sound a book makes when someone drops it on the floor. I forced a breath into my lungs and squeezed my brain back into my head. Somehow, I got my feet under me and I staggered into the hall. Then I screamed.

Norman sat with his back against the wall of the hallway. Blood trickled from his nose in twin red rivers. He held his fingers over his belly, but the red stuff that came out of him wasn't slowed much by his hands. He looked at me and tried to smile. "I tried to stop him … I tried … Kissy …"

"Oh God! Not again!" I tore out another shriek. "Help! Somebody get help! Call an ambulance!"

I saw Mikey rush out of the elevator on his stubby legs. He looked down at Norman with his mouth agape. I snatched his shoulders and gave him a shake. "Call an ambulance! Now!"

"Yeah!"

He raced away, and I turned back toward Norman, who surprised me by wheezing out an attempt at laughter. "Great, my life depends on a running midget."

I stroked his hair and sobbed out a chuckle. "Yeah. He's gonna save you. You'll see."

He struggled to keep breath in his lungs, but he still touched my wet cheek. "You … don't … cry."

"That's right. So you'd better not die. I won't cry for you."

"That's … okay. I love you anyway." Then he closed his eyes and his head slumped forward.

Chapter Fourteen

Lightning stabbed the night, splashing light across the sky and silhouetting the city's crumbling bones. Water fell from the clouds, but there would never be enough rain to wash the blood from the streets into the gutters. With the lights out, I sat with my knees drawn up to my chest in an easy chair, watching the storm lash its fury on the outline of downtown.

In the other rooms of Suite 408, the police did what they do. I could hear their footsteps scampering to and fro and the ceaseless drone of their chipmunk chatter. They spoke to me: who, what, when, where, why? I drew the chair to the window, lit a cigarette, added a brick to the wall with every tobacco breath, and denied them the joy of interrogation. Eventually they gave up the fight and left me to my solitude.

On some primal level I knew he'd come, and he did. He entered the little bedroom, pulled the wooden chair from the desk, and sat next to the window. Pale silver light crashed through the rain-streaked pane and illuminated his face, Paolo's intimately familiar face. He didn't speak right away, and for a while we watched the sky weep over Cincinnati.

I spat the expended cartridge of my cigarette onto the floor, where a dozen of its compatriots smoldered their death throes. I pulled another round from the pack, loaded the chamber, and fired it into my lungs. Paolo watched me through a cloud of tobacco smoke for another minute, then reached into his coat and pulled out a leather object. He opened it and showed me his badge, which he carefully placed on the windowsill. I stared at it for a moment then looked into his ocean-blue eyes.

"Kissy, I've taken off my badge, so for the moment I'm

not here as a cop. I'm here as your friend because I think you need a friend more than you need a cop right now." Even though he waited for me to say something, I didn't answer. Eventually, he went on. "They took him to the hospital. He was alive when the ambulance left, which is good news. I've known two or three guys who had gut-shots and lived, so don't give up on him just yet." I could see him watching me, I could see his concern for me written in his posture. Poorly healed scabs, five years old, tore free and began to bleed somewhere deep inside of me. I drew in another gust of smoke and continued my statue-like vigil.

He hung his head, picked up his badge and stood. "All right, Cassandra. I won't force you to talk to me." He slipped his badge into his jacket pocket. "I'll go for now, but when I come back into this room I'll be a cop again. I don't have a choice in the matter." He stood next to my chair and draped a hand onto my shoulder. "Again, I'm sorry about your friend."

He started to leave, and suddenly I wanted him to stay more than anything else in the world. I threw away my smoke and grasped his hand and held it between my own. "Paolo." My voice rasped like used sandpaper. "Don't go." I closed my eyes and pressed his palm to my face and held it there, a touch I remembered so well. A touch I needed more than I could admit. A touch I'd forbidden myself a long time ago.

With his free arm he brought his chair close to me and sat down. He let me keep his hand and leaned close to me. "Kissy, what happened? Who shot Norman?"

My hands trembled; I knew he could feel it. "I don't know."

He nodded slowly. "Why were you here, in this hotel?"

"Who's asking? The cop or the friend?"

He looked away. "Can't they be the same person?"

"No. You know why."

He nodded. "Because of Mary."

I clutched at his arm in a sudden mania of need. "It's happening again, Paolo! Don't you see? It's all the same! It's my fault, just like before." I squeezed his hand to my chest. "If he dies, I won't be able to bear it. It'll kill me this time!"

"Shh, shh, shh. Kissy, don't give up hope yet." He pulled

me to him; my arms coiled around his body without being told to. He held me close, and I shuddered in his embrace. Tears came, and I cried for all the people I'd murdered. For Norman, for Mary, for Cassandra. The sky wept regrets with me, our bitter tears commingling on the cold unforgiving ground. All through the storm Paolo held me, and I held him.

Finally, I pulled away from him and sat back in my chair. He wiped tears from my face with his fingers. "No more tears, okay?"

"I don't cry."

He smiled a little. "Oh yeah. I forgot." He tucked a stray lock of hair behind my ear. "May I ask you something, as a friend?"

I nodded.

"Are you and Norman a couple? You know, together? An item?"

That made me laugh. "Good lord! No!"

"I see. So, he's just a friend?"

"More like a pet." I spat out a bitter chuckle. "He's helpless, and more stupid than I can describe, but he's also sweet, loyal and totally in love with me."

"Yeah, I saw that the other day."

"That was the last thing he said to me. That he loved me."

Paolo closed his eyes and hung his head. "Oh, God."

"I'm glad you haven't forgotten."

He shook his head, eyes still closed. "No. No, I haven't forgotten. Mary's last words to you were, 'I love you, Cassy.'"

I shook my head. "No, she said 'Kissy' not 'Cassy.' She called me 'Kissy' when we were alone. She said it by accident one day and it made me laugh, so it became her nickname for me."

A knock sounded on the door, and he went to answer it. He stepped out of the room and spoke to someone on the other side. I couldn't discern any of the particulars, but the other voice rose in anxious agitation. Paolo made a reply: smooth rhythmic tones. The other voice interrupted, increasing in agitation and volume. I didn't care, none of the men in the other room meant anything to me. None save one.

Paolo reentered the room and sat down beside me. "We

have a problem. Some people in the other room want to take you down to the precinct to answer some questions.”

“Some people. You mean your people, right?”

He swallowed hard and licked his lips. “No, they’re not my people.”

“Feds?”

“Some of them are, I don’t know about Greene.”

“Do you mean Colonel Greene?”

Paolo rubbed his forehead and stared at me. “How did you know that?”

“I’ve heard the name.”

“Oh yeah? Where?”

“Just around.”

“Jesus, Kissy. Right now this town is crawling with G-men and Army Intelligence, and they won’t even tell us what the game is. Please tell me you aren’t tangled up in whatever it is that they’re after.”

I picked up the pack of smokes I’d been burning through, but it was empty. “I need cigarettes.”

“You are, aren’t you?” He threw up his hands and paced back and forth between me and the window. “Cassandra. Kissy, these men want to put you in a little cell in some godforsaken federal prison! You’ve got to give me something, or I can’t help you.”

I bit my lip and stepped over to him. I had to look up to see his face. “Remember your murder, the one in Mt. Washington?”

“Yeah.”

“The victim was a Nazi, right?”

He expelled a lungful of air. “We think so.”

“You found some literature in the top dresser drawer, right?”

“You were in that house! Kissy, you didn’t kill that man. Did you?”

I grinned. “What do you think?” I paused, holding his eye for a moment. “Right now, the Feds have pushed you out of the game. I can deal you back in, but you have to get me out of here.”

“Are you saying the Mt. Washington murder victim was killed by the Feds?”

I turned away from him. "Are you gonna help me, Paolo?"

"If I do, what's the plan?"

"I know who to shake down for information. We find out who shot Shultz and nail them. We find out who or what the Feds are after, and we give it to them and tell them to get the hell out of town."

He nodded. "You'd make a good cop."

"I'd make a terrible cop because I have one more condition. When we find the guy who shot Norman, I'm gonna bleed him out."

He stood there, watching me. "Well, I see you've not lost your thirst for vengeance. You know I can't agree to that last part."

"I know. When we find the guy, I'll wait for you to leave." I twitched my lips into a grin.

He waved his hands. "A fine plan, but how can I get you out of here? The other room is full of cops and more than a few Feds."

"We'll just have to scam them." I pulled him down and whispered into his ear.

Paolo opened the door and we stepped into the sitting room. Detectives, photographers, Feds and beat cops all hushed themselves into silence. I clung to Paolo's body and simpered as pitiably as I could. I trembled, I whined, and I wailed. His arm draped over my shoulder and he held me tightly. He motioned to another man and spoke up. "Sergeant Hobbes, I'm taking this young lady down to the hospital. I'm worried that, in the condition she's in, she might do herself injury. Please take over here."

A squat, ugly man in a gray suit intercepted our progress across the room. "You aren't taking her anywhere, Belvedere. Not until I say you can." He swaggered toward us.

That was my cue. I let go of Paolo and grabbed my hair in my fingers and I shrieked and shrieked. I dropped to the floor and pounded my fists on it. I looked up at the ugly man and howled like a banshee! My throat burned from the force of my lamentations, but I didn't stop.

The ugly man took a step away from me. "What's the matter with her?" He looked to Paolo. "Can't you shut her up?"

Paolo just shrugged. "She's been traumatized, Colonel. It took me an hour to get her to agree to go to the hospital. For some reason, it seems that she has an unreasonable terror of you. Why would that be, Colonel?"

Colonel Greene's mouth hung open. "I-I don't know!"

Paolo gestured at me with his hands. "Well, she's all yours, Colonel. You may begin your interrogation of the subject."

I kept up my keening wail, adding in some choking and coughing for effect.

"Better hurry though, Colonel, you'll want to get what you can out of her before she swallows her tongue. After that she won't be fit for much besides burying. I'll let you explain to the district attorney how a subject in your custody choked to death."

The colonel's mouth worked, and he looked like he might be ill. "Get her out of here, Belvedere!"

Paolo smiled. "Oh, no hurry. I can wait until you've had a chance to talk to her." He jingled the loose change around in his trousers pocket as if he watched women pitch a fit every day.

"Dammit, Belvedere! Take her out of here! She belongs in the nuthatch!"

"Well, all right. If you're sure you're done with her, Colonel." He knelt and slipped his arm around my shoulder. "Come on, Miss. We'll take you away from here. It'll be just fine now."

My screams dropped to whimpers and gasping sobs. I let him guide me out of the room and close the door behind us.

He pursed his lips and looked sideways at me. "You are amazing."

I showed some teeth. "I know."

Chapter Fifteen

We exited the Aristocrat and stood under the awning for a moment. Paolo pointed down the street. "My car is right over there."

I squinted through the rain. "Does Colonel Greene know what kind of car you drive?"

He blinked a few times. "I don't know. I suppose he could."

"Let's assume he does. We'll have to take a different car." I made a show of looking up and down the street. I pointed to my green Chrysler. "How about that one? It looks about right."

"What are you talking about? I'm not stealing a car!"

I shushed him. "Of course not. I am." Before he could say anything, I swam through the downpour and down the street to my car. I already had the keys in my hand, so within a sawed-off second, I had the door open and the engine purring like a tame tiger. I switched on the headlights and pulled up to the awning in front of the Aristocrat. I rolled down the window and handed him a grin. "Get in, copper."

He stared at me, long enough that I thought he'd refuse to get into the car, but eventually he heaved a titanic sigh, opened the door, and sat in the passenger seat. "We'll have to reevaluate our estimates on how long it takes to hot-wire a car. You must be some kind of pro." I thought he looked sad, and I had to laugh.

"It's my car, dummy." I pointed to the key in the ignition. "I just wanted to make sure it was Paolo the man who was with me. I knew Paolo the cop wouldn't get in a stolen car." I parked about a block away from the Aristocrat and gave him a serious look. "You aren't here as a cop, right?"

"Kissy, it's what I am. I'm a cop."

I shook my head. "No, that's what you do, not who you are. Being a cop is just a job, Paolo, no different from a greengrocer or a ditch digger. It doesn't have to define you. What you are is a man. You've just played policeman so long that you've forgotten how to act like a man. I'm hoping that we can salvage Paolo the man from the wreckage of Paolo the cop."

"Why are you telling me this?"

"Because until this mess is cleaned up, we might have to do things far worse, both morally and legally, than stealing a car. If you can't accept that, you'll have to get out right now."

"You're asking a lot."

I chuckled. "I'm not asking anything. I'm telling you the way things are gonna be. It's up to you, Paolo. Are you gonna be a man or a cop?"

His jaw clenched and he stared through the windshield at the dancing droplets of rain. He suddenly turned to me with a toothy smile on his face. "I'm already in Dutch with Colonel Greene, might as well see this through to the end." He stuck out his right hand. "Partners?"

I shook it. "For now. Say, what kind of car does Colonel Greene drive?"

"Uh, it's white."

I pointed my finger at a Packard parked on the street. "Is that it?"

He squinted through the deluge. "Yeah, I think it is."

"Good." I opened the door and sprinted toward the Packard. I opened my pocketknife and stabbed each tire a time or two. The air hissing out of each one sounded like a basket of angry cobras, and that image set me to laughing. I laughed the whole way back to my car, and brayed even after I got inside.

Paolo shook his head, frowning. "Why did you do that?"

My laughter made it hard for me to speak, and it took a while before I could give him an answer. I finally fought the giggles to a standstill. "Because he fell for that stunt we pulled on him back there."

Paolo's frown deepened. "Huh?"

"Look, the only reason he let us go is because he thinks so little of women that he honestly believed a woman would react to trauma like that. He's an idiot. I also want to keep him off our backs for a while."

"He'll just get another car."

I drove past the crippled Packard with a broad smile on my face. "I know, but that'll take some time. Besides it felt really good." My smile stretched my face to the limit. "*Really* good."

He suddenly leaned his head back and bellowed out his rich laughter. "You are a wicked woman, Kissy Lisbon."

"I need to find an open drug store."

"Why? Are you sick?" He seemed to be waiting for a punch line.

"Well, all that screaming isn't easy on the throat. I want to buy something soothing for it."

"Oh. Try the one on Vine Street. I think it's open until 10:00."

The rain began to slacken as I parked in front of the store. Paolo waited in the car while I ran inside. I came back outside with a cigarette between my lips and a bottle of bourbon in a brown paper bag. Once I'd gotten in the car, I took a tug from the bottle and hissed my pleasure. "That's better."

"You bought cigarettes and whiskey to sooth your raw throat?"

"Yeah, what do you use?"

He threw up his hands. "I remember a time when I couldn't get you to take a sip from a martini."

My brows knit. "Hmm. I don't remember that. You must be thinking of some other person."

"I'm starting to think you're right. So, where do you want to start?"

"I want to go see a lawyer."

He nodded. "Good idea. I have a feeling we'll need one by morning."

"That's not what I mean. I know a lawyer who's in deep with Colonel Greene."

"You do? Bah, Kissy, I think you need to start at the beginning. Tell me everything."

I chewed my lip for a moment. "Okay, but remember, you're not a cop tonight."

He rubbed his forehead and gave a little moan. "I'm

gonna regret this, I just know it. Okay, start at the beginning."

So, I did. I told him the high points, but left out just enough to make sure I stayed in charge. His eyes never left my face, and there were times when I felt certain his eyeballs would roll out of his skull and rattle around on the floor.

When I'd caught him up, he whistled. "When you get in trouble you don't hold anything back, do you? Why do you want to see this Martingdale guy?"

"Because I think Colonel Greene, or one of his goons, shot Norman."

That woke him up. "Why do you think that?"

"Shultz worked for Martingdale, right? When I went to Martingdale's office to find out where Shultz lived, I overheard Martingdale mention that Colonel Greene would be interested to know somebody was looking for Shultz. So, Greene knew Shultz. Shultz ended up dead."

Paolo ran his fingers through his curls. "You think Greene had Shultz killed. Why?"

"I think Shultz was working for Greene. Mrs. McKnight, the lovely old woman you caught me speaking to in Mt. Washington, said that sometimes a white car picked up Shultz. We know Greene drives a white Packard."

He shook his head. "That's all circumstantial. There are hundreds of white cars in Cincinnati. Even if Shultz was working with Greene and Greene had him shot, how do you connect Greene to Norman's shooting?"

"When Norman and I left the Aristocrat this morning, we were being followed. I don't think it was the first time either. There was another guy at the auction."

"So what? Your tail could have been working for the Bund."

I laughed. "When the Bund follows you, they also shoot at you. No, I think this guy worked for someone else. At the time I thought he might be a cop. Now, I think he was a Fed."

Paolo's forehead dented as he thought.

"Tonight, before we left for the Aristocrat, a white Packard nearly ran us off the road. It went in the same direction we did. Toward the Aristocrat."

"Still circumstantial. This could all just be a series of

coincidences. It'll never hold up in a court of law."

I hurled a scowl at him. "Be careful, Paolo, you almost sounded like a cop just now."

He held up his hands in surrender. "I'm sorry, bad habit. I'm just saying that we can't prove any of this. Why would Greene shoot Norman?"

"Whoever shot Norman was in the room where we'd met with Gottlieb earlier. He could have been looking for something. Or someone. Gottlieb, Ruger, or maybe even Heloise Kendall." I threw my dead cigarette out the window. "The guy in that room tackled me with his body. Believe me, he was built like a bull. All I remember about him was his size and his cheap gray suit."

Paolo grimaced as if in pain. "Built like a bull; that's a great description of Greene, and Greene had on a cheap gray suit tonight."

I nodded. "Yeah, I'm convinced Greene shot Norman. To be sure, we have to go to the one person who seems to know what Greene is up to."

"Martingdale."

"Right." We drove through the rain and I parked the car on the street next to Martingdale's office building. A light burned on the third floor, right in the same window where I'd seen Martingdale standing after my last visit to his office. "Looks like he's still here."

"You know, Kissy, he might not want to talk to us."

"Just flash your buzzer at him. He'll talk to a cop."

"Oh, now I'm a cop?" He laughed. "I can't force him to talk. He's a lawyer."

I waved that away. "Once he hears our story, he'll want to talk, believe me." I opened the door and gestured to the stairs. "If not, I'll have to get rough with him."

Paolo stopped on the second-floor landing to frown at me.

I threw him a grin. "Just kidding, officer." I scurried past him and made it to the third floor before he did. I pointed out the door to Paolo. "There it is. Maybe you'd better be the one to knock."

"Because I'm a cop?" He sighed and rapped on the door.

"Mr. Martingdale? This is Detective Belvedere with the Cincinnati Police Department." He shot me a glance while we waited. Nothing. He knocked again. "Mr. Martingdale? I'd like to speak with you." Silence reigned from within. He tried the knob, but the locked door wouldn't budge.

I pointed up to the transom, which was open. I took off my jacket and put my hand on his shoulder. "Give me a boost." Reluctance chiseled itself into his face, but he lifted me until I could pull myself through the transom. I dropped through it and landed on my bottom on the other side of the door. "Ow!"

He rattled the doorknob. "Kissy? Are you all right?"

I turned the lock and opened the door. "Yeah. Just perfect." Darkness swathed the room, except for the sliver of light that escaped around the edges of the door leading into Martingdale's inner office. Paolo handed my jacket to me, but he had my Colt in his hand.

"What's this?"

"A gun."

"Why do you have a gun?"

"Why do you?" I snatched it from him and held it in my hand. "Stay out of my pockets!"

He held up his hands again. "I give up." He knocked on Martingdale's door. "Mr. Martingdale? Police, please open the door." Not response. He shrugged. "Maybe he just forgot to turn off the light."

When I tried the doorknob and it turned easily. I sighed. "This seems awfully familiar." I clutched my pistol tightly in my hand and flung the door inward.

Martingdale sat in his swivel chair with his head leaned back. A neat round bullet hole decorated the center of his forehead.

I turned to Paolo. "You were right, he's not gonna talk to us."

Chapter Sixteen

Just like that, Paolo became a cop again. "Don't touch anything! The entire room is a crime scene." He started to leave the room.

"Where are you going?"

"To call this in. We need to start collecting evidence immediately."

I chuckled. "Have you forgotten that we're in this office illegally? How do you intend to explain that?"

He ran his fingers through his hair a time or two. "This is a murder scene, Kissy!"

"Yeah, he's dead. He's not going anywhere. So, we don't need to be in a hurry to call anyone. It's a safe bet his secretary will call the cops in the morning. We need to see what he can tell us."

He grit his teeth, but didn't leave the room. "I don't like it."

"I don't care." I took a long look at the office, not focusing on any single object, rather just letting the generalities of the place sink in. A bottle of gin and a glass sat on the desk in front of Martingdale. I leaned close to both.

Paolo grunted. "Looks like suicide. There's a gun on the floor beside him."

"What caliber is it?"

He knelt beside the chair. "Uh, .45, revolver. If you're gonna kill yourself, that's the thing to use. Bang, and then it's 'Hello Saint Peter.'"

I leaned close to Martingdale's face. "Paolo. I don't think this guy plugged himself."

"Really, why not?"

"The bullet hole's right in the middle of his forehead." I pulled out my gun and aimed it at the same spot on my own noggin. "See what I mean? How awkward is this?"

He held out his hands placatingly. "Kissy, don't do that. Put down the gun."

"Pay attention, copper." I moved the barrel of my Colt to my temple. "See? This is how you shoot yourself in the head."

"Okay, Kissy. I got it."

I slipped my heater back into my pocket. "Then there's the whiskey."

"Whiskey?" He examined the bottle more closely. "It's not whiskey, it's gin."

"It might be gin in the bottle, but it's whiskey in the glass. Smell it." I broke into a smile.

He took a whiff. "Damn. You're right. It's almost empty, just a drop or two left."

"Also, what kind of suicide has a whole bottle of liquid courage on their desk, and doesn't drink it all? That bottle is more than half full! If it were me, that bottle would be dead before I was."

Paolo shook his head and smiled at me. "What else, Sherlock?"

"Do you see a note? Suicides leave notes, don't they?"

"Usually." He glanced around the room. "Okay, you win. We have a murder here, not a suicide, though it's clearly supposed to look like a suicide."

I placed the back of my fingers against Martingdale's face. "He's not completely cold."

"Rigor?"

I grasped the corpse by the wrist, raised his hand a few inches and dropped it to the desk, which made Paolo clench his teeth again. "Nope."

"All right, so he's probably only been dead an hour or two. I think we need to leave now. He's not gonna tell us much more." He yanked a handkerchief out of his pocket, wiped off the doorknob and pulled it closed behind us, then he did the same to the other door.

"What about the lock?"

He smiled, and with the handkerchief in hand, rattled

the knob. "It locks automatically. I turned the lock it when I wiped your fingerprints off it."

"You're a sweetheart, copper."

"Let's get out of here before somebody sees us." He put his hand on my back as he looked over his shoulder, gingerly guiding me toward the stairwell. We made it outside without being seen, and piled into my car. I fired up the engine and steamed away from the bloody ruin formerly known as John Martingdale.

Paolo took out a notebook and began scribbling in it.

I favored him with a glance. "Still think everything's circumstantial?"

"Well, we don't have proof of any connection between any of the three shootings. That said, it is more than a little suspicious that the only two known associates of Colonel Greene have turned up dead within the last few days. I plan to have all four sets of bullets compared to one another."

"Four sets of bullets?"

"Yeah, Shultz had been shot by two different guns of two different calibers."

I whistled. "Somebody really hated Shultz. I wonder why?"

Paolo glanced over at me. "How do you even know his name was Shultz? We've not found out anything about his identity."

"Really? Well, I have a snapshot of Heloise Kendall that Mrs. Kendall gave me. When I was in the house in Mt. Washington, I found another photograph of Heloise with a young blond-haired man that I assumed to be Shultz. The guy on the floor and the guy in the picture looked alike."

He nodded. "May I see those photographs?"

"Sure. I don't have them with me though."

"Where are they?"

"At my place."

"I'd really like to see them as soon as I can." He suddenly pointed to a ratty little hotel. "Pull over here. They have a public telephone. I'm gonna call in Martingdale's murder." He grinned. "Don't worry, I'll do it anonymously."

As he strode inside, I lit a cigarette. The rain no longer

pelted the world, but a light mist still fell. I took a deep smoky breath and battled the flighty butterflies below my ribs. I tried to drown them with a tug from the whiskey bottle, but they survived the onslaught. Putting the smoke down, I took a deep, if somewhat shaky, breath of pure night air, and let it leak out slowly. "Dammit." I swallowed another mouthful of hooch. "Dammit."

After a few minutes he exited the hotel and slid into the seat beside me again. "They're on their way. I feel better about the situation now."

"I'm so glad." I started the car and we rumbled toward my building. "What do you hope to find in the photographs?"

"I don't know. Maybe something, maybe nothing."

I sucked the life out of my cigarette and flung it out the window. We rode in silence for several minutes. Finally, I looked over at him. "Which hospital did they take Norman to? I want to visit him tomorrow."

"Christ Hospital, I think."

I parked around the corner from Lou's Diner and we crossed the street to my building. He looked up at the crumbling edifice, but kept any opinion he might have formed to himself. We climbed the stairs and I unlocked the door to my room. I flipped the switch and the dim overhead bulb grudgingly flashed to life. Paolo looked around the room and then at me.

"Nice place."

"Stow the sarcasm." I took off my jacket, lit a smoke and burrowed into my trunk.

"No, really. It's great."

"Shut up, copper." I smirked as I handed him the two photos. "I hope you get something out of them."

He stood directly under the lightbulb and took his time looking at each of the two photos. Finally, he lowered them and peered at me. "The corpse you found in Mt. Washington wasn't the same guy that's in these photos."

"What? How do you know?"

"The corpse had a scar, a big one on his right cheek that looked fairly old. The guy in this photo doesn't have any facial scars."

"Let me see." I studied the photo of Kendall and Shultz.

"The corpse had a scar? Why don't I remember a scar?"

"That cheek was pressed into the floor."

"Yeah, but I rolled him. Rigor had set in and he was all stiff."

"Well, I don't know why you didn't see it unless it had flatted out before he got stiff. All I know is the dead guy had a scar, Shultz clearly doesn't."

I sat on my bed. "So, Shultz is alive. Maybe that explains why Kendall hasn't left town."

He sat next to me. "You're really desperate to find that girl, aren't you?"

"I'm not desperate, not yet. But as deep as I am in this mess after only a few days, imagine how far she's in it. She's just a girl. I want to help her."

He leaned toward me and bumped me with his shoulder. "I think you want to save her."

"Didn't I just say that?"

"Nope." He threw out a smile. "You help old ladies cross the street; you save them when they're about to be hit by a truck."

I gave him a frown. "Thank you, Dr. Freud, for that insight." His proximity hit my brain like a gallon of rye alcohol, and the world spun for a moment. I could smell his scent: citrus, aftershave, and hand soap.

"Why is it so important for you to get her home?"

"Why wouldn't it be? He mother paid me to find her, so I'm damned well gonna find her."

"Her mother paid you off, though. Your client has ended your employment."

I stood up. I had to get some space between us. "Jesus, you sound just like Norman! Everything is about the money. Kissy only thinks about money. Why does everybody think I'm mercenary? Am I really so vile that it never enters your brain that I could be motivated by anything but money? That girl needs help, and nobody, not you, not the Feds, and not the US Army nor any of the ships at sea are trying to help her!" I jabbed my chest with a finger. "I'm gonna find her, Paolo. Me. And I don't care if I get another red cent out of old lady Kendall!"

He stood to face me with the bed between us. "Kissy, I'm

sorry. I didn't understand."

I turned my back to him, sat on the bed and fired up another smoke. I poured him a double shot of silence, but he thwarted me by turning on my battered radio. Bing Crosby crooned out "Only Forever" in his dreamy baritone. Paolo came to my side of the bed and took my hands into his. He pulled me to my feet.

"What are you doing?"

He placed a finger on my lips. "Shhh."

He pulled me to him and started to sway. I closed my eyes and felt five years fall away to rot on the floor. My heart hammered furiously beneath my ribs and my breath abandoned me to my own devices. Still, Bing sang and we danced.

I felt his hand on my back, moving in slow circles, something I hadn't felt since ... since the night Mary died. My body jerked and I tore myself away from him. I fell across my bed and scrambled to the other side of it. I pressed my back against my closet door. My eyes closed and my breath hissed between my teeth.

"Kissy? What's wrong?"

"Nothing. Please leave. I'm suddenly exhausted."

He took a step toward me. "Did I do something wrong?"

"No. Yes. I don't know. I just can't dance with you anymore."

He stared at the floor and shook his head slowly, sighing expressively. "It's Mary again, isn't it?"

"Go home, Paolo."

He sighed out his exasperation. "Will there ever come a time when she won't be standing between us?"

"Just go home. Please."

"All right, if that's what you really want."

"It is."

"I'll meet you here in the morning. Say, eight?"

I opened the door and stood next to it. "Fine. See you then."

He put on his hat and walked through the door. He took a step toward the stairs, then turned to face me. "I saved your life by not telling you who it was."

I stiffened. "You think so?"

"I know so. You forget, I knew her too, and you and I both know she wouldn't have wanted you to die trying to avenge her. She cared too much about you to have wanted that."

He had tears in his eyes, which put a lump in my throat that I couldn't swallow.

"You don't have a monopoly on pain, Cassandra. I mourned her passing every bit as much as you did. If I could have died in her place I would have, if for no other reason than I knew what she meant to you." He took a deep breath, and walked down the stairs.

Chapter Seventeen

I stood in the hall as Paolo descended the stairs, and then I turned to the window in the hall opposite them, saw him leave the building and flag down a cab. Just as the car pulled away, I watched him turn around in the seat to look back toward my building. I touched the cold windowpane with my fingers as the hack carried him away from me.

As I paused there trying to rebuild the disassembled parts of myself, I caught sight of something, a tiny speck of glowing orange, like the cherry fire at the tip of a cigarette. Someone stood across the street under the shoe store's awning, and that someone was looking up at me, or at least at my building. "Damned Feds." Slamming my door felt like an appropriate thing to do, but that would earn me another tongue lashing from Mama Jose, and I needed that like I needed a hole drilled in my face.

Paolo's scent lingered in my room. When I closed my eyes, I found it easy to imagine he still stood there in front of me. Of course, when I reached my hand toward his body, I found only his absence. I undressed, sat on my bed and took the little shoebox out of my trunk. I opened it and sifted through the memories it held, most of which were photographs. I picked up the one of Paolo and me at Coney Island. Then the one of us on the Ferris wheel at the State Fair. I went through them slowly, remembering, smiling, weeping.

That cardboard box held more pain for me than I can explain, and when I found the lock of Mary's hair, I clutched it to my breast and rocked back and forth, a study in misery. She'd had the most beautiful blonde hair, golden as a sunrise in Heaven. All that remained of it, all that remained of her, could fit in my clenched fist. I squeezed that lock and wept for her until sleep stole my sorrow.

The howling blast of a black-and-white's warbler tore me out of slumberland. I sat up in the dark and listened to the sound drift away. My wristwatch claimed the sun would be rising soon, so I forced myself to stand up. Photographs littered the floor, so I had to pick them up and put them back in their shoebox. I pressed Mary's hair to my lips for a moment, then put it in the box as well. I scrounged up my robe and covered my nakedness before opening my door. Before continuing to the shower, I took a peek through the window. Sure enough, my tail still stood under the shoe store's striped awning. "Damned Feds." I stomped toward the bathroom for my morning rituals, then returned to my room, dressed, and opened the shades. The sun had cleared the building across the street and stared me straight in the face. I turned my back on it and smoked cigarettes until Paolo knocked on the door.

When I opened the door, he offered me a broad smile. "Good morning, Kissy."

I didn't beat around the bush. "Someone is spying on me."

"What?"

I spat smoke at him. "Are you deaf? I said someone is spying on me."

"Show me."

I took him to the window and pointed to the man under the awning, who spoke briefly to another man and walked away. The new fellow opened a newspaper and tried to look unobtrusive. I'd seen him before, at the auction. "Must be shift-change."

Paolo squinted at the man, then frowned. "I think I know that guy."

My eyebrows took flight. "He's one of yours? A cop?"

He shook his head. "No, FBI. I worked with him on a case back in '39."

"A damned Fed. I thought so."

"He's not a bad guy, Kissy. He's just doing his job."

"Fine. Go down there and tell him to leave me alone." I murdered my used cigarette in the ashtray. "Tell him I don't like being spied on.”

“I’ve got a better idea.” He put on his ‘mischievous’ grin. “Follow me.”

I snatched my jacket and plummeted down the stairs behind him. On the first floor, he turned away from the front door and careened down the hallway toward the rear of the building. I rarely saw anybody except Mama Jose use the back door, and he had to stop long enough to fumble open the locks. Mama Jose stuck her face out of her room.

“Hey! What are you a-doin’ there!”

I tossed her a crooked grin. “Police business, Mama.”

“Police?” Confusion clouded her myopic eyes.

Paolo finally got the door unlocked and we tumbled through it into the filthy alley beyond. He took off again, and surprised me by laughing like a loon. “This’ll be great, Cassy!”

He flashed a smile so boyishly sincere that I didn’t even cuss him for using the wrong name. We went down a block, made a right turn, another block, another right turn, and both again so that we were creeping up behind Lou’s Diner on the corner. The shoe store stood next to that and, in front of the shoe store, the Fed who’d attached himself to me lingered.

Paolo sketched out his plan, simple and direct, then stepped around the corner. I peeked around it to see the show. He put his hands in his pockets and assumed a slow stroll, seemingly not in a hurry at all. The Fed pretended to ignore him and stared the ink off his newspaper.

“Tanner? Is that you?”

The Fed’s head snapped up and his mouth hung open for a second. “Uh, yeah.”

Paolo smiled and stuck out his hand. “I thought that was you. Don’t you remember me? We worked the Rutherford racketeering case a few years back.”

A slow smile spread across Tanner’s face. “Oh okay, of course I remember you, Belvedere. How have you been?”

“I’m doing well, yourself?” Paolo had maneuvered Tanner so that his back faced me and I crept up on cat-feet behind him, lighting a smoke as I went.

Tanner folded his newspaper as he spoke. “Good, things are good.” He stuffed the paper in a jacket pocket. “I never really got to thank you for helping me out back then. I was pretty banged up and I just, well, there's no excuse for being rude."

Paolo waved that away. "No problem. I was just gonna grab some breakfast, why don't you join me? We can reminisce about the good old days and get caught up? What do ya say?" He clapped a friendly hand on Tanner's shoulder.

Tanner smiled but shook his head. "I wish I could, Belvedere, but I'm working right now." He cleared his throat and shuffled his feet nervously.

Paolo contorted his face into a mask of surprise, a little overdone but Tanner didn't seem to notice. "Oh, really? What are you doing?"

Before Tanner could answer, I spat a jet of tobacco smoke over his shoulder. "He's spying on me."

Tanner spun around, his mouth falling open again. He stared at me for a few seconds, long enough to endure another blast of my cigarette, then looked to Paolo who just grinned like a jack-o-lantern. Tanner frowned and hissed out a long, exasperated sigh. "Dammit, Belvedere, you blew my cover!"

Paolo laughed in his face. "Actually, I didn't. Standing on the street all by yourself is maybe a bit conspicuous, especially when one of your men does it all night. Doesn't the FBI have a car you could sit in? Kissy figured you out all on her own."

I pointed my snipe at his face. "What do you want?"

Tanner turned to Paolo. "I could take you both in right now, you know that? For interfering with a federal investigation."

Paolo didn't flinch. "Really? How interesting. I'm sure the DA or police commissioner would love to know that a bunch of FBI agents are running roughshod through Cincinnati. It's customary to inform the locals if you're working a gig on their turf, just so nobody accidentally mistakes you for Al Capone. Be a shame if one of your guys got themselves plugged by a cop, wouldn't it? I wasn't told about you guys playing in our sandbox. Why would that be?"

Tanner sighed again, looking at his shoes for a moment. "You know what? Breakfast does sound pretty good right now. Does your offer still apply?"

Paolo shot me a glance, then nodded. "Yeah. Sounds like

a great idea."

Tanner took a step toward Lou's, but I stopped him by flicking my expired smoke at him. "Not there. You might not survive the food in that joint." We found a diner a block or two away and took a seat in an abandoned corner. We placed our order and Paolo got right down to business.

"Spill it, Tanner. Why are you following my friend here?"

Tanner looked at each of us for a minute before he spoke. "Look, Belvedere, I just do what I'm told. My superiors say, 'Follow that woman,' so I follow that woman."

I leaned toward him. "Fine; why did they tell you to follow me? I saw you at the auction. I know you've been after me at least since then."

He nodded. "I wasn't there to watch you, but I did see you there. We decided then, at the auction, you were someone we wanted to know more about."

Paolo frowned. "Who were you there to watch?"

Tanner held his tongue, so I answered for him. "Gottlieb. Or maybe Braun."

"It's interesting that you know those men, Miss Lisbon." Tanner grinned.

The waitress brought our coffee and I sipped mine before answering him. "It's not a crime to talk to someone in a public place. Is it?"

"It depends on whether the people you're speaking to are Nazi spies or not. We are, after all, at war. Certain unpleasant things happen during war."

Paolo dumped sugar into his coffee. "Things like murder?"

"Yes, undoubtedly."

"I've had two corpses pop up in my town within the last few days. One in Mt. Washington, and one downtown. I think you guys know something about both of them."

Tanner frowned. "I haven't heard about the one downtown. Who was it?"

Paolo whispered the name. "John Martingdale."

"Oh, wow." Tanner sat back and his eyes glazed over a bit. "That's ... interesting."

I mashed out my cigarette. "Why is that interesting?"

Tanner remained silent so long that Paolo began to lose patience. "Look, Tanner. You know me, I'm on your side. We need to work together on this, you need to trust me."

His eyes moved from Paolo to me. "I owe you a lot, Belvedere, and I'm willing to trust you, but I need to know more about your friend. You help me clear up her part in this mess, and I'll help you as much as I can. Deal?"

Paolo leaned his head to me. "Kissy? What do you say?"

"Go ahead, but I'm only answering questions about the case. Nothing personal. I don't like nosy Parkers sticking their snouts into my life."

Paolo looked to Tanner. "Good enough?"

"For now." The food came and he occupied himself with it for a few minutes. His enthusiastic use of the saltshaker rivaled Norman's. "All right, Miss. What is your name?"

"Kissy Lisbon."

"Is that your real name?"

"It's short for Cassandra. The FBI's never heard of nicknames?"

He broke into a grin. "I can neither confirm nor deny that accusation."

"Funny." I turned to Paolo. "Feds are a laugh riot, aren't they?"

"Seems so."

Tanner tucked away his smile and resumed his interrogation. "Who is Eva Weber?"

"Just a name."

"Tell me about it."

I heaved out a mighty sigh and sketched out a rough outline of my night at Shultz's house and how my quick thinking saved me from Braun's bullet. Tanner ignored his food as he listened, his mouth hung open like a baby bird.

"Okay, so why were you at the auction?"

"I found a note in Shultz's pocket with an address and date on it. I thought maybe Kendall was supposed to meet Shultz at that place and time, but it turned out to be the auction. Gottlieb and Braun approached me there, still thinking I was Weber."

Tanner took a bite of his cold eggs. "Did Gottlieb say why

he was there?"

"Yeah, to buy Hirsch's safe."

Tanner's eyebrows rose. "You know about Hirsch?"

"A little. I know he died, and Gottlieb wanted whatever was in the safe."

"Did he say what was in the safe?"

I tossed back the last of my coffee. "Just some paperwork the Bund didn't want to get out."

He shook his head. "You are remarkably well-informed about all of this for someone who blundered into it." He shot me a quick glance. "No offense."

I waved him my non-concern. "Gottlieb said the safe might have the identity of Wulf. He seemed to think that meant something to me. Who's Wulf?"

Tanner threw down his fork. "Unbelievable. That's top-secret information you have there, you could go to Leavenworth for just mentioning it to the wrong person."

Paolo smiled at him. "Sounds like you'd better put her on the payroll, Tanner."

"I'll see what I can do."

I lit a cigarette and sucked in a lungful of tobacco. "So, are you convinced I'm not a Nazi spy?"

He studied me for a moment, then broke into a broad smile. "I'm convinced. I think you've been lucky so far, and I think you still have a lot to tell me, but I don't think you're a Nazi."

"Thank God for small favors." I turned to Paolo. "Do you trust him?"

Paolo seemed to consider it. "I think so. He's always been straight with me. So far, anyway."

I took a long drag as I watched Tanner watch me. "All right, I guess we can tell him."

"Tell me what?"

I blew smoke at him. "You know Martingdale? He was deep in this mess, wasn't he?"

Tanner nodded. "Yeah, as deep as it gets."

"Somebody murdered him but tried to make it look like a suicide. We think it was an inside job."

Tanner looked confused. "What do you mean an inside

job?”

I held his eye for a long moment. “Tell us what you know about Colonel Greene.”

Chapter Eighteen

Tanner finished off his coffee and waved over the waitress for a refill. He waited until she'd moved away from the table to begin. "Colonel Greene. I hardly know where to start. He's a big shot in Army Intelligence. When the war started, the Bund chapters went underground almost overnight. Greene had been collecting information about the Bund for years, correctly predicting that war with Germany was inevitable and that the Bund would be a resource that Germany would exploit against us. President Roosevelt put together a group to deal with domestic espionage and deal with saboteurs and the like. He personally put Greene in charge of that group, and he immediately started tracking down Bund members. The thing is, Greene has no official authority over, or position within, the FBI structure. A week ago, he bulled his way into town and took over the whole shebang."

Paolo's brows knit. "How did he manage that?"

"Avery Brightman, that's how."

"Who?" I looked over at Paolo. "Who's that?"

Tanner heaved a great sigh. "Avery Brightman oversees the local FBI operation. He's a bean-counter that kissed up to enough of the right politicians that he landed himself this sweet little gig. He's smart in his own way, but he's also in desperate need of a backbone. When Green showed up flashing his presidentially appointed credentials, Brightman rolled over and handed Greene the keys to the kingdom." He poured some coffee down his throat and stared at us. "It's war, he says, and during war the ends always justify the means."

I mashed out my smoke. "Does that include murder?"

He nodded. "It seems to. I'm sure Greene would think

so."

"You disagree?" Paolo leaned closer to Tanner, his voice dropping. "You don't like the way he runs the show?"

Tanner shifted in his seat. "I don't trust him. Something strange is going on here. He's got our guys positioned all over the city, but his orders are nonsense. For instance, he has me just standing on the street, watching a building. No car, no hidden position. What he's doing seems to be designed to make sure we're kept out of the way. Then there are the murders. The FBI isn't in the business of murdering citizens of the United States, and while I've never been in the Army, I like to think they aren't either. Hirsch got himself shot. Apparently, so did Shultz. Three enlisted men who served as couriers were found dead just over a week ago. Now you tell me that Martingdale got shot, too. Why were all these men murdered? If they were involved with the Bund and committing seditious activities, we'd want them arrested, not shot. We'd want to interrogate them until we found out who else was working against us. Dead men don't answer many questions. The only conclusion that can be made is that someone wanted to silence them. Why silence them unless you were afraid of what they'd say?"

The waitress cleared away our plates and refilled our coffee mugs. We sat in silence for a long time. Finally, Tanner asked about Martingdale, and Paolo sketched out what we found in Martingdale's office the night before, including our theories about Greene. You could see Tanner's brain twisting in the labyrinth but not finding a way through. He shook his head. "Why kill Martingdale?"

I lit a cigarette and sucked in a lungful of tobacco. "I heard Martingdale mention Greene by name when I was trying to find Shultz's address. He obviously knew him."

Tanner waved that away. "Yeah, they knew each other. Martingdale was on the Army end of the information trail."

"Can you explain that part a little more? I don't quite understand how all of this spy stuff works." Paolo spun a tinkling spoon in his coffee. "Sorry if I seem dense."

"No, it's a murky mess. The contact in the Bund, known as 'Wulf,' would get the skinny on what the Bund was up to, hand it off to Shultz through an unknown intermediary, and

Shultz would deliver it to his 'employer,' Martingdale, who passed it on to Greene through various couriers. Large sums of money then went backwards through the chain, with each fish in the pool getting a bite."

Paolo nodded. "Okay, let's start at the top. Let's go talk to Wulf, maybe he knows something about Greene's business."

I took a long drag on my smoke. "That's not gonna happen."

"Why not?"

I looked between each of them. "Because Hirsch was Wulf, and Hirsch is dead."

Tanner gave me a strange glance, but nodded. "We think so, anyway. The guy at the top of the chain and the guys at the bottom are all dead. That leaves us one link, and we don't know who that person is. I'm not sure if Greene even knows who that guy is, if he does, he's keeping it to himself."

Paolo shot a glance at me. "Shall we tell him about Shultz?" I nodded and he explained about the scar on the ersatz Shultz's cheek and how we doubted that Shultz was really dead. "So, whoever died in Shultz's house, it wasn't Shultz himself."

Tanner ran his fingers through his short, brown hair. "According to Martingdale, 'Shultz' was an assumed name. He told us that when Shultz disappeared."

"When did Shultz disappear?" My coffee had gone cold.

"I'm not sure, a little over two weeks ago. I think."

I nodded. "That fits with what Mrs. Kendall told me about Heloise Kendall and Shultz. Kendall left home around that time. Would that have been about the time Hirsch died as well?"

He closed his eyes and did the math in his head. "Yeah, about the same time. A day later, maybe."

"What happened two weeks ago that set all of this into motion?" Paolo rubbed his forehead with his fingertips. "Something had to have happened to shake up the Bund like that."

"Richter." I puffed out a cloud of smoke.

Tanner's coffee cup clanked onto the tabletop. "Christ! You know about him too?"

I tossed him a grin. "I'm good at what I do. Everyone that

mentions Richter seems to be afraid of him. Wexler said Richter was *active* and had been trained by the Gestapo. I assume that by active he meant that Richter was actively a spy?"

"Exactly."

I spun it all out as I saw it. "Okay, so Hirsch for whatever reason decides to start feeding information about the Bund to the Feds. Maybe Wexler or some other bigwig in the Bund becomes suspicious and calls in Richter, who tries to work out who the informant is. Somehow he decides it must be Hirsch, so he plugs him. The guy working with Hirsch goes into hiding and so does Shultz, which leaves Martingdale as the only guy in the chain who knows all the players. Then he gets bumped off."

Tanner nodded. "Yeah, Martingdale is the problem. It seems unlikely that Richter would have even known he existed, or if he did, why kill him once Hirsch was dead? It's an unnecessary risk to take. The three dead couriers are another problem too, there's no way Richter could have gotten to them. I can't even get their names out of Greene, but he's using their deaths as an excuse to keep a stranglehold on Brightman, and through him, all of us."

"Then there's the attempted cover up." Paolo swallowed the last of his coffee before going on. "Whoever killed Hirsch and Shultz didn't bother to make it look like a suicide. That points to a different murderer. We're also left with the corpse in Shultz's house. If he wasn't Shultz, who was he? Has anyone mentioned a missing person?"

I snapped my fingers. "Yes! Wexler said Richter was missing. He hinted that maybe Heloise Kendall had run off with him."

Paolo turned to Tanner. "Do you have a description of Richter? Did he have a facial scar?"

"I'll get on it, see what I can find out. I'll get a photo if I can. It won't be easy with all of Greene's insane security measures in place. Belvedere, you should know I can't officially offer you anything. At the moment the local FBI office is acting as an extension of Colonel Greene's Army Intelligence unit. There are a few of us that smell a rat, but we can't really do much to help you, not with Greene calling the shots." He turned his face to me. "Miss, if I were you, I'd check into a nice hotel and stay there until all this blows over. Better yet, go visit some relatives in Minnesota or something."

I crushed my cigarette in the ashtray. "I'm not that kind of girl, Tanner. I believe your Colonel Greene shot a friend of mine, and until I find out otherwise, he's the one I'm going after."

Tanner sighed, but nodded. "It's your funeral. But get out of the flophouse. Greene has us watching it, and he knows by now you didn't end up in the nuthatch last night. You're probably both on the list, and he'll have you brought in for questioning. Don't believe you'll be allowed a lawyer or telephone call; the usual rules and civil rights have been thrown out the window. Once he has you in custody, you'll stay there until he decides to let you go. It's war, remember?" He turned to Paolo. "I'm only helping you because I owe you one for '39. That, and I don't like having to tap-dance to Greene's tune. The ends don't always justify the means." He stood. "Get what you need and clear out. That goes for both of you. Where can I get ahold of you?"

Paolo jotted down a number on a slip of paper and handed it to Tanner. "This is the number of a friend of mine. He's a retired police officer; you can trust him. Name's Mason. Stephen Mason."

"Right. I'll find out what I can and be in touch. Right now, though, I have a building to babysit." He turned and left the diner.

Paolo threw four singles on the table. "You heard the man, let's get you packed up." We walked back to my building. Tanner stood under the shoe store awning, reading his newspaper and studiously avoided looking at us. We climbed the stairs and I unlocked the door to my room.

"What should I take? Everything?"

"No, just some clothes. And money, if you have any."

I scowled. "What does that mean?"

His eyes roamed around the room. "Uh, nothing."

"I'm doing just fine, thank you very much!" I didn't want to take the trunk, so I pulled my ratty suitcase from under the bed and stuffed my clothes into it. I pulled out the wad of money I kept in a sock. "See?"

His jaw dropped. "Good God, Kissy. If you have all that, why do you stay in this flea trap?"

"I like this flea trap. Mama Jose doesn't pass judgment, as long as you pay the rent."

He didn't have an answer for that, so he crammed his hands into his pockets and watched me finish packing. "Where do you want to go?"

I thought it over. "Have all the cops left the Aristocrat?"

"Yeah, I think they cleared out not long after we left."

"Let's go there. They won't be expecting that."

He chuckled. "You must like living dangerously."

"I'll drive." I latched my suitcase closed. "You get to carry my luggage."

"As madame says. I shall carry her valise." He bowed and picked it up.

I locked the door and we jogged downstairs. Tanner still stood in place with his newspaper open. Paolo placed my suitcase in the trunk and I drove us to the Aristocrat Hotel. He got us a suite under the name of 'Smith,' and we rode the elevator to the top floor. The elevator operator was an elderly gent with a crooked back, not Mikey. I tipped him a quarter.

The room had the same faded-glory feeling as the room Ruger had had. Paolo put my suitcase in one of the two bedrooms, joined me in the sitting-room, then called his friend Mason to let him know to expect a call from Tanner. When he hung up, he put on his hat and gave me one of his patented grins. "I'm gonna run home and grab a few things and then come back here."

I nodded. "I'm going to visit Norman at the hospital. Want me to drop you off on the way?"

He shook his head. "No, you go ahead. I'll take a cab. Say hi to Norman for me, and I'll see you soon." He kissed my cheek and left the room before I could slug him.

Chapter Nineteen

I circled Christ Hospital like a hungry shark, completing two circumnavigations before parking along the street. I didn't see Colonel Greene's white Packard anywhere, so I judged it safe to go on in. I looked up at the tall red brick building as I approached the main entrance. Somewhere within, on one of the ten floors, Norman either clung to life, or had left it behind him.

I stepped into the lobby and scanned the room for cops or Feds, but didn't see any obvious candidates for either. I went to the desk and asked for Norman's room. When the candy-striper directed me to a ward on the sixth floor, I felt a massive rush of relief, as if a mighty boulder had rolled off my shoulders. Norman, poor bullet-pierced Norman, still drew breath.

Thinking the elevators would certainly be watched, if anyone was watching for me, I took the stairs up to the sixth floor. I walked past Norman's room to the end of the hall. I stood there, looking out a window for a few minutes, before I turned around. Nobody seemed to be paying me any undue attention, so I went back to Norman's room and opened the door. The blinds were drawn, which plunged the room into a gray half-light. Norman's eyes remained closed, his chest rose and fell in the rhythm of sleep. He had bottles of fluid suspended from a pole next to his bed. They dripped slowly, trickling down little rubber hoses and through needles into his veins.

"Norman?" I brushed back the hair from his forehead. "Can you hear me?"

I pulled a chair close to his bed and sat beside him. After a few minutes a nurse came into the room and snapped on the overhead light. She tried on a smile. "Hello there, I'm Nurse Myers. Are you a relative?" In the light, Norman's skin held a grayish pallor that I didn't like.

"Uh, not really. Just a friend. How is he?"

She busied herself straightening his covers and looking at the dangling bottles. "Well, we got the bleeding stopped, but he hasn't woken up since he's been here."

"Is that a bad sign?"

The nurse tilted her head back and forth, as if trying to rattle loose a decision. "We'd be happier if he woke up. Don't lose heart though, sweetie, he's made it through the worst of it already."

"So, he won't die?"

The nurse bit her lip. "Well, we'll do whatever we can to make sure he doesn't."

"That's not really an answer. Will he die?"

She put a hand on my shoulder. "The best thing to do is remain positive. I've seen men much worse off than your friend pull through. Ultimately, it's up to the Almighty." She patted my shoulder and left the room.

"Hear that, Norman? She wouldn't say that you're gonna die, so there seems to be some doubt about the subject. Just like you to make a mess of it. I guess you'll have to get better now and try to die properly later." I leaned close to his ear. "Get better, you dolt." I stood, watched him sleep for another minute, then left the room. I headed toward the stairs and had just about made it there when I heard a familiar voice.

"Hey! Weber!"

I turned and saw Braun heading my way with two of the oxen I'd seen at the party on Bremen Street. Braun's mug, never a pretty sight, burned red and twisted itself up into a puss even a gorilla wouldn't like. He jabbed a finger in my direction and rushed toward me. I darted into the stairwell and up to the next floor. I didn't wait to see if I'd been followed, but stepped into the hall. I moved as quickly as I could toward the other wing, searching madly for another set of stairs. I heard cursing behind me and I saw one of Braun's cronies swinging his head back and forth, but he hadn't found me yet. I opened the door to the nearest patient room, stepped in, and closed it behind me.

The old woman sitting up in bed squinted in my direction. "Clementine, is that you?"

I pressed my ear to the door and heard the heavy footfall of a running man, followed by the shrill chastisement of several irate nurses. The words were indistinct, but the tone wasn't, Herr Kraut had not made any friends on the seventh floor.

"Clementine?"

"No, ma'am. I'm not Clementine; my name's Cassandra. I got myself turned around in this great big hospital. Would it be all right if I sat here and visit with you for a while? Just until I catch my breath?"

The old woman smiled broadly, apparently delighted to have a visitor. "Why sure, miss. My name's Margaret O'Malley." She held out one gnarled paw and I shook it. Over the next several minutes Margaret O'Malley regaled me with riveting tales about her appendectomy when she was twelve, her long marriage to Mr. O'Malley, and her recent bout with dyspepsia. I nodded in the right places and made sympathetic noises when I should, and concluded that my visit with her had been appropriately appreciated.

I opened the door and peered down the hall in either direction. No krauts in sight. I thanked Mrs. O'Malley for her time, and she told me to come visit her again. I crossed the floor to the far end of the opposite wing of the hospital and took the stairs to the ground floor. I exited the building and spun around, looking for a landmark. When I got my bearings, I realized my car sat on the other side of the hospital. I lit a cigarette and casually strolled down the sidewalk. I turned the corner and stopped in my tracks. The three of them, Braun and his goons, stood there, eyes wide and jaws slack.

"Howdy, boys."

Braun's face collapsed into a scowl. "Get her!"

I flung my smoke to the sidewalk as I turned to flee. My feet pounded the concrete, followed closely, much too closely, by the heavier tread of the men chasing me. The mouths of people on the sidewalk hung open in great 'O's as I sprinted past them. The men behind me cursed in German and shouted for me to stop. I reached the corner and hurled myself around it. I dared a glance over my shoulder and found that I had gained a bit of a lead on my pursuers.

Ahead of me, a large delivery truck had backed up to the hospital's receiving area. I swung my feet in that direction and found stacks of wooden crates in front of me. As I leapt behind a stack of boxes, I found something interesting: an iron crowbar. Grinning, I picked it up and held it like a baseball bat.

The three of them had stopped running and I could hear a hasty conversation. They split up, and only one came my way. His breathing wheezed stertorously and I had no trouble timing my swing. The crowbar caught him across the ribcage, higher than I'd anticipated, and sent him tumbling to the ground in a gasping heap. He'd managed to hold on to his revolver, which he haphazardly aimed at me, so I swung the crowbar again, crunching into him just above the wrist. The gun dropped to the ground and his arm hung in an unnatural angle. He clutched it to his broken ribs, his mouth working like a catfish.

I dropped the iron and picked up his heater. I spun the chamber: six rounds, .38 caliber. "Thanks." I walked on cat-feet back the way I'd come, hoping the other two had moved on by now. I peeked around the end of the truck and saw Braun standing on the sidewalk with his back to me. In the other direction several pedestrians were animatedly describing my footrace to a couple of beat-cops. *This just gets more fun by the second.*

I turned around, opened the delivery truck's cab, and climbed into it. The keys were in the ignition, so I started it up. I'd never driven a truck like that, but I managed to put it in gear. I misjudged the acceleration and tore away from the hospital like a whipped racehorse. I turned into the street and heard the squealing tires of oncoming traffic. Crates flew out of the back of the truck, smashing open and being crushed by cars desperately trying to stop. I hooted with laughter and gave a long blast of the air-horn.

Braun and his remaining crony watched me pass them, then dashed toward a black Ford. I was a block away when they pulled out behind me. Braun sat behind the steering wheel while the other kraut leaned out of the window. I heard a crack and the mirror on my side of the truck shattered. I hit the accelerator, ground a few gears, and avoided traffic as I turned south onto Sycamore Street. The krauts hung onto me, hammering lead into the truck every few seconds.

The warbling wail of a black-and-white sang from behind Braun's car. The cops were following one of us, or both of us. In the broken remnants of the mirror I saw Braun's gun hand turn to aim his gat at the cop car. The windshield on the black-and-white spidered with cracks and fell back, but didn't entirely stop chasing us.

My truck hurled down the street but somehow I managed to avoid the streetcars, automobiles and pedestrians. The cops finally started shooting at Braun's car and he screeched his wheels as he roared onto a cross-street, his sedan almost tipping in the process. The cops decided to follow their car instead of my truck. I grinned and tried to downshift. Gears slammed together with a metallic crunch. I didn't know if a bullet had hit some vital part of the truck's works, but when I tried to slow down, the brakes screeched like drowning cats and did little else.

Black smoke billowed from the engine compartment, obscuring my view of the street, but not my view of the river, which hurtled toward me. I tried the brakes again, but got no response. People at the edge of the water scrambled out of my way as the truck careened off the end of the landing and crashed with a titanic splash into the river.

Water rushed into the cab as the truck sank. I forced the door open and swam away from it. I dragged myself to the shore where a couple of helpful bystanders helped me to my feet. I still had the kraut's revolver in my hand, but I put it into my jacket pocket before it alarmed anyone.

A freckle-faced boy looked me over. "Are you all right, lady?"

I patted my wet hair. "No, I lost my hat."

An older man looked at the truck with his hands on his hips. "Damnedest thing I ever saw. Lose control of it?"

I laughed at that. "I never really had control of it. The krauts were shooting at me."

The old man's eyes widened. "Krauts?"

I nodded. "Yeah, krauts. Spies. I'm with the FBI. You folks, none of you ever saw me. Understand?"

They all nodded solemnly. "Yes, ma'am."

"Great. Thanks for your cooperation."

I felt a tug on my sleeve and looked down. A dripping wet little girl had my hat in her hand and a smile on her face. I took the hat and seated it, with as much dignity as I could muster, onto the wet mess of my hair. "Thanks."

One of them, the boy I think, called me a cab, which pulled away just before the cops arrived. I told the cabby to take me to the Aristocrat. I had to tip him five dollars before he stopped complaining about the wet seat. I went to my room, took off my dripping clothes, and scalded the Ohio River off my body in the shower.

When I had dressed again, I sat in an easy chair, smoked a cigarette and realized Paolo hadn't shown up. I burrowed through the drawer of the bureau until I found a telephone directory, and dialed Paolo's number. The bell rang twice before someone answered it. "Belvedere residence."

The voice was not Paolo's, so I improvised. "Mr. Belvedere?"

"Yes, who is this?"

"Ah, yes, Mr. Belvedere, this is Maude with Victory Cleaners, your tuxedo is ready to be picked up. The balance owed is $2.15."

"Fine, that's fine. Thank you." The line went dead.

I concluded that someone had Paolo.

Chapter Twenty

I sat on the sofa with a pack of smokes in my hand and an ashtray on the coffee table, but the cigarette between my lips hung there, unlit. My eyes stayed focused across the room on the silent telephone until the sun started to set. "Dammit."

I crossed over to the telephone and dialed Mason's number. The bell buzzed four or five times before he picked up. "Yeah?"

"Mason?"

"Yeah, who is this?"

"My name is Cassandra; we met at the precinct ball a few years ago. I was with Paolo Belvedere."

"Cassy, of course I remember you! What can I do for you?"

"Well, I'm helping Paolo with a case, and I know he called you earlier. Have you heard from him since?"

He paused before continuing. "Not exactly, no."

"What does that mean?" I finally lit my cigarette.

"I could get into trouble for telling you this, but the Feds nabbed Paolo. A friend of mine who's still on the force called to tell me that not an hour ago."

I closed my eyes and spat out an exasperated sigh. "Do you know what they're charging him with?"

"Not really, but I figure it's probably interfering with a federal investigation or something similar. That's what the Feds do when local police officers become annoying."

"That's just great."

I heard a lighter flick on his end of the line. "Cassy, that friend Paolo mentioned called about ten minutes ago. All he said was 'It was Richter.' I hope you know what that means."

"I do. Thanks, Mason."

"You're welcome, Cassy. I'll be here if you want to call again." He sounded eager.

I thanked him again and hung up. I slipped into my jacket and put on my hat. I plopped the kraut's .38 into my jacket pocket and my own Colt into a trouser pocket. The elderly operator still worked the elevator. I had him take me to the ground floor, where a young woman with luxurious golden hair stood behind the lobby desk. I asked if she had a city directory. I found the address I was looking for, and wrote it down.

My car sat waiting at the hospital, exactly as I'd left it. I fired her up and tore across town toward the crumbling mansions of Clifton. Darkness fell as I ascended the hill; the lights of downtown twinkled like yellow stars below. I found the Lafayette Avenue address without too much trouble, but I circled the block a couple of times, just to make sure nobody was watching. Everything looked quiet, so I parked across the street, slipped my hand around the hickory grip of the .38, and approached the house.

I rang the doorbell and readied myself to jab my heater into his ribs. The door swung open and a blonde girl around nine years old stood looking up at me. "Hi. Who are you?"

I tried to hide the gun behind my leg and I stammered through an explanation of my presence. "Uh, hi there. I'm looking for Mr. Wexler."

The girl rolled her piercingly blue eyes at me and bellowed out at the top of her lungs. "Dad! Someone wants to see you!" She looked me up and down. "Why are you dressed like that?"

"It's comfortable."

"You look like a man though."

"Do I?" I managed to slip the revolver into my pocket without her noticing. "I think it's a good look for me."

She frowned. "It's really not."

Dewitt Wexler came down the stairs dressed in a cardigan. He had the stump of a cigar in one hand and his eyebrows rode high on his forehead when he saw me. He put a hand on the girl's shoulder. "Go help your sister with the dishes, Marlene."

Marlene scowled. "It's not my turn!"

"Go. Now."

She pointed at me. "Who is she, Dad?"

"A friend. We have business. Now go."

She waved at me. "Nice meeting you. I bet you could be really pretty if you put on a dress!"

"Uh, thanks." I watched her disappear into the labyrinthine guts of the house.

Wexler directed me into a study, where he sat behind a mammoth antique desk. I closed the door and remained standing, my hand in my jacket pocket. He mashed his cigar out in an overflowing ashtray. "Well, what do you want? Are you here to squeeze more money out of me, Fraulein Weber?" He put a hard emphasis on the name.

"So, you figured me out. I'm not Eva Weber."

"Obviously, since there is no Eva Weber. Now, what do you want?"

"Richter's dead."

He froze. "How do you know?"

"I know. It was his body in Shultz's house."

"If that's true, it's bad news for you. And for me."

"Why?"

He pulled the stopper out of a decanter and poured himself a drink. "Richter came to town with four men, all of them killers. If Richter's dead, they're with Braun, and Braun wants you dead." He swallowed a mouthful of bourbon, then chuckled. "Braun's taken a fairly serious dislike to you."

"I'm good at making friends like that. Richter's men, they're the ones who shot at me the night of the Bund party?"

He nodded. "Braun almost blew his stack when they told him you were a phony. I'd leave town if I were you." He refilled his bourbon. "These men are serious trouble."

"Everybody keeps telling me to clear out of town! What about you? Why aren't you leaving?"

"I am. We're taking a trip. We leave tomorrow, and I'm not sure when we're coming back. Little lady, I want out. Out of the whole mess, and most definitely out of the Bund. I have a family to think about. I'm just an accountant, and I want out. We're going to visit Havana for a while."

"Why? Tell me what the hell is going on."

He leaned back and stared at me. "Who are you, missy? What's your angle? Still looking for that lost puppy?"

That made me smile. "Oh yes, I haven't forgotten her. I have other priorities now. Someone shot my friend, almost killed him. That's a debt I intend to pay. In blood. First things first though. Tell me about your deal with Colonel Greene."

Wexler didn't seem surprised by the name; he just shrugged. "Not a lot to tell. He passed information to us from Washington, we passed it along to the proper people who transmitted it to the Reich. Less trouble with the Feds in Cincinnati than in New York or Washington."

I flopped down into a chair opposite Wexler and tugged at my lip. "So, Greene sold military secrets to the Bund?"

He shook his head. "No. He sold them to the Reich, the Bund just acted as couriers."

"For which you got paid."

"Well, of course I got paid." He gestured around the room with his stubby hand. "The money was good, and the risk was minor because Greene was able to protect us."

"So, Greene got paid too."

Wexler swallowed another slug of bourbon. "Yeah. What I got was chicken feed next to the Colonel's cut."

"Fine, so what went wrong?"

"Hirsch."

"What about Hirsch?"

"He'd been working with the Feds, on the sly, feeding them anything he could about the Bund and anything he heard about what the Reich was up to. Hirsch probably didn't ever know much, but the Feds took everything he said as gospel truth, and they acted on what he told them. They shut down more than one active operation here in the States. I heard he even had a stupid code name." Wexler frowned and shook his head slowly.

"Wulf."

He chuckled. "Was that it? Wulf. German for wolf, right? He wanted to be a wolf in Bund clothing? We became suspicious when the Feds started leaning on us harder than usual, figured we had a rat. That's when Braun called in his buddy Richter.

When he got to town everything fell apart." He poured more whiskey into his glass. "Richter started feeding false information to various people within the group, and when a certain warehouse in Chattanooga got raided by the Feds, by a process of elimination, he knew Hirsch was the rat."

"So, Richter shot Hirsch."

"Yeah."

"All right, who shot Richter?"

Wexler shrugged. "Got me. Maybe Shultz? I can't figure why Richter would be in Shultz's house, unless Shultz was working with Hirsch."

"What was in the safe?"

"The safe? What safe?"

"Hirsch's safe, the one Gottlieb and Braun were bidding on in the auction on Saturday."

He leaned back in his chair, staring at me. "I don't know what you're talking about, little lady."

"Oh, come on. I saw Gottlieb and Braun at an auction in Over-the-Rhine, an auction that was selling off Hirsch's things. Gottlieb said he was there to buy Hirsch's safe."

Wexler blinked at me for a few seconds before tossing back another ounce of bourbon. "First I've heard of it. Makes sense though."

I frowned. "How so?"

"We figured Gottlieb must be up to something when he vouched for you. Now, that could have just been a stupid mistake on his part, but Gottlieb isn't the sort of man to make stupid mistakes. If he was in it with Hirsch, he might believe there was something in Hirsch's safe that would get him killed."

I tugged at my lip again. "Would Colonel Greene want what was in that safe? Could Hirsch have found out about Greene's treachery? Maybe he was trying to bleed him for a payout?"

"Got me. I can tell you that something is gonna happen real soon. Something big. The Reich is smuggling men into the country. Hell, they might already be here." He swallowed more whiskey. "I didn't sign up for that. I want out."

I watched his jowls shake. "Saboteurs? Where are they going?"

Before he could answer I saw his jaw drop and his body tense. The first bullet shattered the whiskey decanter on its way to Wexler's heart. I dove for the floor just as a second round crackled through the air above my head. Wexler sloughed off his chair and onto the floor, his lips wetly red. His mouth moved as he tried to speak. "Trin ... Trinidad Hotel ... Gottlieb ..." His breathing stopped and his eyes glazed over.

Marlene Wexler ran into the room. "Daddy!" I heard a laugh from outside the window and I threw myself at the child. I covered her head with my hand as machine-gun fire tore the room apart. The bookshelves behind Wexler's desk exploded in a blizzard of shredded paper and splintered wood. The barrage seemed to go on forever, but it finally stopped and I heard Braun's voice calling out. "So long, Wexler!" Then I heard screeching tires on the street. I sat up and probed Marlene's body for bullet holes. Finding none, I raced to the window, but the car was too far away for me to note the make, model or license plate. It almost flew down the hill.

Marlene clutched her father's hand, moaning. "Daddy! Daddy, get up!" Her older sister came into the room and also fell to the floor, weeping. When their mother appeared, a willowy redhead, she started screaming and pulling at her hair.

I held the .38 in my hand and climbed out of the room through the shattered window. I paused for a moment, turning to meet Wexler's wife's pleading gaze. "It was Braun. Get your girls out of here before he comes back!" Her slack jaw tightened and she nodded, then herded her children out of the room.

I looked around and saw curious neighbors peeking from behind their blinds and curtains. I dashed to my car and fired up the engine, stomped on the accelerator and sped down the street in the direction they had gone. Cross streets blurred by as I descended the hill toward downtown, but I couldn't find Braun's car. I pounded the steering wheel with a clenched fist. "Damn you, Braun. You've got a lot to answer for."

I stopped at a drug store and bought two packs of cigarettes and a bottle of gut-fire. The clerk watched my hand shake and looked up at me. "Guess you need a drink pretty bad, huh?"

"Guess so." I stopped in the public telephone booth and

opened the directory, found the Trinidad Hotel, and wrote down the address. The clerk tossed me a smirk as I left. I told him what he could do with himself.

I sat in my car, sipping the rye out of the bottle. I thought of Wexler's wife, now a widow, and her two daughters. I thought of Norman, clinging to life in a hospital bed. Then I thought of Paolo, rotting in an FBI holding cell.

I spoke to the bottle. "Gottlieb, you're gonna get a visitor, and I'm gonna get some answers. Otherwise, one of us is gonna die."

Chapter Twenty-One

The Trinidad Hotel turned out to be one of those garish theme motels that cling to the edges of towns like barnacles on a garbage scow. The walls sported pink flamingoes, painted by someone who'd never seen a pink flamingo, and a sickly yellow sunset that peeled off the brick in strips. Despite its down-at-the-heel appearance, the parking lot beside it had very few empty spots. More than one of the cars in the lot rocked like seasick ocean waves.

I parked next to a rusty chain-link fence and stood leaning against the car, smoking a Camel. I pulled out the .38 caliber and spun the chamber, then I slipped the magazine out of my Colt; both full. I snapped it back in and dropped it into my trousers pocket. I held the .38 tightly, watching the streetlights glint up and down its barrel. Even as an instrument of death, you couldn't deny its elegance, its coldly expressive beauty. I slid it into my jacket pocket and started toward the flamingo-clad front door.

A redhead with too much makeup on her leathery face smiled broadly as I approached the desk. "Hello, welcome to the Trinidad. How can I help you?" Her speech held quite a dollop of backwoods Kentucky in it.

"I'm looking for a friend of mine, but he's with a group and I don't know which name he's registered under."

She opened the register and flipped to the current page. "That shouldn't be a problem. What's his name? We'll start looking there."

"Gottlieb."

Her flame-red fingernail traced its way down the page. "No Gottlieb registered. Do you know another member of his party?"

"Yeah, Ruger."

The fingernail slid down the page again. "No, sorry."

I pounded the desktop. "Dammit."

The redhead frowned until I worried that her lipstick would smear her dress. "Do you know another name?"

My brows knit and I tried the only other name I could think of. "Kendall?"

"Hmm, aha! Here we go, Kendall, Heloise."

"Yes! That's her. My friend is her uncle."

"Room two-oh-three. Upstairs." Her lips pulled back in a horsey smile that looked anything but genuine.

"Thanks." I started for the stairs, climbing slowly and listening for any footfalls other than my own. I stopped on the second-floor landing and pressed my ear to the door. I didn't hear anything, so I turned the doorknob and opened the door a crack, just enough to peek through. I watched for a couple of minutes, seeing only the dusty concrete floor and gaudy teal paint flaking off the walls. I pulled the .38 out of my pocket, gripped it tightly and opened the door.

I didn't see anybody, so I trod the concrete on cat-feet until I stood outside the door of room 203. I strained to hear anything in the room, but silence reigned. I knocked on the door, three swift raps. "Who is it?" Ruger's voice.

I sprinkled some Kentucky into my own voice. "This is Charlene from the desk, I have a telegram for Miss Kendall."

"A what?"

"A telegram, sir."

I heard him cursing as he approached the door. I held the .38 up and watched for the doorknob to turn. When it did, I shoved the door inward with my shoulder. It crunched into Ruger's face, knocking him to the floor. He looked up at me, dazed and bleeding from his lips and nose. I saw his eyes drift away from me and onto something behind me. I spun around just in time for Heloise Kendall, the woman I'd been searching all over creation to find, to take a swing at me with a wooden stool. I managed to duck it, but I dropped the gun.

She lunged at me, tackling me to the floor. She pounded her fists onto my face as if she were kneading dough. I walloped her twice across the chops with my knuckles and the fight went out of her. I rolled out from underneath, scrambled to my feet, and aimed a kick into her guts. She grunted and didn't move.

Ruger had gotten to his feet and bent to pick up my revolver. I slammed my knee into his face, and he fell to the floor. I snatched up the .38 to cover them both, but they weren't moving. I checked the bedroom, bathroom and the kitchenette, but didn't find Gottlieb. I dragged Kendall across the room and dumped her into an easy chair. I sat on the bed, with Ruger's motionless form on the floor between us. I fished out a cigarette and stuck it between my swelling lips. Kendall's eyes opened as I lit my smoke. "Who are you?"

"That doesn't matter. I know who you are, Miss Kendall."

Her eyes widened. "What do you want?"

That made me laugh. "Well, at first I only wanted to find you. Now, things are complicated, and, darn it, I just hate when things are complicated." I pointed my revolver at her. "So, here's what's gonna happen, I'm gonna ask you questions, and you're gonna tell me the truth. Got it, sweetheart?"

She stared at the gun for a minute, then tossed me an angry scowl. "Go to hell."

I chuckled. "Your poor wrinkled mother would be horrified to hear that kind of language come out of your mouth. She'd sniff and thump her purse in her lap."

Her mouth hung open. "You know my mother?"

"Yeah." I probed at the nascent shiner under each of my eyes. "She paid me to find you, to stop you from marrying Shultz." I pointed to Ruger with the barrel of the gun. "I guess this is Shultz?"

"There is no Shultz. That was just a name Joe used with our boss."

I nodded. "So I've heard. Ruger carted messages from Hirsch to Martingdale, right? Gottlieb arranged it all, and everybody got a fat payday from the Feds? That sound about right?"

She crossed her arms over her chest and remained silent.

"You don't have to confirm it; I don't care. Helping the Feds root out Nazi spies during wartime sounds as patriotic as hell, but it doesn't add up. Gottlieb wanted Hirsch's safe, and he was at the auction with Braun. That tells me that Braun knew about the safe too, and he also wanted what was in it. Braun called in Richter to kill Hirsch, then Richter ends up dead. Want to know what I think? I think Gottlieb and Braun were working together, and they had Richter kill Hirsch, then they bumped off Richter so they could split what was in that safe. So, that means the paper in the safe was the spendable kind. Cash. I think there must have been a boatload of it. How close am I?"

Kendall smirked. "Close."

"I thought so. How is Gottlieb in it with Greene?"

"Who?" Her brow furrowed. "Who's Greene?"

I blew smoke out of my nostrils. "He's Army, but now he's running all the Feds in town too. He's deep in this mess, but he's cleaning things up fast. Wexler's dead. So's Martingdale."

She pressed her hands to her mouth. "You're lying! Tell me you're lying!"

I shook my head. "Sorry pumpkin, but I'm not lying."

She covered her ears with both hands. "My God, no! John was such a good man!"

"I would almost believe that, except that he had his finger in the pie, too. He got his cut from the Feds. Or was it the Army? Maybe both?" I nudged Ruger with my foot. "Either way, he got his final payment in lead. Your boyfriend here could be next."

She started. "What do you mean?"

I mashed out my smoke in the ashtray on the nightstand. "Look, Gottlieb will use Ruger for a scapegoat, or install some new ventilation in his ribcage. Either way, you and he won't be sipping martinis in Miami when this is all over."

"Joe is Gottlieb's nephew! He wouldn't do that to family!"

I chuckled. "I wouldn't put it past him, but let's suppose for a minute you're right. You'd still have to deal with Braun. Do you think he'd shy away from plugging your precious Joe? I just saw Braun cut down Dewitt Wexler with a Tommy gun, right in front of his daughter. He'd drill you both and then order ice cream from room service."

She bit her knuckle and drew her knees to her chest. In that pose, she lost a decade and looked almost as young as

Marlene Wexler. "What should I do?"

"That depends." I winced as I poked at my swollen lower lip. "Is the money here?"

"Why does that matter?" Her eyes narrowed as she watched me.

"Because if you don't have the money, they won't be able to kill you. They'll suspect that you know where it is, and that'll keep you alive. That might be the only thing that keeps breath in your lungs, pumpkin."

She sat up straighter. "What if we do have the money?"

"They'll kill you both, split the money and take a powder."

She chewed her lip as she mulled that over.

"Look, Heloise, your boyfriend is gonna wake up pretty soon, so you need to make a decision right now. Give me the money and live, or keep it and get shot by Braun. Choice is yours."

Kendall popped up off the chair and went around to the far side of the bed, dropping to her knees. I stood as she moved, keeping my revolver aimed at the floor. She pulled a Gladstone bag from under the bed and heaved it onto the comforter. "Here, this is all of it." She opened the bag and rooted through its contents.

I put a hand on her shoulder. "You did the right thing, Heloise. If I were you, I'd go on home. Take your mother to visit some distant relatives for a while." I stared at the bag, which bulged with greenbacks. I exhaled slowly, then reached out my hand to take it.

She yanked her hand out of the bag and pointed a little .32 caliber revolver at me. "You must think I'm stupid!" She sneered and stepped closer to me until the barrel of her gun almost touched my ribs. "You're not taking the money. You're wrong about Gottlieb, too. He'd never turn on us."

I threw her a crooked smile. "Maybe you're right." I took a step toward her and pressed the barrel of her gun into a spot between my breasts. My heart thumped, only a few inches away from the bullet in the .32's chamber. "So, now what? Are you gonna pull the trigger? Put a hole in my chest and watch me bleed out on the floor of your hotel room? They have your name in the register at the desk. The police will certainly find that information useful when looking for the cold-blooded killer who murdered me."

She jabbed me with the barrel. "Shut up!"

I shook my head slowly. "You asked me if I thought you were stupid. Right now, I'd have to say yes, I think you're an empty-headed little twit." I stepped closer and she retreated a pace. "I'm trying to save your worthless Nazi hide, but you're complicating things. Like I said before, I really hate complications." I moved forward again, and she stepped away from me until her back found the wall.

She poked me with the heater again. "Stay back!" Her voice quavered almost as much as her chin.

"No. Either pull the trigger or drop the gun." She stared at me, eyes wide and wet, but held the gun in place.

"Let me help you, Heloise." I put my hand over hers and thumbed back the hammer. "You need to cock it before it'll fire. There you go. Now you can murder me." I watched her eyes, icy blue eyes, but found no killer in them.

I felt her tremble through the barrel of the gun, and I reached out and took it away from her. She didn't resist. I uncocked the hammer, swung open the cylinder and emptied the bullets onto the floor. I snapped it closed and held it in my hand. "When will Gottlieb be back?"

Her chin quivered. "An hour, maybe two."

"Fine, I'll call him then. I need to talk to him, and I'm sure he'll want to talk to me. One more thing; thank you for not killing me, Heloise." I swung the gun at her face then, as hard as I could, and she fell onto the bed and didn't move. I looked down at her and shook my head. "Twit."

I heaved the bag across the room and out the door. I hurried down the stairs, through the lobby and out of the hotel. I staggered to my car, wrangled the bag into the passenger seat, and fired up the engine. I drove slowly across town, as I certainly didn't want to get pulled over with a bag of cash in the car.

I parked outside the Aristocrat and tried to look nonchalant as I headed towards the elevator. Mikey smiled as I stepped inside. "Top floor, Mikey." I dropped the bag on the floor as we rose.

Mikey looked up at me. "How is your friend? The one who was shot?"

"He's holding his own. Thanks for asking."

"I hope he heals up soon. He had a nice laugh; I'd like to hear it again." He was silent for a minute before he spoke again. "Are you here to see Mr. Ruger, ma'am?"

"No, I have a room." I looked down at him. "Anyway, Ruger checked out."

"Yes, ma'am, he did, but his uncle seems to be staying on the fourth floor. I took him down not twenty minutes ago. I thought perhaps you still had business with Mr. Ruger or his uncle."

I chewed my lip for a moment. "No, my business with either of them is almost finished. I'll be checking out first thing in the morning. Could you arrange to have a bellboy fetch my bags at around 7:00?"

He nodded. "Of course. I'm sorry you're leaving, ma'am."

"You're a sweetheart, Mikey." I tipped him a buck. "Do me a favor, don't mention to Ruger's uncle that I'm staying here. It might hamper my business with him."

Mikey nodded, a tiny, knowing grin on his face. "Certainly ma'am. Anything you want." He gave me a wink as he sank down the elevator shaft.

I dragged the bag down the hall, unlocked my room door, and shoved the Gladstone inside. Once I'd locked the door, I spat out a luxurious sigh and threw myself into a chair. I smoked two Camels before I finally opened the bag. The folding green inside it came in thousand-dollar bundles. I stacked them up as I counted. Ten thousand, twenty-thousand, thirty-thousand, forty-thousand, fifty-thousand. It didn't stop there; the piles grew until the count made it to five hundred thousand. "Half a million dollars. Half a million dollars." The butterflies in my stomach took flight every time I said the number. "Half a million dollars."

I counted each bundle again as I put it back into the Gladstone. Then I tallied the dead. "Three Army couriers, Hirsch, Richter, Martingdale and Wexler. Seven dead men. How many more murders will this bag of money buy?"

Chapter Twenty-Two

The sun had risen, peaked, and started looking for someplace soft to land before I got out of bed. I felt like someone had beaten me with a sackful of bricks, but I consoled myself by counting the little bundles of green paper a few times. I had just stashed the money in the bedroom closet when the door to the suite opened. I snatched the .38 off the nightstand and cocked the hammer. Two thumps sounded, and then I could hear footsteps coming toward me. Someone had gotten into the suite.

"Kissy?" Paolo's voice.

I exhaled a breath I didn't know I was holding and uncocked the revolver's hammer. "Paolo. You scared me half to death." I stood up just as he opened the bedroom door. He saw the gun and took a step back.

"How about putting the gun down, Kissy? I'm on your side."

I slipped it into my jacket pocket and carried the jacket with me into the sitting room. "How are you here? Mason said you'd been nabbed."

He nodded. "Yeah, I was. By Tanner. He needed to talk to me. What happened to your face?"

"I ran into a door."

"A door?"

"We'll talk about it later. You weren't arrested?"

He chuckled. "Not really. Just brought in for 'questioning,' but Tanner did more answering than asking. He finally got some information out of the Bureau. He had to go above Director Brightman's head, but he has a friend in

Washington that gave him some answers.”

“Let me guess … we’ve had it all wrong?”

He sighed. “I wish we did, but we got most of it right. Except the part about Greene.”

“What about Greene?” I leaned forward and snuffed out my smoke in the overflowing ashtray on the coffee table.

Paolo took off his jacket and loosed his tie. “Greene’s job involved feeding false information to the Nazis through the Bund. He’d pass on wildly inaccurate troop numbers, manufacturing capability and other such info through Martingdale to the Bund, and through them to Germany.”

I sighed. “We already knew who was in the chain.”

“I know, but we thought Greene was a traitor. He really isn’t. Neither was Martingdale; they both worked for Army Intelligence.”

“Fine. What went wrong?”

He shook his head. “Do you know what an oxymoron is?”

I sat back in my chair and gave him a cold stare. “Yes. I’m not completely brainless.”

He held up his hands in surrender. “Well, ‘Army Intelligence’ might just be the most moronic of all oxymorons. They classified the entire mess ‘Top Secret’ and left the Feds out of the loop. But for some reason, Hirsch had an attack of guilt and spilled what he knew about the exchange of information between the Army and the Bund to the Bureau, and they thought the same thing we did: that Greene was a traitor.”

That made me laugh. “Typical governmental efficiency. Nobody ever connects the dots.”

“Things started to break down about three weeks ago when Richter came to town. He found the leak and plugged it up with a bullet. Only after Hirsch got shot did the Army and the Feds have a sit-down. That’s why Brightman gave the Colonel free reign.”

“All right, but Tanner said Greene’s got Feds running all over town doing a whole lot of nothing.”

Paolo nodded. “Yeah, he’s still trying to convince the Bund he’s working with them.”

“Think it’ll work?”

He shrugged. “It might, but I doubt it.”

I pulled another Camel out of the pack. "Why don't they just arrest all the guys in the Bund and get it over with?"

"Because they're desperate to find some sort of list."

"List?"

"Yeah, a bunch of names on a list."

"Whose names?"

He rubbed his eyes. "Tanner's friend didn't know, and Greene's not gonna tell us. This is all such a mess. I'm absolutely lost."

I huffed out a lungful of smoke. "I'm not. I think I know whose names are on that list." I filled him in on my trip to Wexler's house and about the German saboteurs making their way to America.

Paolo started pacing around the room. "Saboteurs? Here in Cincinnati?"

"No." I shook my head. "Wexler just said they were coming to America."

"Did he say how?"

I hissed out a deep breath. "Braun perforated him before I got the whole story, but the saboteurs' names must be on the list. Do we know who has the list?"

"We know Hirsch had it at one point, but we don't know who has it now."

The cogs in my brain spun and I almost heard them click. "Hirsch had the list when he died?"

"Yeah, as far as we know. He died before he could pass it to the Feds."

"Where would someone keep something that valuable?"

Paolo threw up his hands. "I don't know. In a bank vault? Maybe a safe." His pacing halted and he turned to look at me. "The list was in Hirsch's safe!"

"Yeah." I mashed out my snipe. "And Braun and Gottlieb bought the safe, so they had the list."

"What do you mean 'had'? Wouldn't they still have it?"

"I don't think so. I know Gottlieb has suddenly come into a great deal of money. I think he and Braun sold the list to somebody and split the money between them."

Paolo frowned. "Who'd want to buy the list? It's only valuable to Greene, and he hasn't found it yet."

"I know who we can ask."

"Do tell." He tilted his head and gave me a funny look.

"Gottlieb."

He laughed. "You had me going, Kissy."

"I'm serious."

"Why would Gottlieb talk to you?"

"Because I have his money."

Paolo's jaw swung open and he stared, speechless.

"Better shut your jaws before flies start breeding on your tongue." I pointed to my battered face. "Remember that door I told you about?"

He nodded.

"It's named Heloise Kendall." I sketched out the salient points of my visit to the Trinidad Hotel and my confrontation with the woman I was paid to find.

He just stared at me as I spun out the story, and I stared right back, sinking into the warm, familiar depths of his painfully blue eyes. When I finished, he offered me a wry smile. "It's nothing short of a miracle that you haven't been killed. I leave you alone for a few hours and you get shot at, beat up and steal a fortune."

"I also crashed a truck into the Ohio River."

"What!"

"Never mind. The bag of sawbucks is what matters."

He scratched his head. "How much did you get?"

"Three hundred thousand." I didn't even blink as I lied to him.

He whistled. "That's a lot of money."

"Yeah, and I'd bet every cent of it that Gottlieb wants it back. He'll talk to me."

"All right. We need to know who bought the list, make sure he tells you that."

I sat at the desk and pulled the telephone close to me. I took a deep breath and made the call. The bell only rang once before someone answered.

"Ja?"

"Gottlieb? It's me."

"Fräulein Lisbon. You are quite a thorn in my side. You haff my money. I vant it back."

"I know you do. I'll give it back to you. First things first though. I know you had a list, the one you found in Hirsch's safe. A list of Nazi saboteurs sent to America."

A long pause. "Ja. The list vas in the safe. You are a remarkably vell informed young lady, Fräulein."

"Who did you sell it to?"

"Vhy does that matter?"

"Was it Colonel Greene?"

Another pause, followed by a long sigh. "No, fräulein, it vas John Martingdale."

"Martingdale?" I looked up at Paolo's frowning face. "Gottlieb, Martingdale is dead."

I heard a quick intake of breath on his end of the line. "Truly so, Fräulein?"

"Yeah. He came down with a bad case of murder. Shot in the head."

"Mein Gott. That vas not supposed to happen. He vas a good man. A good friend."

"Why did Martingdale want the list? Did he tell you?"

"Nein. I had only haff of the list. Herr Braun has the other haff."

"Martingdale didn't buy Braun's half of the list?"

"Nein. That vas supposed to happen tonight."

"Where?"

"Vhy vould that matter now? Martingdale is dead, ja?"

"Yeah, but whoever shot him probably did it to get the list. That means they'll still want Braun's half of it too. I'm betting he'll Shanghai Braun like he did Martingdale, so he'll keep Martingdale's appointment with Braun."

"Vhat is your interest in the buyer, fräulein? Vhy do you care?"

"Maybe I'm just a patriot, Gottlieb."

I heard him snort out a laugh. "Yes, perhaps you are, but I think that is not the reason."

"No, it's not." I tightened my grip on the receiver until I could hear its parts squeaking in protest. "Someone shot my friend in the guts. He's barely alive, and I think the bum that shot him is the same bum that shot Martingdale. I mean to fit him for a Chicago overcoat and plant him in a cow pasture.

That's my interest in your buyer, Gottlieb."

Gottlieb cleared his throat. "Fräulein, you are a woman of a quality I hadn't imagined." I could hear the smile in his voice. "You fascinate me."

"I'm flattered. Now, where is Braun meeting the buyer?" I scribbled an address on a notepad. "Yeah, I got it. Eleven o'clock tonight." I wrote the words 'Elsinore Tower' on the notepad as Paolo looked over my shoulder.

"Now, Fräulein, vhat about my money?"

"Give me an hour to stash it in a place where you can pick it up. I'll call you when I've got it ready to be picked up."

"You are a cautious one, ja?"

"People have a tendency to die around you Bund types."

He laughed. "Truly so, but I haff left the Bund. I vill take my money und retire."

"I'll call you in an hour." I hung up the phone and took a deep breath. "How'd I do?"

Paolo grinned. "You did fine. You'd make an excellent cop."

I gave him a dirty look. "Hey, don't be insulting, copper."

He tore the address off the notepad. "Okay, I need to make some arrangements. I'll need to have someone waiting to pick Gottlieb up when he tries to get the money. We'll also want as many guys around Elsinore Tower as we can manage to hide. Cincinnati Police will pick up Braun and his buyer." He almost bounced around the room as he spoke.

I snagged a cigarette out of the pack and lit it. "So, just like that, you're a cop again?"

He gave me a look that I couldn't decipher. "Kissy, I never stopped being a cop." He put his hand on my shoulder. "Can't you understand that? It's what I am."

I shrugged his hand away from me. "Go on then. Be a cop. Just like you've always done."

"Cassandra. Please, I don't want ..."

"Just go, Paolo." I didn't look at him. "I'll tell Gottlieb to pick up the money at the Union Terminal luggage claim office. I assume you can do the rest?"

He spoke softly. "Yes."

"Good. Now get the hell out of here."

"I'll need to take the money. It's evidence."

"It's in the bedroom closet. Take it and go." I wrapped my arms around my knees and watched him fetch the Gladstone bag.

He opened the door, but paused before he left the suite. "I want you to know, I still feel the same about you now as I did back then. Nothing has changed."

I looked up at him and huffed a jet of smoke in his direction. "I don't care."

He winced. "Goodbye, Cassandra."

I didn't say anything, and he eventually pulled the door shut behind him. I stood up and pulled on my jacket, padded over to the window and looked down on the street below. I saw him flag down a cab and ride around the corner and out of sight. I touched the glass with my fingertips, covering the spot where I'd last seen him. "Goodbye Paolo."

I'd call Gottlieb like I said I would, but after that I had a long night planned. Paolo and his cronies would spend that long night hiding in the bushes around Elsinore Tower, but I'd be meeting Braun's buyer all the way across town, at the Fritz Brothers' Trucking Company down by the river.

Chapter Twenty-Three

I seated my hat carefully on my head and looked at myself in the mirror. The bruises on my face had blossomed into a riot of black and blue blotches. I frowned at my reflection. "At least you'll make the undertaker earn his money, Kissy old girl." I stepped into the sitting room and dropped the .38 into one jacket pocket, and the .22 Colt into the other one. My pockets bulged a little, but not so much that anybody would notice unless they were specifically looking for bulging pockets.

I left the room and locked the door behind me. On the off chance that I lived through the night, I figured I'd want to find my things where I'd left them. I rang for the elevator, which clattered its way up the shaft. Mikey opened the gate and threw me a polite smile. "Good evening, Miss Lisbon."

"Hello, Mikey."

We fell past a floor or two before I had the nerve to ask him for the favor I needed. "I was wondering if you could help me out, Mikey."

"Of course, Miss Lisbon."

"We're friends now, you can call me Kissy."

He smiled up at me. "All right. What can I do for you, Miss Kissy?"

I handed him a note with the Fritz Brothers' Trucking Company address written on it. "Remember the fella I was with earlier?"

He nodded. "Tall guy, curly blond hair. Moved like a cop."

"You really don't miss much, do you? He's a cop; his name is Belvedere. In a few hours he's gonna come here looking for me, and I think he's gonna be in a bad mood when he does.

Just give him that note and tell him that, one way or another, he'll find me at that address tonight." I took a deep, ragged breath, and exhaled slowly, just glad to have finally gotten all the words out.

He studied the note for a few seconds. "I have to ask. Are you in some kind of trouble, Miss Kissy?"

"Oh yeah." I grinned. "You have no idea how much trouble I'm in. Just give that note to Belvedere when he gets here."

"How do you know he'll come looking for you?"

"He's a cop, methodical and completely predictable. He'll be here, believe me."

Mikey slipped the paper into his pocket. "I'll make sure he gets it." The elevator landed in the lobby, and Mikey stuck out his hand. "Good luck, Miss Kissy."

"Thanks." I shook his hand, then crossed the lobby on rubber legs. I piled into my car and pulled the rye bottle out of the glove box and took a mighty tug on it. Once the fire in my guts got to roaring about right, I turned the key and the engine shuddered itself awake. I took another bite of whiskey before shutting the bottle back up in the glove box and pulling away from the curb.

I made it halfway to Christ Hospital before the skies opened and dropped a deluge on the city. The fat raindrops hit the windshield hard, making a crackling sound. Within a few minutes I felt like I sat behind the wheel of a tugboat instead of an automobile. The splashing river of water on the street reminded me of the flood that drowned Cincinnati five years earlier, in 1937. Those memories always led to Mary though, so I did what I always did when bad memories surfaced: I lit a cigarette.

I parked as close as I could get to the hospital's front door, but I still felt liked a drowned rat before I found a roof to hide under. I pressed through the doors and a candy-striper, a little wisp of a redhead, started to tell me that visiting hours were over. Then she saw my face, and gave me directions to the emergency room. I squelched my way down the hall wondering if I really looked that bad. The redhead seemed to think so.

This time, I took the elevator to the sixth floor and passed the nurses' station on my way to Norman's room. They didn't stop me, but I could hear them whispering behind me. I spun around to face them, but instead of saying anything I just smiled and mashed out my smoke in a sand-filled ashtray, then strode down the hall into Norman's room.

A tiny lamp on the windowsill struggled to illuminate the space. I pulled up a chair and sat next to Norman, who didn't move or open his eyes. I wondered if he could. I took his hand, which felt cool to the touch.

"Norman, I don't know if you can hear me or not, but I came here to say a few things." I looked at his face, but nothing in it had changed. "I'm going to get the guy that shot you. I got a hunch who it was, and I'm pretty sure I'm gonna see him tonight. Braun's gonna be there too though, and he doesn't like me too much." I chuckled at that. "I guess most people don't like me too much. Not you though; for some reason, you stick around. That's probably just a symptom of your idiocy ..."

"Kissy." His eyes opened and he gave my hand a squeeze.

"Hey, Norman."

"I got shot."

"Yeah."

"No, I mean I got shot, and you're still calling me an idiot. You're always so nice to me." He smiled, weakly, and his eyelids drooped for a moment. "Who's been knocking you around?"

"Heloise Kendall."

He coughed out a laugh. "That broad really doesn't want to go home, does she?"

"No." I laughed with him. "She really doesn't. I think she's a lost cause."

"Be sure to bill her mother for your medical expenses. Oh, she paid you off already. I forgot."

I frowned. "Yeah, she did. I still don't know why."

He sighed and closed his eyes. "She wanted you out of the way, that's why." His breathing sank into a deep, even rhythm.

"I think you're right. But why?" I looked at my wristwatch, quarter till nine. I gave Norman's hand another squeeze. "Hang in there, pal." He didn't reply.

The door opened and a man in a white coat stepped into

the room and flipped on the light. He didn't seem to notice me for a few minutes as he fussed with the bottles of fluid above Norman's head. Then he must have seen me out of the corner of his eye, because he introduced himself. "Hello, I'm Dr. Evans."

"Nice to meet you." I didn't feel like giving him my name.

He raised his eyes and when he finally got a good look at me, he gasped. "My God! What happened to you?"

"People keep asking me that. I ran into a door."

He lifted my chin and examined my puffed-up mug. "Must have been one mean door."

"Meanest one I've ever met."

He prodded beneath my eyes with his fingertips, gentle but persistent. "Does that hurt?"

"Well, it's not exactly gonna make me burst into song, doc, but I can live with it."

"Hmm. I don't think anything's broken." He jerked a thumb at Norman. "This guy the one that's been popping you in the eye sockets? No wonder you shot him."

I had to laugh. Norman couldn't beat up a sickly puppy. "No, doc, I got that one tamed about right. Would you believe me if I told you a girl did this to me?"

He whistled and shook his head. "I hope whatever you were fighting for was worth it."

"Probably not." I jerked a thumb toward Norman. "How is he? He woke up, but only for a few minutes."

"I think he's through the worst of it now. He's been awake off-and-on for a couple of hours now. We pulled the lead out of him, did a debridement of the wound, and patched him up. We're using the newest penicillin treatment to stave off any infection, and we're keeping him hydrated. All told, we're optimistic he'll eventually make a complete recovery."

I exhaled a blast of pent-up air and sat back in my chair. Relief washed over me until I thought I might drown in it. "I'm grateful for all you've done for him, doc."

"Well, try to not let him get shot again, okay? How did that happen, anyway? Robbery?"

"No, a Nazi shot him."

Dr. Evans' brow furrowed. "We're a long way from the

front."

"Maybe we're not as far away from the front as you think, doc. There are all kinds of big shots in this worn-out burg. All of them are crooks, some of them are murderers, and a few of them are Nazis. Any one of them would jump at the opportunity to fill you full of bullet holes just as soon as look at you. Welcome to Cincinnati, home of big shots and bullet holes." I tried to shake the disgust out of my skull, but it must have liked it in there because it hung on. "In just the last few days I've found two guys shot dead and watched another one get blown to hell by a Tommy gun in front of his own daughter."

"Jesus."

"No, doc, the war is right here, in this town. When this started, I thought it was about high-minded ideals, you know, democracy versus fascism, that sort of thing. But I found out that it's not. It's just about money. Isn't everything about money? Want to hear the really sad part? I think it relieves me to find out that it all comes down to money. I understand money."

"Who are you, lady?"

I took off my hat and ran a hand through my hair. "I don't really know, doc. I haven't known for five years, but if I ever find out, I'll be sure to let you know." I put my hat on my head again and stood up. I gave Norman's hand a farewell squeeze. "Take care of him, will ya?"

The doctor had a puzzled expression on his face, but he nodded. "I'll do my best."

"That's good enough for me." I gave him a jaunty salute and left the room.

I tugged at my lip as I rode the elevator to the ground floor. What Norman had said about Mrs. Kendall kept rattling through my brain. By the time I made it to my car, I'd decided to pay a visit to Mrs. Marian Kendall. Since I figured I'd probably catch some lead with my lungs later in the evening, I decided to go to Kendall's place right away.

I fished my grubby little notebook out of my pocket, checked Kendall's address, then aimed my car toward the Fairview neighborhood. The rain hadn't let up while I'd gone visiting in the hospital; it still tumbled from the sky in five-gallon buckets and turned the gutters into raging torrents. My headlights couldn't pierce the wall of raindrops, so I had to slow to a pace that would set a tortoise to laughing, but eventually I got there. I parked across the street and sat watching the house. Light poured from a bay window, illuminating a porch and tidy front yard. I lit a smoke and savored the taste as I shivered in my wet clothes. The relentless rain didn't seem interested in letting up, so once I'd sucked the life out of my Camel, I opened the door and splashed through the wall of water to the relatively dry patch of Kendall's porch.

I peeked in the window and saw the crevasses of the old woman's puckered face. My knuckles had almost made it to the wood of the door when I heard voices from behind it. I pressed my ear to it, but I couldn't make out anything intelligible. The old lady's throaty rasp made her easily identifiable, while the second voice sounded higher. Younger. I risked another peek through the bay window, and then I pulled the .38 out of my pocket.

Heloise Kendall sat eating cake in the chair next to her mother.

Chapter Twenty-Four

I knocked on the door and stepped to the side, out of view. I heard voices inside, then the clicking of a turning lock. The inner door opened followed by the screen door. As Heloise Kendall took a step out of the house, I pressed the snub-nose of the .38 into her face, dimpling her skin. She froze.

"Good evening, Miss Heloise."

Her eyes rolled toward me, but she didn't move otherwise. "What do you want?"

"We have some fat that needs chewed." I moved to face her, dragging the gun's barrel across her cheek until it rested on the tip of her nose. Her eyes came together as she tried to focus on the blue steel, making her look cross-eyed. "Back into the house, just don't get in a hurry. Move." She held her hands in front of her and backed away from the door, I kept pace with her, the .38 still poked into her snoot. I steered her toward the sofa and gave her a shove when she got close enough. She went down like she had no bones.

I turned to face the mummy-fleshed face of Marian Kendall. "Fancy meeting you here, ma'am."

Kendall offered up a generous helping of her puckered frown. "You. Some private eye you are! I paid you, so what do you want?"

"Yeah, I know you did. That's why I'm here. Who told you to pay me off? Come on, I'm due to be shot to death later and I'd rather not be late, so spill it."

She extended her talon and snatched a snipe from a pack of Luckies on the end table next to her. She lit it and took a long drag, spouting smoke toward me. "I don't know what you're talking about."

I snatched off my hat and leaned toward her, stopping when our noses were within whispering distance. "I'm not in the mood to stand here bumping gums with you all night, sister. Look at my face. Your baby girl did this to me and I've been in a real pisser of a mood ever since, so unless you want me to slap the skin right off your face, you'd better figure out what I'm talking about."

"It was Gottlieb!"

I turned to Heloise. "Gottlieb? Spill it, all of it."

"You told him that you were looking for me, so he had me call Mother to arrange for you to be paid off. He gave her the money." She started weeping, the pitiable weeping of a little girl. "He just needed you to go away."

"Why?"

"I don't know. He just talked to someone on the telephone, and after that he needed you to go away."

I sat in an easy chair that faced the sofa. "What did he talk about when he was on the telephone?"

"The money."

I tugged at my lip; my brain felt like it was trying to open a locked door. "The money?"

"Yeah." She pulled a hanky out of her bosom and honked her nose into it. "He said he got a better deal."

A better deal? I show up, and suddenly Gottlieb gets a better deal? I frowned for a moment. Why would that be? Then it hit me, and I felt almost as stupid as Norman on a bad day. I, Kissy Lisbon, had nothing to do with anything. Eva Weber's sudden appearance, however, had changed everything for Gottlieb. Suddenly the daughter of a high-ranking Bund member had shown up in Cincinnati just when Gottlieb and Braun were planning to sell their halves of the list. With the specter of an increased Bund presence in town, they could conceivably demand a greater payout from their mysterious buyer. The only downside: if the Bund or the buyer found out I wasn't really Weber before the payout, the whole thing could fall apart, so I had to go. Gottlieb tried to buy me off, Braun tried to pop a handful of slugs between my ears.

I motioned to Kendall to pass me one of her cigarettes and I lit it with one of her matches. I sucked in the tobacco's ghost and held it for a few seconds. I turned back to Heloise. "How much more did he get?"

"Double."

That set me to coughing. "Double?"

"Yeah."

"That's gotta be a record, even for me. The half-million dollar lie." I laughed, but neither of them did. "What's your cut?"

Heloise licked her lips and shot a glance at her mother. "Joe and me get a hundred thousand."

"Still gonna marry him?"

She nodded like her head was on a spring. "Yes, absolutely." Her mother's scowl deepened until I thought her desiccated skin might crack and fall off her face.

"Best wishes." I took a deep breath and let it out slowly. "Now, tell me about Richter."

"Who's Richter?"

"The dead guy in Shultz's house."

She chewed her lower lip and gave her mother another sly glance. The elder Kendall made a disgusted noise in her throat and fired up another smoke.

"I'm waiting." I spun the cylinder of the .38 idly, making it click ominously.

Heloise took the hint. "I went to have my measurements taken for my wedding dress, but I got done early. When I got back to Joe's house I heard shouting inside, so I took off my shoes and tiptoed inside. Joe kept his revolver behind the radio, so I picked it up." She honked into her hanky again, which had to have been full by that time. "The guy, Richter? He had a gun pointed at Joe, and he shouted at him in German. I thought he meant to shoot Joe, so I shot him first. In the back."

"Twice?"

She nodded, blubbering by then. "Joe called his uncle, and Gottlieb came right away. We all thought the guy was dead, but as we stood there trying to decide what to do with him, he started coughing, so Gottlieb pulled out his gun and shot him in the head." Heloise couldn't talk anymore, she just sat there heaving great moist sobs. Her mother had finished her cigarette and huffed her way through another while her daughter spun out her story.

I mashed out the nub of my own cigarette. "So, you just left him there and told Braun it was Shultz?"

She nodded.

"How did the marker end up on the floor? Did Gottlieb get it from Hirsch?"

"No." She sniffled and wiped her nose with the back of her hand. "Richter had it."

I scratched my head. "Why did Richter have it?"

She shrugged. "I don't know."

I spat out a sigh. "I hate loose ends. All right, so the three of you slink away from the scene like spineless slugs, then what?"

"Joe called Braun and arranged for a ride, so Braun would be with Gottlieb when they find the body."

"Why bother?"

"Richter was Braun's friend."

"And he didn't recognize his dead friend on the floor?" I raised an eyebrow. "Come on now. That doesn't seem likely."

She surprised me with a smile. "Gottlieb couldn't believe his luck either. It turns out Braun doesn't like seeing dead people, so he didn't get too close. He just accepted it when Gottlieb said it was Shultz."

"A killer with a weak stomach? Who'd have thought?" The memory of Braun shooting Wexler ran like a newsreel through my mind. "He doesn't have a problem slinging lead though, does he?"

"No, he's killed all kinds of people. Joe told me to stay away from him. I think he's afraid of him."

"Did you see the list before Gottlieb sold it to Martingdale?"

"It was just a piece of paper. I didn't get a good look at it."

"Dammit." I hissed out a breath and gingerly rubbed my eyes.

"Who killed John Martingdale?" She'd shut down the waterworks and now she wrung her soggy hanky between her fingers. "Who was it?"

"I don't know who pulled the trigger, not for sure

anyway. But as for who got him killed, that I can explain. You did. And Gottlieb. And your precious Joe Shultz or Joe Ruger or whoever he is today. All of you got John Martingdale killed, because you played a dangerous game with dangerous people, the kind of game where somebody always winds up in the boneyard eventually. Did any of you ever take into consideration that we're at war? Tell a few lies to Germany and get paid. Tell a few lies to Uncle Sam and get paid. How many soldiers have painted the ground red with their life's blood so you could get paid? How much money is a soldier's life worth to you? You sit there and weep for John Martingdale because he was your friend, but how many wives weep for husbands they'll never see again because you got them killed? His death is as much your fault as the guy who shot him. I hope you never forget that."

Heloise stared at me, stunned, and I briefly wondered if I'd gone a bit too far. Sure, she disgusted me, but I really didn't have any proof that the misinformation Martingdale fed the Bund had gotten anybody killed, and if it did, they were probably Germans. They were the enemy of the moment, but it still didn't seem right to condemn rank-and-file soldiers to death for a payout, even if they were Nazis.

"Where is Joe anyway?"

"He went to pick up the money from the train station."

I shot a glance over at Heloise's mother, who regarded me with an odd expression that seemed half contempt and half admiration. Her lips had quirked up just a little in what could almost be described as a smile.

I smiled at her. "I take it you are still opposed to their marriage?"

"Very much so."

"Well, I'm sure everything will work out in the end." I stood up and tucked my heater away in my jacket pocket again. "I've got to run along now. I'd recommend staying away from the Bund, for obvious reasons, and stay away from the police too. They might not look too kindly on someone who shot a man in the back, even if you had a good reason. It'll lead to some very uncomfortable questions at the very least. As a matter of fact, you probably shouldn't talk to anybody ever again."

Heloise sniffed. "Joe and I are leaving as soon as he gets back with the money."

I grinned. "I hope you don't have to wait too long." If Paolo's men did their job, Joe would already be on his way to a nice comfortable cell downtown. "Goodbye, ladies, have a wonderful time spending your ill-gotten gains." I put my hat on my noggin and opened the door. I paused and looked right at the old lady. "By the way, I found your daughter, and she's home. So, now my arrangement with you has ended. I'd mail you a receipt, but I think we'd both rather keep this off the books."

"She's still marrying the kraut."

I chuckled. "Is she? Tell you what, I'll refund all of your money on their wedding day, how's that sound?"

Heloise suddenly stood up. "Go to hell!"

"Oh, I've made reservations for that trip. Made them a long time ago." I took one last glance at Marian Kendall, who gave me one of her mummy-scowls, as I left through the front door.

The rain had slowed somewhat, from a monsoon to a mere downpour. I pulled my hat low over my eyes, raised my jacket collar, and made a run for the car. I splashed away from the curb and parsed what I'd learned through my brain. The size of the web of deceit that Gottlieb had woven would impress liars and spiders alike.

I drove toward the river, toward the probable scene of my murder. The guy who shot Norman wanted Braun's half of the list, so I figured he'd show up to get it. If he didn't, well maybe Braun and me could just play pinochle for an hour or so, and part as friends.

That seemed about as likely as finding a square-dancing polar bear serving drinks in the Bahamas. No, tonight someone had an appointment with the great hereafter. I just hoped that someone wasn't me.

Chapter Twenty-Five

The Ohio River surged, a swollen silver worm, wriggling past the drowned-rat façade of downtown. Rain still fell by the gallon, steadily pounding on the windshield of my Chrysler. The wipers labored to push the water out of my field of vision, but only succeeded in making the blur a little less blurry. I drove past the Fritz Brothers' garage, a tumbledown brick number with a rusty tin roof. Three mammoth garage doors stretched across the side of the building, one of which looked to be open enough for light to escape from within.

I parked under the roof of an abandoned filling station and pulled my raincoat from the trunk. As I buttoned it up, I watched a car creep through the slop toward the garage. It shut off its lights and I lost it in the gloom. I patted my coat pocket, reassured by the Colt's hard presence. The .38 I kept in my hand as I galloped across the street, dodging puddles and leaping over impromptu tributaries of the Ohio. A row of trucks, all of them old and most of them reduced to broken down heaps, decayed between the garage and Carr Street. I squatted behind one of these behemoths as I peered through the rain.

Two men sloshed from the car and through the open garage door. One of them had the build of a silverback gorilla, and the other one, though smaller, moved with a familiar cocksure swagger. "Braun." The hiss of falling water ate the name even as it hissed through my teeth. They stood just inside the garage, twisting their heads to enjoy the view. An icy finger of water found its way down my back, causing me to shiver. I scanned the exterior of the garage and found a man-door and the end farthest away from Braun's rusting vehicle. I took a quick peek in either direction, then made a run for it.

The doorknob turned, but the door wouldn't open. I gave it a hard tug, but it held firm. I peered through the glass window of the door but could only make out the vague outlines of a desk or table inside. I put my shoulder into the door, which served to slap a deep bruise onto my skin but didn't move the door. "Deadbolt." I could either break the glass, or drown where I stood, so I took off my hat, balled my fist around the revolver, and punched out the window.

From where I stood the shattering glass sounded like a freight train barreling into a mountain of beer bottles, but the constant wheeze of the rain must have beat the sound into the ground because nobody came running. I felt inside the door and unlatched the deadbolt. Water streamed off me and pattered on the bare concrete floor. I found the desk and snapped on a little lamp that lurked on top of it. The room looked worse in light: a greasy, cluttered mass of paper and the guts of engines.

A door to my left led out of the room, creaking like a coffin lid when I opened it. A single row of lights burned high above the floor on the far side of the cavernous garage. I snaked my way to the back wall and moved on cat-feet toward the arc of sodium light that fell from above. As I got closer to them, I could hear Braun and his associate arguing.

"Listen, Braun. The police were crawling all over the lawyer's office. I'm tellin' ya, they got him all buttoned up in a cell downtown."

"You don't know anything, Affen, so just shut up."

The big guy bristled. "Maybe I ought to just pop you one for being a mouthy cuss." He balled up one fist and showed it to Braun. "You ain't nobody to me, Braun. I work for Richter."

Braun glanced at his wristwatch, then deigned to regard the other man. "Bring that meathook any closer and I might decide to be less than friendly with you, Affen. Richter's gone. Either the Feds got him or he's floatin' face down on his way to New Orleans. Either way, if you want paid, you do what I say. Right now, I say stand there and shut up. Got it?"

Affen's simian brows fell over his eyes. "Yeah, I got it." He clenched and unclenched his fists, and I could see on his mug what he wanted to do to Braun. I could almost smell it. I felt a smile stretch across my face as I imagined Affen taking Braun apart an inch at a time.

Braun checked his watch again. "He's late though."

"Yeah, I figure that makes sense."

"I'm gonna call him. Wait here, Affen." Braun steamed his way toward the office, passing close enough that had he turned his head to his left, he'd have found my bones shivering behind a stack of tires. His pace didn't allow for sightseeing, though, and he didn't see me. I hunkered lower, knowing he'd be headed in the opposite direction in only a minute or two.

"Braun!" Affen's voice boomed through the building.

I heard Braun cursing, then he slammed open the office door. He cursed all the way back to the open garage door. "Martingdale isn't answering his telephone. What are you bellowing about?" He hoofed his way toward Affen. "Well?"

Affen gestured out the door where a figure in a broad-brimmed hat and gray raincoat approached. Braun put his hands on his hips. "Well, it's about time, Martingdale."

The man whisked off his hat. "I am not Herr Martingdale."

"Gottlieb? What the hell are you doing here? Where is Martingdale?"

"Herr Martingdale is dead."

"What? Who shot him?"

"That is a good question, Herr Braun. Herr Wexler is dead as vell. You wouldn't know anything about that vould you?"

Braun waved that away. "Wexler was a bean-counter. He said he wanted out, so we let him out." He snorted at his own humor. "Ask and ye shall receive, right?"

"This vas not supposed to end this vay."

Braun shook his head. "Who the hell cares, Gottlieb? The Bund is scattering like rats, and you know why. I just want my money so I can get out of the way before everything blows up."

"Who told you to kill Herr Wexler?"

"Look here, Gottlieb. I don't answer to you anymore. The Bund said to shut Wexler up, so I shut him up. No big deal. One last job for old times' sake, and I have to tell ya, I enjoyed it. Wexler was a gutless slug. I never liked him."

Gottlieb ran his hand over his bald pate. "He had a family."

Braun laughed. "So he'll have someone show up at his funeral, good for him." He stepped closer to Affen. "So, if Martingdale is dead, where is my money?"

"I do not know, Herr Braun. Martingdale vas eager to get the list, und I suspect whoever killed him vanted the list as vell. They vill vant it still, ja?"

Braun spat out a long sigh. "They'd better come. If I don't get my money, Gottlieb, I'll just have to take yours. I'm damned well gonna get paid, and I don't much care where the cash comes from."

Gottlieb's hand darted into his coat and came up with a Luger just like that, but Braun moved just a second faster. His .45 roared and Gottlieb fell to the ground clutching at the newly plowed tunnel in his shoulder. Braun kicked the Luger across the room and loomed over Gottlieb's face.

"Gonna plug me, Gottlieb? Gotta be faster than that, you kraut bastard!" He kicked him in the guts. "You're just like Wexler, a useless sack of sauerkraut." He latched on to Gottlieb's lapels and dragged him over to the wall, where he propped him up. "I think I'm gonna take your money even if the buyer does show up. How do you like that, Gottlieb?" He laughed.

I crept closer to them, crouching behind a partially disassembled engine block. I held the gun in both hands and lined the barrel up with Braun's head. Pull the trigger, that's all it'd take, and the open wound of Braun's existence would be stitched up nicely. Squeeze, pop, and then oh-so-red blood running all over the floor. My grip tightened, but not enough.

Braun knelt to face Gottlieb. "Hey, does that hurt?" He balled up a fist and socked Gottlieb in the shoulder, causing him to howl like a dying cat and fall on his side. "I guess it does." He propped Gottlieb up again. "All right, enough fun. Where is your half of the money? Tell me and I'll call an ambulance for you. Otherwise you'll bleed out. You hear me Gottlieb?" He grasped the bald man's face and gave it a shake. "You hear me, Gottlieb?"

"He's done for." Affen lit a cigarettes. "Don't waste your

time."

Braun stood up, looking down at Gottlieb with his hands on his hips. "What a shame. Hear that, Gottlieb? Affen thinks you're worm-meat. You should tell me where your money is. What good is money to worm-meat?"

Gottlieb coughed and looked up at Braun. "*Geh zum Teufel.*"

"What?" Braun looked at Affen. "What did he say?"

Affen grinned. "He told you to go to the devil."

"Oh yeah?" He aimed a pair of savage kicks into Gottlieb's stomach.

Amazingly Gottlieb laughed. He sucked in a long slow breath and spat it out at Braun. "*Geh zum Teufel!*"

Braun snapped off a pair of shots into Gottlieb's chest. His back arched once, then he lay still.

"Say hello to the devil for me, Gottlieb." Braun threw his head back and tossed out an evil screech that seemed to be his version of a laugh. He went through Gottlieb's pockets then, taking his watch, his checkbook and even his pocket change.

The throbbing hum of an engine approached the building, and Affen went to peer through the rain. "Car."

Braun sauntered away from Gottlieb's body to stand directly under the sodium light. "Who is it?"

"I dunno, but they're coming in." He stepped away from the door and pulled his gat out of his jacket pocket.

Braun rubbed his hands together. "Must be the buyer."

Two men in pinstriped suits rushed into the room, each one packing a Thompson sub-machine gun with a drum magazine. They aimed their bean-shooters at Braun and Affen. "Nobody moves!"

Braun scowled. "What the hell is this?"

One of them drove the butt of their Tommy gun into Braun's liver, doubling him over. "I said nobody move! Are you deaf?"

Braun gasped and struggled to remain standing. "I'm Braun. I'm here to sell ..."

"Shut up! I don't give a good goddam who you are!"

Affen dropped his heater and raised his ham-hocks into the air. He stood stock still in an effort to keep his hide in one piece.

Braun seemed to adhere to a different school of thought. He stood upright, gasping for breath, but still tried to take control of the situation. "Tell him I have it."

The Tommy gun crashed into his guts again, and this time he fell to his hands and knees. From my hiding spot I could hear him laboring to breath, and I can't tell you how I enjoyed every second of his agony. He fought his way to his feet and held his hands level with his shoulders. This time he stayed mute.

One of the men jabbed Affen with the barrel of his gun, forcing him to stand next to Braun, who still sucked air like a man with broken ribs. Maybe they were broken. He looked up when the car door slammed shut outside. I heard the splish-splash of approaching footsteps and there he stood. The buyer sauntered into the garage with a smirk on his face and a cigar in his hands.

It was Colonel Greene.

Chapter Twenty-Six

Greene took off his hat, flung the water off it, and crammed it back on his head. He offered Braun a smile. "Don't ya just love Ohio weather? It's either raining, snowing, or it's hotter than hell." He chuckled and as he lit a cigarette, he noticed Gottlieb's leaking pelt. "What happened here?"

Braun kept his hands raised. "He drew on me, so I had to put him down."

"Yeah, can't have that nonsense going on, can we? Who was he?"

"Karl Gottlieb."

"Gottlieb? That's Gottlieb?" Greene's eyebrows crawled up his forehead.

"Yeah. So what?"

"I can't tell you how slippery that son of a gun was." He took a last drag from his snipe and flicked it toward Gottlieb. "We tried for years to get ahold of him."

"Who are you?"

"Who am I?" He stepped and faced Braun. "Why Mr. Braun, I'm hurt that you don't recognize me. I'm Colonel Alfred Greene. I've made you a rich man these last few years."

"Not rich enough. Are you here to buy the list?"

An oily smile stretched across Greene's mug. "First thing's first, Mr. Braun." He took a couple of steps away from Braun and looked Affen up and down. "Who is this?"

"My name's Affen."

"Oh, is it?"

"Yeah. It is." Affen stared the Colonel down. "Who the hell are you?"

Greene took a deep breath and sighed. "I've already

introduced myself. Clearly, you weren't paying attention. If you were one of my soldiers, I'd have you flogged."

Affen snorted. "Try it, little man."

Greene waved that away and he returned to Braun. "Is he anyone to you?"

Braun licked his lips. "No. Not really."

Greene raised a hand and wiggled a finger toward Affen. One of Greene's men took a step forward and unloaded fifty or sixty rounds from his machine gun into Affen's apelike frame. He stumbled backward into a truck's fender as he got blown apart, blood, bone, and flesh flying away from him in a gory red cloud. He squelched when his bulk hit the floor. That's a sound I drink to forget.

Greene turned his grin toward Braun. "How do you like that?"

"He had it coming." Braun shrugged.

Greene brayed out a laugh. "I like you, Mr. Braun. You're made of stern stuff. I think I can do business with you." He clapped him on the shoulder. "Put your hands down, dammit. You look ridiculous."

Braun did. "So, you do want the list?"

"I do."

"You have the money?"

"Of course."

"Then let's do it. I'm a busy man."

Greene snapped his fingers, and one of his men ran out of the garage. "So am I, Mr. Braun. I have a plane to catch. On a good day it takes thirty minutes to get there, but in this downpour, it'll probably take an hour or more just to find the airport."

"Maybe you should have taken a boat instead."

"You could be right." Greene took a satchel from his lackey and opened it up. Braun peered inside, his lips drawing back in a toothy grin.

"That looks about right."

Greene closed the satchel. "Not so fast, Braun. The list, if you please."

"Right." He dug around in his jacket pocket and finally scrounged up a slip of paper. "Here ya go, Colonel."

Greene pulled out his own slip of paper, took Braun's, and examined them both. Each of them had one ragged edge, which Greene held close together. He spent a couple of minutes comparing them, then he smiled at Braun. "Looks like the genuine article."

Braun grunted. "Sure, it is. I'm not gonna cheat ya. I've been called a lot of things, but cheat ain't one of them."

"Not every man has as much integrity as you." Greene kept a straight face somehow.

"I guess not." Braun gestured to the list in Greene's fingers. "You gonna arrest those men? Keep them from blowing something up? They're bringing explosives with them. They're coming ashore on Long Island. Some of them anyway."

Greene's eyebrow raised. "Are they?"

"Yeah. They'll have explosives, blasting caps, timers. The whole show."

"How do you know that?"

"Hirsch told Gottlieb. He told me."

Greene shook his head and scowled. "Hirsch talked too much. He told the Feds too much, told Martingdale too much, and he told you too much. It got him killed." A feral grin stretched across Greene's face. "He begged me not to kill him."

"No kidding?" Braun shifted his weight from one foot to another.

"Yeah, who'd have thought an iron-willed lawyer like Martingdale could turn out be such a yellow-bellied coward? Not that I mind killing cowards, you see. The way I figure it, when a man swears an oath to someone unworthy of his loyalty, a coward for instance, he dishonors himself and becomes less than a man. He becomes an animal. Even worse, he's infected by that dishonor, so he's like a rabid dog. And where I come from, we put rabid dogs down. Just like you put Mr. Gottlieb down. Right?"

Braun nodded, with evident reluctance. "Yeah."

"Your man, Affen, I had to put him down, too."

"But Martingdale?"

Greene spread out his hands. "It had to be done. He knew too much and suspected more."

"Well, now you have the list. You can arrest the spies

when the submarine gets there.”

“This list?” Greene held the two halves of the paper in his hand and lit them with a match. They curled into black wisps and floated to the floor. “No, I have other plans, Mr. Braun. I just wanted to make sure nobody else got the list.”

“I don’t understand.”

“Nor are you supposed to.” Greene reached into his jacket pocket and withdrew a snub-nose .38, the same caliber of slug they pulled out of Norman’s guts. Braun started to take a step back, but Greene didn’t hesitate. He put two rounds in each of Braun’s kneecaps.

Braun collapsed to the greasy floor, clutching manically at his knees. “Aaah! Stop! I didn’t do anything!”

Greene stood smiling over him. “That doesn’t matter. You’re just a rabid dog, Braun.”

“No! I’m a man! I’m not a Nazi!”

“Oh? Really? Perhaps I’ve made a mistake.” He glanced around the garage, his eyes finally stopping on an enormous tank of gasoline. He motioned to one of his men, who immediately ran over to it and opened a valve. I could smell it immediately and watched it spatter across the floor.

Greene lit a smoke and bent to tuck the butt in a crack on the floor. “If you’re not a dog, Braun, I have no need to put you down clean. Don’t worry though, when that gas tank goes up I’m betting you’ll be blown to bits and won’t even feel a thing.” He snatched up the satchel of cash and started to walk out the door.

Braun pulled a smaller gun, it looked like a Derringer, from the pocket of his red-spattered trousers. He fired it twice, hitting one of Greene’s goons in the back of the neck. He went down like he’d been poleaxed.

Greene whirled and fired another round into Braun, this time into his right shoulder. He fell back, groaning. Green tilted his head and watched his man writhe on the floor for a few seconds, before putting a round between his eyes. He scowled at Braun. “When you get to hell, say hello to Hirsch and Martingdale for me.” He and his remaining man left through the garage door. I heard a car fire up and splash away through the rain.

I finally left my hiding place and crept over to Braun. His

ragged breath hissed in and out. He bled freely; the dark red blood that meant your life could now be measured in minutes. I stood there for several seconds before he saw me.

"Oh, Christ. It's you."

"Hello, Braun. You're looking good."

"Pull me out of here." He gasped air into his lungs. "Pick up the cigarette. I don't want to burn."

"Tell me the names on the list, and I will."

"Hurry!"

"The names, Braun. I need to know them."

He blinked up at me. "Dasch. George Dasch."

"Who else?"

"Harm ... Harm. Heinrich ... Har ..." He blinked one last time, then lay still. I closed his eyes just as the stream of gasoline approached him. I didn't bother trying to move him. Instead, I tore through the garage door and across the lot. I took cover behind the rusted-out hulk of a deuce-and-a-half. Then I heard the swoosh of the gas igniting, and a second later the fuel tank exploded. I crouched and covered my head as burning debris sailed over and all around me. When I looked up, the Fritz Brothers' Trucking Company had one less garage to worry about. The roof had been obliterated and everything else crackled as it burned.

Smoldering bits of the roof smoked beside me, hissing in the rain. I tiptoed through the conflagration and crossed Carr Street to the abandoned filling station, where my car waited for my return like a loyal dog. I leaned against the fender and tried to pull a snipe out of the pack, but my hands shook too badly and I couldn't manage it. So I just stood there, shivering and shaking like a palsied old man, when I had places to go.

I heard the howling warble of the black-and-whites, and within a couple of minutes I watched them descend on the fiery remains of the garage like a pack of hyenas. The long red trucks came a minute or two later, but they didn't do anything when they got there. The damage, it seemed, couldn't get much worse, and even with their miles of hoses they couldn't offer much more water than what the sky threw down at them.

A car roared to a stop next to mine and a man jumped out of it. "There you are! What the hell are you doing?" Paolo didn't sound happy.

"Trying to light my cigarette. Feel like helping?"

He slammed the door of his car and steamed toward me like a locomotive. "This isn't a joke! You led me on a wild-goose-chase and now I look like a fool!"

"Are you gonna light my smoke or not?" I finally managed to get one between my lips.

He hissed a lungful of air between his teeth, but dutifully struck a match and set fire to my tobacco. "You're a real piece of work, Cassandra. You lied to me."

I huffed out a jet of blue smoke. "Yeah. Are you surprised?"

"I shouldn't be."

That made me smile. "No, you sure shouldn't be."

"Why did you send me to Elsinore Tower?"

"To get you out of my way. I don't need a cop hanging around."

He gestured broadly toward the inferno across the street. "Really? I think you're right, Kissy, you need a psychiatrist! Or maybe a nanny!"

"I needed a friend."

He ran his fingers through his blond curls and took several deep breaths. Finally, he leaned against the car next to me. "Can I have a drag?"

"I thought you quit."

"So did I." He snatched my cigarette and took a long puff before handing it back to me. His eyes closed and he held his breath for a handful of seconds. "Thanks."

"Anytime, copper."

"Stop calling me that."

"I will when Paolo comes back."

He shook his head. "You're so damned stubborn."

"So are you."

"What happened over there?"

"Who's asking? Officer Belvedere or Paolo Belvedere?" I tossed my spent butt into a puddle.

"I'm the one asking." He grinned.

"Gottlieb and Braun are dead."

He glanced at the fire. "In there?"

I nodded.

"Kissy, I think you'd better tell me everything."

"In a minute. How long does it take to get to the airport from here?"

"Lunken? About ten minutes if we take Columbia Avenue. Why?"

I frowned. "That's not right. He said it'd take half an hour normally, twice that because of the rain."

"Who said that?"

I tugged at my lip. "Could he have meant a different airport?"

"Who might have meant a different airport?"

"Greene."

He turned to face me. "Colonel Greene?"

"Yeah. He bought the list from Braun. With lead."

Paolo heaved a huge sigh. "Thank God."

"No. Greene killed Martingdale."

"What?"

"He bragged about it to Braun. I also watched him order his men to kill Braun's goon. He's got his own agenda, Paolo, and it's not in America's best interest. He's headed to an airport that's thirty minutes away from here."

Paolo's brow creased as he thought. "He might have meant Watson Field. It's northeast of town. It'd take about that long to get there."

I opened my car door. "Do you know where this place is?"

"Yeah." He got in the car. "More or less."

"Let's go." I turned the key and my Chrysler snarled to life. "When we get there, we're doing things my way."

Paolo shook his head. "I hope Watson Field has insurance."

Chapter Twenty-Seven

The lateness, the night, the foul weather, or some other providential power kept most of the traffic off the streets and out of my way. I stomped the accelerator to the floor and the engine screamed like the hordes of hell as we tore through town on our way to Watson Field. Paolo alternated between demanding an accounting of what happened in the Fritz Brothers' garage and reciting the twenty-third Psalm.

"Why didn't you just shoot him, then?"

"He had two goons with machine guns with him! Besides, I wanted to find out as much as I could about his game. My jaw damned near hit the floor when he burned that list."

"So, it's not about money."

"Everything is about money. We just don't know how it's about money yet. It doesn't matter; I'm still gonna plug him."

"No, Kissy. I can't let you do that."

"He shot Norman!"

"You don't know that for sure. Even if you did know it unequivocally, I can't let you shoot him."

"Damn it, Paolo, we've been through this before! This time I know who I need to kill, and you'd better not stand in my way!"

"Norman is alive, Kissy."

I swallowed around the lump in my throat. "Mary isn't."

Out of the hinterlands of my vision I saw him wince. "I know that. You didn't think I'd forgotten, did you?"

"I think you want to forget; I think you try your best to forget." I felt one rogue tear escape from my eye. "I can't forget. I see her face every time I close my eyes—unless I pour a pint of rye down my neck first. I see her, laughing, happy, alive ... then blood ..." I couldn't go on.

"Cassandra, it wasn't your fault. Because of the flood, everything fell apart. People got beaten half to death for stealing eggs, for God's sake. The whole town was in chaos."

I stared straight ahead, the telephone poles careening past the car. "I saw him."

"I know you did." I could barely hear his voice.

"I heard the shot and ran outside. She held her hand out in front of her, staring at it like she'd never seen it before. Her blood covered it, blood from the hole in her chest. It ran down her fingers and onto the sidewalk, just twenty feet from the edge of the floodwaters. When she fell, I caught her, and that's when I saw him. He still had the gun in his hand, and he had a sneer on his face. Two other men ushered him into a car and they drove away. It was too late for him though; I saw him. You'd followed me out the door, so I know you saw him too."

"Yes."

"I know you knew who he was."

"Yes."

"He meant to gun me down, not Mary. He shot the wrong girl. I swore then, and I swear again right now, I will find him, and I will kill him. Just like I'm gonna kill Greene for shooting Norman." My knuckles had turned white on the steering wheel. "You just need to tell me his name, Paolo."

"You know I can't. It'd make us both murderers. I've been in firefights as a cop, and I've shot a couple of hard cases that wouldn't come in without a fight. One of them even died." Paolo rubbed his eyes with the heels of his hands. "Hell, he was just a punk kid running moonshine up from Kentucky, but he had a gun and I have no doubt he'd have killed me if I hadn't have shot him first. You don't know what it's like living with that kind of guilt. I pulled the trigger and now some mother's son won't be at the table come Thanksgiving." He turned to look at me. "Let it go, Cassandra. Let me arrest Greene, and I guarantee you he'll spend the rest of his life rotting in a prison cell."

"I tell ya what, you give me the name of the guy that shot Mary, and you can have Greene."

Paolo threw up his hands. "I give up, Kissy. There's no getting through to you at all. The woman I loved, the woman I asked to marry me, wasn't a remorseless killer obsessed with vengeance at any cost."

I tossed him a scowl. "That woman is dead. She died five years ago when you refused to help her."

"Dammit, I was saving your life!"

"All you saved was the husk. Everything else died when Mary's heart stopped beating."

He remained quiet for several minutes before he spoke again. "It always comes back to this point, doesn't it? Me doing what I think is right, and you hating me for it. I can't win. No matter what I do, I lose."

"Sounds like being a cop is a real pisser." I clenched my teeth on my cigarette.

"It is when you're around." He pointed through the bleary windshield. "Slow down, the airport's just ahead."

I turned onto the road he indicated, and we drove past a jumble of little shotgun shacks until the airport finally appeared out of the rain. I turned off the car's headlights as I pulled into the parking lot beside the double-hangar. Two other cars sat in the lot as well as a large fuel truck. I parked behind the truck, out of sight of the other cars.

Paolo spun the chamber of his .45 double-action Army revolver. "I know what you want to do, Kissy, but I'm asking you to remember what's at stake. We need to interrogate Greene. Hundreds, thousands, maybe hundreds of thousands of lives are at stake. We need to take Greene alive."

I shot him a dirty look. "You're just saying that so I won't kill him."

"Is it working?"

"Not really." I said it, but even as I did, I knew it was working. I'd seen the newsreels of the Dunkirk evacuation, those tattered and bloodied men fleeing from the tide of Nazi expansion in Europe. Those soldiers weren't American, but I could easily imagine that they were. How could I weigh my vengeance against the lives of hundreds of thousands of servicemen?

Paolo opened the door and stepped out of the car. I waited a few seconds before joining him. We peered around the edge of the fuel truck. "Paolo? Are you being serious?"

"About what?"

"About needing to interrogate Greene to save soldiers' lives?"

He blinked. "Yeah, Kissy. I'm being serious. Not everybody is endlessly running a con. We need to know what he's up to. That means we need to bring him in alive." He carefully studied the cars parked next to the hangar. The Colonel's white Packard sat there, sporting brand new tires, and beside that stood a maroon Chevrolet. Paolo frowned. "That's Avery Brightman's car."

"The guy in charge of the local Feds?"

"Yeah. Why would he be here?" He crept over to the cars and peered into them through the glass. He hurried back and crouched down beside me. "There's a dead guy in Greene's car. Young fella, pinstriped suit. He's been popped in the back of his head."

"Greene's gun-hands both had on pinstriped suits. He shot one of them back at the garage. Looks like he doesn't want any loose ends."

"Yeah, he's cleaning things up real good."

A pair of voices carried through the rainfall, and we pressed ourselves against the hangar wall.

"You can't take off in this downpour, Colonel." Paolo looked at me and mouthed the name 'Brightman.'

"It's only a little water. Besides, it has to let up sometime. It can't rain all the time."

Brightman chuckled. "Okay, if you say so Colonel."

"You're gonna take care of that mess, right?"

"Yeah. I'll send Pressman out to pick up the car. He'll know what to do with Corporal Wills."

"Thank you, Avery."

"No, thank you, Colonel. I'll be ready on the 12th."

"So will I. I'll make sure I'm with the president when everything starts to happen. We'll see what that lily-livered cripple has to say then! He'll have no choice but to follow my recommendations. Drive safe, Avery."

"Will do." Brightman dropped into his Chevrolet and rumbled out of the parking lot. Greene stepped into view and opened the trunk of his car. He pulled out the satchel of cash and a leather suitcase and reentered the hangar.

I whispered into Paolo's ear. "Looks like he's leaving town. Whatever we're doing, we need to do it now."

Paolo held up a finger and peeked around the corner of the hangar. "Whatever's going on, Brightman might be in it too." We could hear Greene thumping around in the hangar, just on the other side of the concrete from where we stood. Paolo pointed down the wall, toward the far end of the hangar, and we sloshed through the standing water as quietly as a couple of rampaging hippos. As we moved up the short side of the building Paolo sketched out his plan. "We'll get inside, make sure he's alone, then we flank him. We know he's armed, so be careful."

I nodded, but he startled me by pressing his hand against my left cheek.

"Kissy, if it comes down to a firefight, shoot to wound. Aim for his legs. We need him alive."

I rolled my eyes. "So you keep telling me. I got it, okay?"

The hangar didn't have the huge doors that some other airports had; the front of the structure simply gaped open. Several one- and two-seater planes skulked in the darkness. We tiptoed inside. Whatever nefarious business Greene had at the airport was in the adjacent hangar. The two hangars connected to one another by a smaller structure that housed the business office and a variety of workbenches and toolboxes. From where we stood, we could see into this area through a row of grimy windows. A single desk lamp burned, and Colonel Greene stood beside it, talking into a wall-mounted telephone. His left side faced us.

"No. I said I needed Jacksonville, Florida, not Jackson, Mississippi! I'm trying to get ahold of Commander Holt, Naval Air Station, Jacksonville. Yes, Florida!" Greene slammed his fist against the wall. "Florida! Florida!" His cigar migrated from one corner of his mouth to the other. "Finally. Commander Holt, please."

I shot a glance at Paolo, but his raised eyebrows didn't answer any of my questions.

After waiting a minute or two, the connection seemed to finally get made. "Gerald? Is that you? Thank God! I've been trying to get through for ten minutes. Yes, it's done. Looks like the fifteenth or sixteenth, so make sure Ponte Vedra Beach is nicely deserted. Well, I don't know. Schedule a training exercise somewhere else. Look, no, that's your problem, Holt. Just get it done. There'll be four of them landing there. They're all meeting here in Cincinnati, on Independence Day." He laughed. "No, a total coincidence, unless the *Abwehr* has a sharper sense of irony than I give it credit for. Just be ready on the fifteenth or sixteenth. I'm on my way back to Washington. I have a meeting with the Secretary of War, and then the president. Despite a few setbacks, everything here is on schedule."

Paolo moved across the floor on his hands and knees until he made it to the far side of the doorway, then he stood up and pulled out his gun. He peeked around the corner and shot me a nod.

Green continued his conversation. "Avery's taking care of that. The Bureau's up to its nose in anonymous tips. They won't pose a problem. No. No. No, look Holt, I've got to go. We'll talk after everything. Yes, goodbye." He slammed the receiver onto the hook and spat out the stump of his cigar.

Paolo stepped into the room with his gun trained on Greene. The Colonel's mouth widened into a 'O' and his brows rode high on his forehead.

"Colonel Alfred Greene! Don't move! You're under arrest for murder, conspiracy, and treason!"

Chapter Twenty-Eight

"Belvedere? What the hell are you doing here?" Colonel Greene didn't raise his hands or even seem intimidated by Paolo's .45 Colt.

"I told you, Colonel, you're under arrest."

Greene laughed. "What? You don't have the authority to arrest me. Just who do you think you are?"

"I'm the guy that's gonna put you behind bars, Greene. You're a murderer and a traitor."

Greene laughed again. "Oh really? Who says so?"

"I do." I stepped into the room with my stolen snub-nose .38 glued to Greene's forehead. "I saw you kill Braun and his man, Affen. I saw you shoot your own man just because he got wounded. I saw you burn down the garage."

His smile wilted and fell off his face. "You. You're that broad we found in the suite at the Aristocrat instead of Gottlieb. I see Belvedere didn't take you to the nuthatch. What did you do, offer to bed him if he let you go?"

"That's enough, Greene! It's been hard enough to keep her from killing you this long; don't antagonize her."

He waved his hand and made a dismissive sound in his throat. "If all you've got is the testimony of one lunatic, Belvedere, you've got less than nothing, and you know it. Now put down that bean-shooter before I start to get sore."

"Nothing doing, Greene. You're under arrest for murder, conspiracy and treason."

He took a step toward Paolo. "You wog bastard! We're at war! You have no idea what's going on here. Far from arresting me, I'm arresting you, *both* of you, for interfering in an Army Intelligence operation. Now put that gun down."

I cocked the hammer back on my gat. "If he doesn't arrest you, I'm gonna put a hole in your stomach and watch you bleed out, nice and slow, but if the bleeding starts to slow up too much, I'll just drill you again. That ought to keep us occupied for a while, don't you think?"

"You're a nasty bit of work. What'd I do to you?"

"You shot my friend in the guts."

"You mean the genius at the Aristocrat? He must run, what? One-ten when he's packing an anvil?" He laughed. "You should have left that one in the cradle, dollface. He's not grown up enough to play in the big leagues."

"So why did you shoot him?" Paolo took a step and stood shoulder-to-shoulder to me.

Greene shrugged. "Who cares? I can shoot anyone who gets in my way. Even wog detectives and nutty dames." He poked a new cigar between his teeth and rummaged through his pockets for a match. "But I tell you what, Belvedere, I'm gonna let you take me in, just to teach you a lesson in how the world really works. With one phone call, I'll have your badge and you'll find yourself in a very unpleasant prison cell at Ft. Leavenworth, but you'll have learned a valuable lesson. Hell, they might even let you out in time for the '72 World Series." He lit his smoke and tossed away the match. "How does that sound?" He crammed his hands in his coat pockets and smiled broadly.

"How about I just put you down like a rabid dog, Greene?" I watched his smile fade and felt my own light up. "How does that sound?"

He tore his hands out of his pockets and held up a hand grenade. He'd pulled the pin, but the lever was still in place. If all the Saturday matinee war movies had it right, it wouldn't detonate unless he let go of the lever.

"Now, drop 'em. Both of you!"

Paolo started to place his cannon on the ground. "No, Paolo. Stand up."

"That's a grenade, Kissy."

"I don't care. He's not getting away."

Greene laughed. "Your name is Kissy? Oh my God! Could either of you be more pathetic? Drop the heat, sister. I'm tired of playing with you two crumbs.”

“No.” I kept the gun’s sights in his face.

“I’ll drop it, don’t test me.”

“You won’t. You value your own hide too much to drop it.” Then he did something I honestly hadn’t expected: he dropped the grenade. He spun around and darted across the room and out the door. I squeezed off a couple of rounds, but by then Paolo had his arm across my chest, shoving me out the door we’d come through. I missed Greene both times and I hit the floor hard. Paolo scrambled to haul me behind the cinder block barricade the wall provided.

The blast shattered the glass in every window in the room, it rained down on us from above. My ears rang with the echo of the blast and the world wobbled when I tried to sit up. Paolo sprawled across me, an unmoving lump that I struggled to move. I managed to roll him onto his back. His face bled from half a dozen little cuts. I patted his cheek.

“Paolo?” He didn’t open his eyes, so I belted him across the chops. “Paolo!”

His eyes snapped open, but they wouldn’t focus on anything, so I grabbed his face and gave it a shake. “Paolo, wake up.” His eyes fluttered for a moment, then closed. I held his face between my hands. “Come on, Paolo.” Before I knew what I was doing, I pressed my lips against his, a kiss I’d denied myself for five years, a forbidden kiss from a lifetime ago, a kiss so familiar that I suddenly felt like I’d come home.

I pulled my lips away from his and saw him staring up at me. “Hello to you, too.”

“Are you awake now?”

“I sure hope so, but I’ve had this dream so many times that I’m not sure.”

“Good. Get up, Greene’s getting away.” I stood and helped him to his feet. “I didn’t think he’d drop the grenade.”

He rubbed his temples with his fingertips. “I noticed. Let’s not underestimate him again. Okay, Kissy? I don’t think my skull can take the pounding.”

I picked up his .45 and handed it to him. “Come on!” We raced through the ruined office and out the far door into the second hangar. No sign of Greene. We paused long enough to peek around the corner of the hangar. His Packard had disappeared, but the body of Corporal Wills floated in a pink puddle of bloody water. The good Colonel had taken the time to find my car and shoot out both front tires.

"Turnabout is fair play, right Kissy?" Paolo grinned.

"Now what do we do?"

"You have a spare tire, right?"

"Yeah, that still leaves us one tire short. Can't cops count?"

"Open the trunk, Kissy."

"Greene's getting away!"

"No, he's already gone, which is where we need to be before he comes back with a whole platoon of sharpshooters. Now, open the trunk." I did, and Paolo changed the tire. We briefly considered calling a tow truck, but we decided that we didn't need a record of our being there, so we ended up calling his old friend Stephen Mason, who brought us a tire.

Mason lingered just this side of seventy, his snowy hair being the only indicator of his age. Otherwise, he could have passed for a man of fifty. "No, Belvedere, I don't want to know what's going on. I'm helping a friend, and that's that. I haven't seen any perforated corpses because I can't get involved in murders and such nonsense. I'm retired."

Paolo finished tightening the lug nuts on the tire Mason had brought and spat out a harsh laugh. "Yeah, and you're losing your mind from boredom."

"Not at all. I collect stamps, you see."

Paolo slammed the trunk closed. "Fascinating."

"I'll keep my ears open though. Give me a call tomorrow, and I'll let you know what I've heard, assuming I hear anything."

Paolo shook his hand. "Thanks, old man."

"Watch your back, young pup." I gave him a hug which made him grin like a lecher. "Keep an eye on him, Cassy."

"It's Kissy now." I jerked my head toward Paolo. "He's a passel of trouble, isn't he?"

"Always has been." He climbed into his truck, waving as he drove away.

Paolo offered me an ample dose of his frown. "*I'm* the

passel of trouble?"

"Yeah." I lit my smoke and started the car. "Get in, copper."

He did. "We need to hole up somewhere for a while."

"Let's go back to the Aristocrat. We still have a suite there. The hounds'll be poking their noses into every fleabag motel in the city, but they aren't bright enough to look in the high-class joints."

"Fine." He rubbed his forehead. "I feel like my head's been split open with a chisel."

The rain slackened to a drizzle as I drove. I expected to pass a pack of howling black-and-whites, but I didn't see any at all. Paolo rested his head against the passenger window, his eyes closed, and I couldn't tell if he'd fallen asleep or not. I pulled into a spot on the street and turned off the engine. He didn't move, so I leaned in for a closer look. His breath came and went with clockwork regularity, so I at least knew he hadn't gone to the great police precinct in the sky.

I whispered his name. "Paolo?" He didn't seem to hear me, so I pressed my hand against his face. I moved my fingers through his curly blond locks, which had mostly dried. The glacier that had crusted over my broken heart, shifted, just a little. I'd seen him asleep before, run my fingers through his hair before, but I'd never felt the yawning expanse of regret that clutched at my soul before. He moved his head and I yanked my hand away from him.

"Hey, sleeping beauty. We're here."

He opened his eyes and squinted at me. "Already?"

"Yeah. Let's go, already. I want to get out of these wet clothes."

We crossed the lobby, but nobody saw or cared. The old man with the crooked back took us up the elevator. Paolo leaned against the corner of the elevator. He held his head in his hand. The old man gave him a curious look but didn't say anything.

"Too much gin with dinner." I stared the old coot down until he shrugged and resumed his vacant stare. He rattled open the gate and I helped Paolo stagger down the hall. "Damn, this headache just keeps getting worse."

I unlocked the door to our room and helped him inside.

"Get in the shower and warm up. You'll feel better."

He grunted and headed for the bathroom. I peeled off my soggy clothes and hung them up, hoping they'd have the decency to dry themselves by morning. I wrapped myself in a fluffy white robe and sat on the sofa, burning my way through a pack of Camels.

Paolo came in wearing a robe of his own. I smiled up at him. "Feel better?"

"Yeah." He sat at the desk and pulled the telephone closer to him. "I'm gonna call the precinct."

"Why?"

"To see how much the bounty for our heads is worth."

I mashed out my smoke. "Have fun. I'm taking a shower." Once under the showerhead, I scrubbed the stink of the fire and the grit of the hangar floor off my skin. The scalding water burned away the last twenty-four hours and the room had filled up with steam before I felt anything close to my normal, upbeat, cheerful, self. I brushed my hair and, for a change, left it down. I put my robe back on and went looking for Paolo.

He sat on the sofa with a tall glass of bourbon in his hand. He handed it to me. "Well, I called them."

"How bad is it?" I took a swallow of the whisky and handed the glass back to him.

"Brightman's issued warrants for our arrest. He's strong-armed both the city police and the sheriff's department to bring us in at any cost." He poured the rest of the bourbon into his guts. "Dead or alive."

Chapter Twenty-Nine

The sky rained itself out, but the stubborn clouds lingered over the city, choking out the sunlight and stifling the breeze. The air felt muggy, the heat and humidity conspiring to create the unique misery that is Ohio weather. I flung myself on the sofa and had just started tiptoeing around a nap when a knock at the door roused me.

I picked up my .22 and stepped toward the door. "Who is it?"

"Laundry."

I dropped the gun into my trousers pocket and opened the door. I'd almost forgotten that I sent two of my suits and one of Paolo's out to be cleaned and pressed. I tipped the girl a quarter and carried the clothes into the bedroom to hang them up. On impulse I went through every pocket, desperately hoping to find a cigarette. No dice.

I sat down at the desk and stared at the last two cigarettes in my possession. I needed a smoke in a bad way, but until Paolo came back with more provisions, these two had to last. "Willpower, Kissy, willpower."
I waited almost another minute before giving up.

I poked one of the snipes between my teeth and lit it with a match. The tobacco flowed into my lungs and for a few seconds, I had only good things to say about the world. I sat back and relished it while I could.

I heard a key in the lock followed by the door opening and Paolo cursing. He had a carton of cigarettes, two bottles of hooch, and a paper bag of sandwiches from the deli precariously balanced in his arms. He unceremoniously dumped everything on one of the high-backed chairs opposite the sofa. "Have I ever told you how much I hate shopping for other people?”

“Yeah, you griped about it for an hour before I threw your carcass out the door.”

“I did not.” He flopped himself into an armchair and I could tell by the look on his face he had bad news. “It’s pretty bad out there. They’ve got black-and-whites patrolling all over, and they’ve at least doubled the number of cops on foot. Brightman’s throwing everything he can at us.” He pulled a newspaper out of his jacket pocket and tossed it to me. “Read the front page.”

I opened it up and read the headline out loud. “Spies in the Queen City!” I shot him a glance. “I didn’t know you were a spy.”

“Keep reading.”

“The Cincinnati Police, working in conjunction with the Hamilton County Sheriff’s Department and the FBI, are looking for a pair of mad-dog killers who have rampaged their way through the city, leaving a string of dead bodies behind them. Sheriff Fred Sperber told the *Post* that the FBI has requested the help of both his department and the Cincinnati Police to locate and arrest Detective Paolo Belvedere, a detective in the Police Department and an unknown female accomplice who may go by the name Missy ...” I rolled my eyes. “Missy? When have I ever gone by Missy?” I skimmed through the rest of the article. “So, they’re blaming us for their messes? Martingdale, Wexler, Gottlieb, Braun, Affen, and even Corporal Wills.”

“Looks that way.” He slumped further in his chair, gnawing on a ham sandwich. “I had to avoid a beat cop I know. His name’s Boyd, a good egg, but he’d have tried to arrest me. At least they’re not gonna find you, Missy.”

I tugged at my lip. “Tanner knew my name, so did Brightman. Why would it be wrong in the paper?”

“Probably just some half-deaf reporter misunderstanding Sperber. Kissy isn’t such a common name when you think about it.”

I lit another smoke. “Well, they got our descriptions mostly right. Are you really six foot one?”

“Six foot two.” He rubbed his temples with his fingertips.

“Head still hurt?”

"Like I got smacked with a king-sized sledgehammer."

"Go take a nap. I have to make some telephone calls."

He squinted at me. "What kind of phone calls?"

"The kind where I ask for a number and talk to someone on the other end."

He waved that away and stood up. "We'll need to find a good lawyer. You might as well start looking for one this morning."

"You can give up if you want to, but I'm not. Greene hasn't won yet."

"Kissy, we have literally every cop, deputy and Fed in the city looking for us. Not to mention the United States Army. Brightman's probably already asked the governor to call up the National Guard to help look for us."

I shrugged. "None of that compares to what we have."

"Oh yeah, what do we have?" His puzzlement creased his forehead.

"Guile."

"Oh good! We have guile! I'd forgotten about guile! Long live guile!" He padded into the bedroom and closed the door.

The first call I made was to the front desk to ask if they could spare a bellboy to run some errands for me, which they could. I told them I'd call for him when I'd finished making the arrangements. Then I telephoned Woolworth and described to the manager what I wanted. I added that I'd send someone to pick the items up, so have them ready. I called for the bellboy and gave him a $20 bill and a quarter for the bus. I told him he could keep the change, which I figured to be near $6.00, if he didn't tell anybody. He whistled as he left the suite.

I considered my next move carefully. Greene presented a difficult problem because of his position as an Army Intelligence officer, but more directly because of his influence over Avery Brightman. Brightman was the big shot in the local Bureau office, and he issued the warrants for our arrest, but he also carried Greene's water. Brightman, from what I knew about him, sounded like a spineless bucket of goo, which made him the weak link.

I looked for the Bureau's telephone number in the local directory, but it wasn't there. I dialed the operator.

"Operator, number please."

"I need to speak to the FBI."

Silence for a year or two. "I'm sorry, I need a number."

I sprinkled some backwoods into my talk. "Look here, just between you and me, because I think I can trust ya, I need to speak to them Feds because I think I know where them spies from the paper are a-hidin'."

"Ma'am, I can connect you to the sheriff's department or the city police."

"Naw, I'm not a-wastin' mah time with the likes of them. Them's the ones that locked up my Jim last year for jaywalkin', course he was a little lit up from a bad jug o' shine ..."

"Ma'am, I really think you should talk to the police ..."

"I know you knows the number, jus' poke that pigsticker in the hole and let me talk to 'em. I won't talk to anybody else, you unnerstand?"

I heard her sigh. "One moment, I'll connect you to their switchboard, but I can't guarantee they'll talk to you."

"Thank ya." I head a couple of clicks, then the bell.

"FBI, Cincinnati Office, how may I direct your call?"

"Agent Tanner, please." More clicks, then another tolling bell.

"Tanner."

"Hiya, Tanner. Still watching my flop-house?"

His voice dropped to a whisper. "Kissy, where are you?"

"I'm safe. You don't believe all this hogwash, do you?"

"No, of course not, but Kissy, Brightman is determined to bring you in, dead or alive, which really means dead."

"So I've been told. Was that Brightman's idea, or Greene's?"

"He doesn't live up to his name, but he's not a traitor either. At least I don't think he is."

"I think he's in it with Greene."

Tanner paused a long time. "Why do you say that?"

"He was with Greene at that little airfield north of town last night. I heard him tell Greene that he'd take care of Corporal Wills' body. Said he'd send some ace named Pressman to make Wills' body go away."

Another pause. "That doesn't mean what you think."

"Do you have a guy named Pressman who does that sort of thing?"

"Agent Pressman is a crime scene investigator. He looks for evidence at the scene of murders and the like. Brightman just meant that he'd have Pressman and his team process Wills' body."

"So, you think we can trust Brightman? Is he clean?"

"As clean as any of us are."

"That's not at all reassuring, Tanner."

"If Greene is what you say he is, Brightman is the only man in town who can legally do anything about it. And Kissy, anything you do has to be done legally."

That made me laugh. "That's no fun."

"Sorry, them's the breaks."

"Well, I guess I'm gonna have to go to work on Brightman."

"How?"

"I don't know yet. Is he there right now? In the building?"

Tanner laughed. "No. You know how some men like to drink, other men like to get hopped up? Well, Brightman's vice is baseball. He's got season tickets for the Reds and never misses a home game. He always says he's going to lunch, but everyone knows what he's really up to. He just left for Crosley Field twenty minutes ago."

I shot a glance at my wristwatch. "Is he alone?"

"As far as I know."

"We might have to pay him a visit."

"Be careful, Kissy. If you get caught, I doubt you'll live long enough to stand trial."

"Will do. Give me your number before I go." He did. "Okay, time to get to work." I hung up the receiver. The Cincinnati Police got my next call. I asked to speak to someone in charge and I got connected to a Major Shearwood.

"How can I help you, Miss ..."

"It's 'Missus,' so don't get any ideas. My name's Inez Winterthorp, and I live on Gilbert Avenue."

"Yes, please go on."

"Well I read in the paper that the police are looking for spies. Last night there was a whole passel of cops beating the bushes around that damned Elsinore Tower. Was them spies in the tower?"

"Uh, no ma'am. That was an unconnected search."

"Was it? Cause I saw that man you're looking for, what's his name? Belvedere? Yes, Belvedere. I saw him at the arch last night."

"Yes, as I said, the search at the tower was unconnected ..."

"That's bull, Sonny, and you know it! The paper said that Belvedere fella shot someone in a garage down by the river, is that right?"

"I didn't read the paper, ma'am ..."

"Well, that's what it said! You can trust me on that! What I want to know is how he shot all them people at the river at the same time I saw him at the tower? Can you explain that to me?"

"No, I really can't discuss ongoing investigations."

"The dame he's all dizzy over, I seen her too. She just stood there smoking butt after butt. She had on a man's suit too, which just ain't right."

Major Shearwood didn't say anything for a minute or so. "Now, you're sure you saw them both at Elsinore Tower?"

"Sure I am. Didn't I just say so?"

"Yes, you did."

"I guess someone's been lyin' to you boys." I lowered my voice to a near-whisper. "I bet it was them Feds. They all seem like sinners to me." I suddenly screeched into the phone. "Sinners! All of 'em!"

I heard him curse on his end of the line. "Mrs. Winterthorpe, can you give me your address?"

"Sure I can. 1700 Gilbert Avenue."

"Thank you. I have to go, but I'll be in touch."

"Goodbye." I hung up the phone and chuckled. 1700 Gilbert Avenue was the address for Elsinore Tower. How many times could I send the cops running up there before they caught on? I guessed around fifty, more if the sheriff got in on the action.

I'd burned my way through another cigarette by time the bellboy returned with my packages. I asked him if the tip did him fine, and he just showed me his teeth. I took everything into the bathroom and closed the door. I did an inventory. Dress, check. Shoes, check. Hat, check. Everything else, check.

I stripped to my bones and climbed into my lady-clothes, frowning at the way off-the-rack items fit. The slate-blue dress matched the shoes well enough. The hat only came in white, as did the gloves, but the handbag couldn't have been a better match to the dress. I declared myself pleased. My hair hadn't seen a brush in a dog-year, so when I set to work on it I had a fight on my hands. I finally got it tamed and looked at myself in the mirror. Besides being a lot on the skinny side, I thought I looked passable, if far more feminine than I usually did. I remembered what Norman had said when I'd last worn a dress. You almost look like a woman! I'd never be as pretty as Mary had been, but I thought I could turn a few heads. I put on some red lipstick and opened the bathroom door.

Paolo had my uneaten ham sandwich in one hand and his jaw in the other. "Kissy, you look gorgeous!"

"Close your mouth, Paolo." I set fire to a snipe and gave him a grin. "I had your suit cleaned. Get dressed."

"Where are we going?"

"To a baseball game."

Chapter Thirty

"You should dress like this more often."

I parked the car in the Crosley Field parking area. "You think so?"

Paolo eyed me up and down. "Yeah, I really do."

"Put your eyeballs back in your head. I'm dressed like this to avoid going to the electric chair, not give you a peep show."

He looked at the stadium. "We'll never get in there. It's sure to be watched."

"Here. Put this on your hair." I scrounged through my handbag and handed him a can of pomade and a comb.

One of his eyebrows took flight and he stared at me like I had a weasel poking out of my nose. "This is your big plan? Hair jelly?"

"Yeah. Get on with it, Paolo. We don't have all day."

"So, I slick back my hair, and that's gonna be enough of a disguise to get us past the cops, through the gate, and all the way to Brightman?" He slimed up his hair and ran the comb through it. "I think you've lost it this time, Kissy."

I heaved a huge sigh. "Oh, ye of little faith. Can't you just trust me? This is my game, Paolo. I've been playing it for a long time."

As we waited, I saw exactly what I wanted to see: a pack of three boys lurking around the stadium, perhaps hoping to find a way to sneak inside and watch the game free of charge. Today they got dealt a pat hand. I whistled and motioned to them. They approached the car warily.

"You boys interested in seeing the game?"

The tall one kicked his toe into the dust of the parking

lot. "It's half over now."

"Fine, are you boys interested in seeing half of the game?" I looked at them each, tall one, short one, fat one. "I'm buying if you're interested." They said they were interested.

"You'll have to help me out though."

"How?" The fat one had bad breath.

"Well, you see, my husband here sent our three boys off to military school in Switzerland, and I miss them so very much. So, I'll pay for your tickets if you call me mom and this bum dad when we're at the gate. Make it loud, have an argument if you can. That's what our boys always do."

"Lady, you're crazy!" The short one.

"Yeah, but if it gets you boys a ticket who cares, right?" They all nodded.

"I slipped on my sunglasses. "Okay, let's go. Paolo, put on your sunglasses." The five of us walked toward the ticket gate. A pair of uniformed beat cops stood by the gate looking bored. The boys didn't disappoint me.

"Mommy, can I have Cracker Jack when we get inside?"

"You don't need any candy, Russell! You're too fat already!"

"Mommy! Sean called me fat!"

"You are fat, Russell."

"Mommy! Now Stephen called me fat too! Tell him I'm not fat! Dad! Stop them from calling me fat!"

I patiently ignored all of them, just like any mother would. I paid for our tickets and herded my bickering brood through the gate. We walked right past the cops without them even twitching a whisker. I rewarded each of my ersatz sons with a whole dollar and sent them on their way to the candy counter (which I'm sure their real mothers appreciated). When I turned to Paolo, I found him shaking his head.

"How did that work? Those cops didn't even look at us."

I smiled behind my cigarette. "We weren't who they were looking for."

"But we were."

"No, we weren't. What are they looking for?"

"You mean *who*, not what. They're looking for us."

"Don't tell me what I mean. What are they looking for?"

"I don't understand." His brow trenched behind his dark glasses.

"They're looking for a man with curly blond hair, and a woman wearing a man's suit. I'm wearing a dress, and you have straight brown hair."

"I do?" His hand crept to his skull. "No, I don't!"

I chucked. "The pomade's still wet, which makes your hair look almost brown, and it took out the curls. So, yeah, right now you have straight brown hair."

"Okay, what about the kids?"

"The folks the cops are after don't have any. So, as soon as we show up with a trio of snot-nosed sons, we no longer fit the description of what they're looking for, so they stop looking at us."

"Why?"

"Because it's impolite to stare. Didn't your mother teach you anything?"

He raised his hands in surrender. "Okay, you win. Now what?"

"Now we find Brightman, of course."

"Right."

"That could take a while, though. This place holds over twenty-nine thousand people." I glanced around. "Where do we even start?"

"Well, I like to sit right behind home plate when I come to watch a baseball game."

"Right behind home plate?"

"Yeah, that's where you get the best view. So, if Brightman is as serious about baseball as Tanner says he is, that's where we'll find him."

We ambled our way through the stadium until we stood at the top of the aisle-way leading to home plate. Sure enough, Brightman occupied a cozy spot with an empty seat on either side of him. Paolo's mouth turned down. "He must have season tickets for three or four seats. Look at all that prime baseball real-estate going to waste!"

It was the top of the fifth, and the Giants already had three runs up on the Reds. Johnny Vander Meer struggled mightily on the mound, but he'd left his arm at home, so his day didn't look likely to improve. Even the home plate umpire, Beans Reardon, looked dissatisfied with the mediocre quality of Vander Meer's torpedoes. When you disappoint the ump, you're not gonna have a good day. Avery Brightman sat on the edge of his seat, shoving handfuls of popcorn into his mouth and lobbing verbal grenades at the visiting team. Paolo sat in the empty seat on one side of him, and I sat on the other side.

Brightman didn't even look at us before he shot off his machine-gun mouth. "These are my seats, bought and paid for. So scram, both of ya!" He crammed more popcorn into his maw. "You call that a ball? Can we get an ump that wasn't born without eyeballs! Christ's sake!"

Paolo leaned toward him. "Hello, Mr. Brightman."

He finally deigned to look at Paolo.

"Belvedere? You're under arrest!"

Paolo smiled. "That's not such a good idea, Brightman."

"Why not?"

"Because the beautiful young lady sitting to your right might lose her temper, and trust me, you don't want that to happen."

I poked the barrel of the .38 into his side, deftly concealed by my new handbag. "We need to talk, Avery. Do you mind if I call you Avery?"

"Uh ..."

"I prefer talking in a more secluded spot. How does that sound?"

Brightman threw his popcorn onto the ground and sat back in his chair. "You'll just shoot me if I agree to go with you. So why should I cooperate?"

I gave him my best smile. "Why, Avery, I'm starting to think you don't trust us!"

"I won't be led to the slaughter like some meek sheep. If you want to kill me, you'll have to do it right here." He focused his eyes on the pitcher's mound.

I gestured all around us. "If we were really the murderous monsters you told everybody we were, we'd plug you where you sit, and take out as many of these other people as we could, aiming especially for the women and children."

His eyes bugged out until they almost pressed against his

glasses. "You wouldn't."

Paolo chuckled. "Of course not, because everything you've been told about us is a dirty lie told to you by a liar and murderer."

"Greene?"

I pulled the snub of the .38 out of his guts. "Now you're making sense. So, can we talk someplace a little emptier?"

He nodded and together the three of us climbed the stairs and left the grandstand. We wandered outside until we found a lonesome bench on the sidewalk and sat down, like three ducks in a row.

Brightman ran his fingers through his thin hair. "Now, what did you mean by Greene being a murderer?"

"He killed Braun."

Brightman grinned. "You'll have to do better than that, lady. Braun was in the Bund, and as far as I'm concerned, that makes him the traitor."

I lit a cigarette. "I saw him shoot his own man in the head."

"Corporal Wills? Greene tells it differently; he says you shot Wills."

"I'm not talking about Wills. He shot a different man in the head at the Fritz Brothers' garage rather than take him to the hospital. Braun shot the guy, then Greene finished him off. His own man. Interesting how you could believe I shot Wills at the airport when Greene and Wills got there before we did."

He waved that away. "You say he got there before you did. That's not proof. We pulled a nice .38 slug out of Wills' brainpan. A .38, just like the one you have in that little purse, Lisbon."

Paolo frowned. "Have you compared it to the bullet in the other guy? The one at the garage?"

He shrugged. "That place went up like the Hindenburg. Our guys are still picking through the ashes. If we find a corpse that has a bullet hole in it, we'll check the lead against what we pulled out of Wills. If for no other reason than to prove you two did it."

I mashed out my dead snipe. "Have you checked it against the slug they pulled out of John Martingdale?"

Brightman blinked. "Why would we?"

"Because Greene shot him, too."

"No." Brightman shook his head. "Why would Greene want to kill Martingdale?"

"Because Martingdale had half of the list. You know the list I mean?"

He nodded. "Yeah. He has both halves now."

"No, he doesn't."

"I saw them last night, at the airport! Both halves!"

Paolo shook his head. "Maybe not. Hear her out."

"I was hiding in that garage; I saw the whole show. Braun gave Greene the list and then he burned it. I saw him burn it, Avery."

Brightman's brow furrowed. "You're lying."

"Not this time. He took the list, compared the torn edges with the half he took from Martingdale, then burned both."

"Why would he do that? That's nonsense! The names on that list are invaluable to both the Bureau and Army Intelligence. For him to burn the list would be, would be …"

"Treason?" I plucked another smoke from the pack and lifted a match to it. "I'm telling you the truth, Avery. I saw Greene burn the list."

Brightman stared hard at me so long that I thought about charging him for the privilege. "You can't prove a word of it, either of you."

"What will it take to convince you?"

"If the bullet we took out of Wills matches Martingdale, you'll have my attention."

"But not your trust?" Paolo rubbed his jawline.

"I need more. You've not given me much to work with, Belvedere. There's not even anybody we can interrogate to corroborate your story."

"I think I can remedy that." I huffed out a lungful of tobacco. "Greene called somebody named Commander Holt in Florida. Where was it, Paolo? Do you remember?"

"Naval Air Station, Jacksonville."

I nodded. "Yeah. Can you arrange a chat with this Holt fella?"

"Yes, we can."

"Good. Ask him what's gonna happen at Ponte Vedra Beach on the fifteen or sixteenth of this month, and why he's scheduling training exercises designed to avoid that beach."

That seemed to get his attention. "Ponte Vedra Beach?"

"Yeah." Paolo shot me a glance. You know it?"

Brightman licked his lips. "I've heard the name. Did he happen to mention any other locations while you were eavesdropping?"

I've spent years reading people's faces, and I saw right then that we had him. "He didn't, but Braun mentioned another place when he was talking to Greene."

"Where was it?" He licked his lips again.

"Long Island."

Brightman closed his eyes for a moment, and his mouth quirked up just a little. By the time his eyes opened, his smile became real.

"What is it, Brightman?" Paolo's eyebrows scraped the sky.

"The New York office raided a Bund meeting room a month ago. They found a half-burned list, place names, not people. Both Ponte Vedra Beach and Long Island were on that list, along with about a dozen other sites alone the Eastern Seaboard."

That made almost as much sense to me as a soup sandwich. "So, now you believe us?"

He kept right on smiling. "I'm leaning toward it. By now your Commander Holt has scheduled his training exercise, and if it looks like it'll leave Ponte Vedra Beach unguarded on the days you mentioned, you'll have earned my trust."

Paolo and I looked at each other, sharing a huge grin.

"There is just one other thing I'll need from you."

"What is that?"

He looked right at me. "I'll need that .38 you're packing around. We'll need to compare it against the slug that killed Wills. Just to be sure."

I handed it to him without thinking twice.

Chapter Thirty-One

We spent the rest of the afternoon waiting. Brightman seemed to think that he could verify our story by simply asking Commander Holt's superiors to examine the schedule of their training exercise. Sounds simple, but with Uncle Sam, nothing's ever simple. So, we waited.

Brightman had asked for a phone number where he could reach us, but this girl wasn't born yesterday, so we cooked up a convoluted relay scheme that had the FBI calling Lou's Diner and asking for Amelia Earhart. When that happened, Lou would call the Aristocrat, which was our cue to call Brightman's office. I had to promise Lou a sawbuck for his trouble. Lou's all heart.

The call came in just as the sun started to set. Paolo crossed his fingers as I waited to be connected to Brightman. "Avery? It's me."

"Miss Lisbon, I have good news, for you anyway."

"Do tell."

"Commander Holt spilled his guts about everything. It seems that you and Belvedere were right about Greene."

"And the bullets?"

"Both the one we pulled out of Martingdale and the one that came out of Corporal Wills' brain were a perfect match. Moreover, neither of them came from your .38. You might be interested to know that the bullet that came out of your pal Norman Osterhagen, also matched the other two rounds."

I exhaled a long, pent-up breath. "So, how about cancelling those arrest warrants you swore out on us?"

"Already done. We've also issued a shiny new arrest warrant for Colonel Alfred Greene. You're both off the hook for murder. Now, do us a favor; stay in whatever hole you're hiding in until we have Greene in custody."

"What about Ponte Vedra Beach and Long Island?"

"That's been taken care of too. You don't have to worry about that. We'll nab the saboteurs before the submarine's stink has been blown off them. You have the thanks of the FBI, Army Intelligence, and the US government, unofficially, of course. This mess can't ever get out; it never happened. None of it ever happened. Sorry, but I doubt you'll get a medal, Miss Lisbon."

"I don't want a medal, Avery, I'm just happy I'm not taking the hotsquat in the big chair. That's all I really need from good ole' Uncle Sam."

"Consider that done. Look, I've gotta go. Thanks again." He hung up before I could say anything more.

I looked up at Paolo. "Everything checked out, we're no longer public enemy numbers one and two. Congratulations to us."

"That's great news!" He flung his arms around me in a bear-hug. He lowered his head, and I knew he meant to kiss me. I stepped out of his embrace.

"No, Paolo."

He held up his hands. "Sorry. I'm just so relieved, that for a second I forgot you hate me."

I patted my pockets in search of my Camels. "I don't hate you Paolo, not really."

"You don't?"

"No. But until you stop protecting Mary's killer, I can't be with you."

"It's not him I'm protecting, Kissy. I'm protecting you. It's always been you."

I found my cigarettes and set one on fire. "I don't need your protection, Paolo. People drop dead in this town a dozen at a time, as the last few days have shown. What's one more stiff amongst so many? I'm a clever girl, I won't get arrested."

He shook his head. "That's not it. I'm not worried about you getting arrested." He came to within a foot of where I stood. "It's what'll happen in here once you've killed that man that worries me." He placed his fingertips on my chest. "The Cassandra I loved wasn't a killer, and even though you say that person is dead, I don't believe it. I think you've just buried her beneath five years' worth of liquor and cigarette ash. Mary is dead. Killing the guy who shot her won't bring her back, and it won't let your soul rest any easier." He took my hands in his, cocooning them in his warmth. "Revenge is a hollow pursuit. It's an empty promise. What do you think you'll feel after you've killed him? Satisfaction?"

"Justice. I'll feel like I found justice."

"No, Kissy, you'll be a murderer. I've arrested murderers and they've told me about the sick feeling they get in the pit of their stomach once they realize what they've done. Some of them call it an agony in their soul, and how it eats away at them a little every day. That's how you'll feel, Kissy, after you've killed a man."

I turned my back on him. "Go away, Paolo. I don't want to see you anymore."

I heard him sigh, then open the door. "Goodbye, Kissy."

"Goodbye." I couldn't watch him leave. Once he had, the room suddenly felt cavernously empty. Maybe it wasn't just the room. I kicked off my shoes and sat smoking cigarettes as the moon rose. The sounds of a city falling asleep drifted through the open window, honking cars, wailing sirens, barking dogs and the full symphony of noise that only a big town can produce.

A soft tapping knocked the sleep out of me. I stabbed a squint through the gloom, but I didn't see anything. Another knock. "Miss Kissy? It's Mikey."

I slipped my feet into my shoes but didn't bother to tie the laces. I yawned until I thought I might swallow my own head, but luckily, I didn't. "Coming, Mikey." I unlocked the door and pulled it open. A balled-up fist about the size of a charging rhino slammed into my guts. My wind hissed out of me in one titanic huff, and it felt like my lungs wouldn't inflate again. I looked up into Colonel Greene's sharklike eyes. He held Mikey by the scruff of his uniform jacket, hurled him to the floor and slammed shut the door shut.

"Lisbon, you filthy whore. You're through gumming the works."

My bellows tried to find enough breeze to work my voice-box, the best I could manage amounted to one choked word.

"Greene ..."

"I've been out looking for you, Lisbon. Imagine my surprise when I saw your boyfriend strolling out the front door of this hotel! I knew wherever he was, your wretched hide wouldn't be far away. The dwarf was very reluctant to bring me to you. Are you bedding him too?" He aimed a kick at me, but my legs caught most of it. "It wouldn't surprise me. You're a dirty traitor, you know that? You don't have a clue what you've done, do you?"

"What ..."

"Roosevelt's gonna shut down my counterespionage unit. He says the Feds can handle that job! The Feds are a bunch of bumbling idiots! We can't leave the security of our country in the hands of a bunch of civilians!" He wiped the contempt off his chin. "Civilians! Civilians! Civilians!" He punctuated each repetition of the word with another attack on my bones with his boot.

He stroked the iron gray stubble on his head. His hand came away wet. "If the saboteurs had managed to blow something up, kill a few red-blooded Americans, well, maybe then that crippled-up old man would understand. He'd be forced to understand! We'd force him to declare martial law until the war was over! The Army would run the show, guarantee obedience from every citizen!"

I finally wrestled some air into my lungs and pulled myself onto my knees. I held my innards together with my left arm. "Sounds a lot like Nazi Germany to me, Colonel."

He grinned. "The Germans pushed the Allies off the edge of Europe. How many Brit corpses are bloating in the North Atlantic? Hitler's won every battle, overcome every obstacle, and why? Because he understands that obedience and security are essential during war. Berlin's thousands of miles away, and it's us, here in America, who are worrying about sabotage! Not the Germans, no, they *understand* the need for national security." His eyes grew distant for a moment, and for a second, I could almost see the swastikas in his eyes.

"You should have been in the Bund. You're more of a Nazi than any Bund member I met."

He drew back his fist and walloped me a good one across

the chops. I fell backward onto the floor and tasted blood. I brought my hand to my face but found a wet mess instead. My hand came away bloody from my lips, nose, or both.

"I am not a Nazi!" He glared at me. "What I am is a fugitive from the government that I've served for three decades." He stuck his bulldog mug at mine. "Because of you. A stupid, interfering bitch!" He shook his head like he couldn't understand how I'd managed to stop darning socks long enough to muck up his grand scheme.

He pulled himself up to his full height, but kept his scorn pouring down over me. He pulled a snub-nose .38 out of his pocket. I'd seen it before, and I knew what he liked to do with it. He held it up, putting it on display for me. "Know what this is, Lisbon?"

"A gun."

"Wrong. This is your death. It's been the death of many men over the years, but you'll be the first woman it's put a hole in. Of course, after I kill you with it, I'll have to retire it. It won't be a weapon fit to kill a man with anymore." He put on a sad face. "Won't be worth using on a sick cat, really. It'd be an insult to the cat. You understand? Killing you with it will disgrace this fine weapon. It'll forever after be unclean, tainted by your filthy blood. Your traitorous, female blood."

Brightman had taken away the .38 I took from Braun's man, and my Colt Ace slumbered in my jacket pocket across the room on the sofa, either fifteen feet away or fifteen-thousand miles away. Once Greene finished his philosophy lecture, he'd use some lead to plow a few holes through me, that much I knew, but there wasn't a way to get to my gun.

He hitched a great sigh. "Are you a religious woman, Lisbon? I'll let you say a prayer if you want. Just make it quick."

"Just pull the damned trigger, Greene. You're putting me to sleep with all the hot air."

He chuckled. "You got guts, for a woman. Too bad they'll be strewn all over the floor in a minute." He jabbed the barrel at my head. "Such a shame. About what this'll do to the gun, I mean."

I swore I wouldn't look away, and I didn't. I stared right up the barrel and waited. I saw his fingers tense and I wondered if I'd hear the blast, or would everything just go dark, like switching off a lamp? I'd figured I'd ask the Grim Reaper when he showed up.

Colonel Greene and I shared a moment of complete surprise. Mikey hadn't moved since he'd hit the floor, except that he had, and we'd just both missed him scavenging the letter-opener from the desk and jab it into the colonel's calf. He pulled it out, with a sadistic twist that excavated a crimson trench through Greene's leg, and jabbed it into his leg again. Greene bellowed like a bull and aimed a kick at Mikey's head. This time when he hit the floor, Mikey really didn't move.

I leapt to my feet, but Greene saw me and swung his gat in my direction. I rushed at him, slamming my head into his abdomen, which felt like I'd just hit a concrete barricade. He lost his balance and fell to the carpet. The .38 skittered across the floor, out of our reach.

I snatched a handful of his collar and pulled myself onto him. I straddled his chest and went at his face like a well-greased piston, ramming my coiled fist into his snoot. I felt my knuckles crackling like twigs, but his nose crumpled and spouted the red stuff like a spigot. He swung a rogue backhand and caught me on the chin. The room convulsed, danced the jitterbug and narrowed into a tiny point of red-hot agony that twirled through my skull and oozed out my ears. He fired another salvo at my face and I buckled, becoming nothing more than a reeling sack of turnips. He shoved me from his legs and struggled to stand.

As he drew his legs under him, I saw the letter-opener still lodged in his calf. I shot my foot out and crunched into it. The blade came out the far side of his leg and he shrieked like a burning banshee. I scrambled away from him, managing to get onto my knees. I saw my jacket, neatly folded on the sofa, neatly concealing my Colt Ace automatic. I lurched forward on my hands and knees until I could snatch the jacket. It fell on the floor with a thump, and I dragged it toward me.

I fumbled through the pockets until I found it. I pulled it out and rolled onto my back. Greene had made it to his feet by using the desk chair as a crutch. I pointed the gun at his clockwork and pulled the trigger. Nothing. I hadn't cocked the slide to rack the first round!

Greene grinned, his teeth pink, which made him look like a shark that had just gnawed through a school of fish. I frantically tried to cock my Colt, but with my bloodied and broken fingers, I couldn't get a good enough grip. He lifted the chair over his head and staggered toward me. I had just enough time to tuck into a fetal ball before he smashed the hardwood into my bones. The pain lit me up, and I gasped from the impact, equal parts misery and outrage. The chair, one of those annoyingly well-crafted things that hotels sometimes had, cracked but didn't break. He lifted it for another assault, but when he did, he left his breadbasket unguarded. I found my feet and launched myself headfirst into him.

He grunted and staggered back, dropping the chair and embracing the meat below his ribcage. Moving with every droplet of speed I could find, I seized the chair and swung it in a swift arc that terminated at the side of his head. He kept to his feet somehow; some demon lent him enough fortitude to remain standing, but the chair had sprouted claws which tore his face open, and he bled. I swung the chair again, but its days as a weapon had passed into memory, so it just disintegrated against his body. He did take another step back though, pressed against the window.

I bent to pick up his .38 from the floor, wiggled my broken finger through the guard and cocked the hammer with my thumb. "It's over, Greene. It's over and you lost." My words sounded thick and muffled because of my swollen lips.

He wiped some blood off his face and spat a thick red gobbet at my feet. "You don't have the guts and we both know it. You're not fooling anyone, Lisbon."

I glanced at the gun I held in my hand. "You shot Norman with this gun, didn't you?"

He didn't answer, but he did offer up another pink grin.

"The way I see it, Colonel, some men dishonor themselves, and when they do, they stop being men and become dogs. Rabid dogs, and where I come from, we put down rabid dogs." I took a step toward him. "You're a dog, Greene, a filthy Nazi dog that somebody needs to put down."

He laughed then. "Then do it! You think you're a tough

guy? You're a woman, not much of one, but that's still all you are. You're pathetic. A little girl trying to play the part of a tough guy, but you did what women always do: stick their noses in the business of their betters. You aren't anything more than a gossiping bitch. If you had any guts at all, you'd pull the trigger, and have it done."

"You know what? You're right." I squeezed the trigger and drove a round past his head, which shattered the glass behind him. He clutched at his chest, an expression of complete surprise on his face. I took another shot and put a hole through the window to his right. He didn't like my apparent willingness to hurl lead at him, so he charged across the ten feet between us and wrapped his meathooks around my hands and the gun. I got my shoulder into him and forced him to take a step back, but I couldn't wrestle the gun out of his hands, nor could I let it go. He had my fingers pinned and the more I fought, the more trapped I got.

He roared an inarticulate syllable and gave my hands a jerk, in one last attempt to tear my fingers off so he could get the gat away from me. Something popped, which I felt more than I heard, and Green let go of me. He clawed at his face, part of which didn't exist anymore. The scorching blast of the .38 had caught him at the jawline and blown apart the opposite cheek. He tried to hold his face together, but ichor ran between his fingers in thick red rivers as he staggered away from me. When the backs of his legs met the windowsill he leaned back, lost his balance, and tumbled out the window. He didn't scream on the way down, but I clearly heard the meaty squelch of his sudden arrival on the sidewalk below.

I dropped the gun and dragged myself over to the phone and asked the operator to connect me to the only voice in the world I wanted to hear. As the bell rang, I lit a cigarette and sucked a painful gust of tobacco into my lungs.

Paolo sounded sleepy when he answered the telephone. "Hello?"

"Paolo?"

"Kissy? Are you all right?"

"Greene's dead. You were wrong, I didn't feel a goddam thing."

Chapter Thirty-Two

Norman rode in his wheelchair like a triumphant Roman emperor. Why shouldn't he? He got gut-shot but pulled through, which I think would legitimately cause anyone to celebrate. He waved to the other patients in their rooms as he rolled down the hallway. "Goodbye, Helen! Goodbye, Bill! Goodbye Lester!"

I marched along behind him, having had my own wheelchair ride only two days earlier, just a floor or two below where he spent the last two weeks. I spent a few days of my own in Christ Hospital, mostly because I didn't have the energy to put up a fight. They stitched, bandaged, splinted, or casted seemingly every inch of my body. A week after Greene's beating, the swelling had gone down, but my skin could pass for some impressionist's painting of midnight. My bruises had migrated from purple, to black, to blue, to a stomach-curdling welter of browns, yellows, greens, and a particularly nauseating shade of ocher. Four of the soldiers on my right hand still walked with crutches, while my left arm and the cast that embraced it slept in a hammock that dangled from my neck. My nose had to be set, which they did with a pair of chopsticks. The less said about that, the better. All told, I looked like I'd gone twenty rounds with Joe Louis, but I never went down for the count.

I fetched my car, while Norman sat in his chair, chatting with the candy-striper who'd been pushing it. I pulled up to the curb and opened the door for him. He made a big production out of getting into the car, and I'd burned through half a cigarette before he managed it. He waved goodbye to the hospital as I pulled away. "So, what do we do now, Kissy?"

"I thought I'd take you home for a while, then I have something to show you."

"What is it?"

"A surprise." I smiled. "One I think you'll like."

"Oh yeah?"

I nodded. "I hope so, anyway." I drove toward downtown. I looked over at him and saw his frown. "What's wrong?"

"I thought you said we were going home. This isn't the way home."

"Sure it is."

"Kissy, it's not. How hard did you say he hit you again?"

I laughed. "He hit me plenty hard, but I know the way home." I pulled into a parking lot of the Majesty Arms apartment block and shut off the engine. "Here we are."

Norman just stared at me. "Have you lost your brains? Why are we here?"

"Because we live here, Norman."

"We do? Since when?"

"Since yesterday." I huffed out smoke. "Unless you'd rather go back to Mama Jose's flophouse ..."

He craned his neck up to see the top of the building. "No, I think this'll do. Can we go in?"

"Sure, pal. Let's go." We found the front door and entered the lobby. The tiled floor looked new and sparkling clean. The automatic elevator spit us out on the fifth floor. I stopped at room 503 and unlocked it with a key on a string. We stepped inside the apartment and I gestured around the room with my splinted fingers. "What do you think?"

His eyes bugged, his mouth hung open and he spun in slow circles. The green satin sofa and two armchairs flanked a low coffee table, and paintings of sailboats hung on the wall. "Kissy! How can we afford to live here?"

I waved that away. "We'll get to that later. Follow me." I led him to the bedroom, which had a double bed, a dresser with a mirror, and a tall cherry wood chest of drawers. I opened the closet and pointed to the three new suits that hung inside of it. "I hope they fit. I had to guess your measurements. We can have them altered if we need to." I pointed to the chest. "Your socks and underthings are in that. The bathroom is over there. Wash the stink of the hospital off of you, and put on one of the suits. The blue one, I think."

"Now?"

"Yes, now." I threw him a smile. "Get moving." I left the room and closed the door behind me. I waited until I heard the water start up before I went down the hall to my own place. I changed into one of my own new suits, no easy feat with splinted fingers and a broken arm, but I managed. I had five new suits of my own, hanging in the closet, plus the one I had just put on. I seated my new hat, a fedora like the one Humphrey Bogart wore in *The Maltese Falcon*, and found Norman, looking sheepish in his new suit. "You shine up like a new penny, Norman."

He grinned. "I do, don't I?"

"Ready for the surprise?"

"This wasn't the surprise?"

I shook my head. "Not at all."

"There's more?" His eyes had the hungry gleam of a child.

"Yeah. Follow me."

He locked the door to his new home and slipped the key into his pocket. "Where are we going?"

"You'll see." I drove into downtown proper and parked outside a particular building, a place of business. "Here we are." He kept looking around, not understanding at all.

"Where are we?"

"You'll see." I led him up a flight of stairs, which neither of us could climb very fast, and down a hall. I stopped in front of a door with a large glass pane in it. Letters on the glass spelled out 'Kissy Lisbon & Associates', and beneath that, 'Private Investigators'.

"Surprise!"

Norman's eyebrows raised. "You're putting me on, right?"

"No." I laughed. "It's no joke."

"This was just a con job, Kissy! It's not real! You're not a real private eye!"

"The city of Cincinnati disagrees. I have the papers to

prove it. I am a private eye, and so are you." I smiled and cuffed him on the shoulder. "Congratulations, Norman!" I opened the door and we stepped into our new offices.

Norman put on a half-frown and followed me inside, then he hurled a groan at the floor. "Oh, no! Not that guy!"

"Good morning, Mr. Osterhagen, Miss Kissy." Mikey Malone, former operator of elevators, grinned at us from behind his Remington typewriter.

"He's our secretary?" Norman shot me an uncertain glance.

"He's our partner."

"Now I know you're kidding, Kissy." Norman flopped into a chair

"I'm not kidding, Norman. Mikey saved my life, and in case you forgot he also saved *your* life."

Norman shook his head. "When did he save my life?"

"He called the ambulance for you after Greene had shot you. Don't you remember?"

"No. I sure don't." He looked Mikey up and down. "Uh, thanks."

"Certainly, Mr. Osterhagen." He smiled and resumed his hunt-and-peck typing. "I placed the newspaper ad like you asked, Miss Kissy."

"Thanks, Mikey. We'll be run ragged with snoop jobs within a week. Won't that be fun, Norman?"

He rubbed his abdomen where he'd been perforated by a .38 slug. "Fun? I got shot, Kissy!"

I jabbed my thumb, the only mobile digit on my right hand, toward him. "Listen to this guy, Mikey. Gets a bit of metal stuck in him, and he never stops complaining about it." I poked a snipe between my teeth and lit it with my new Zippo lighter. "Tell you what, Norman, I'll trade you your one measly bullet hole for my bruises and broken bones. Deal?"

Norman's mouth worked for a few seconds before his voice box caught up with it. "We were just supposed to find a runaway girl."

I nodded. "Yeah, and I found her. Job done."

"And Nazis, Feds, cops, and colonels with guns." He ran his hand through his hair. "I don't understand what happened.

Any of it."

I spouted smoke from my nostrils. "It's really simple, if you want me to explain it to you. Before the war, nobody saw anything wrong with Hitler; in fact, quite a few Americans admired his take-charge approach, including Colonel Greene, Gottlieb, Braun, Hirsch, Wexler and too many others to name. That's how the Bund got started, as a place for Americans of German heritage to get together, shoot the bull, and reminisce about the old country. Harmless as pie until Germany invaded Poland. Then the Bund became something different." I mashed my burned-out smoke in a ceramic ashtray.

"When the Nazis started eating up Europe, Hirsch and Gottlieb had a change of heart, so they contacted the Army and eventually got referred to Greene's intelligence unit. Hirsch, as a big shot in the Bund, had access to all the juicy gossip, including the stuff coming out of Berlin. He'd pass it to Gottlieb, whose nephew Ruger worked in Martingdale's law office. Ruger gave the goods to Martingdale, who handed them off to an Army courier to give to Greene. False information was fed back to the Bund by reversing the process. Everybody along the way got a paycheck from good ol' Uncle Sam.

"After a while though, Hirsch became suspicious that the false information being passed to the Bund from Greene wasn't false at all, and of course it turned out he was right. So, without telling Gottlieb, Hirsch contacted the FBI, and started informing them of the Bund's activities too. Unlike Greene, who had a vested interest in doing nothing to upset the milk cart, the Feds acted on what they learned, which alerted the local Bund that they had a rat in their cheese-wheel.

"One of the last bits of info Hirsch ever got his hands on was a list of eight saboteurs who were being ferried to America aboard two U-boat submarines. Four to land on Long Island, and four to land in Florida. Once their feet were on dry land, they were to meet up right here in good ol' Cincinnati, where the Bund would shelter them and help them blow up munitions factories and the like. Unfortunately for Hirsch, a Nazi spy named Richter filled him full of peepholes before he could get the list to the Feds. After that, Gottlieb wanted out of the spy racket but needed money, so he arranged to sell the list to

Martingdale. He needed Braun's help to get the list, because Richter was the shoot-first sort of fella, but he and Braun were drinking buddies from way back. Braun was able to distract Richter long enough for Gottlieb to find out where the list was stashed. In return, Braun got half the list and half the money from the sale. With me so far, Norman?"

His eyes had a faraway look in them. "Yeah, got it."

"Gottlieb sent Ruger to break into Hirsch's place, just to mess it up, so when the list came up missing Richter would suppose someone had stolen it. Unfortunately, Richter saw Ruger leaving Hirsch's place and followed him back to his house. Ruger had found the thousand-dollar marker that Wexler had issued as cheese to lure in their rat, but dropped it as he fled Hirsch's house. Richter assumed Ruger was his man and meant to plug him. Heloise Kendall walked in on Richter waving his gat around, and she put two rounds in his back. Gottlieb came over and finished the job.

"Enter Eva Weber. That's when I showed up claiming to be Eva Weber, the daughter of a chieftain in the New York Bund, and Gottlieb saw a chance to make even more money by turning up the heat on Greene. That backfired because Greene got so scared he almost soiled his olive drab drawers, and he came to town with a presidential appointment and a powerful need to silence a goodly number of people. He knew about the list from Martingdale, but also knew that if the Feds managed to end the sabotage operation, his own counterintelligence unit would be in jeopardy. There would be no more free money, and no more position of authority for poor Colonel Greene.

"He took the list Martingdale bought, then killed him. He'd previously killed the three couriers who'd worked with Martingdale, and he later shot two others, including one named Corporal Wills. He killed Braun, who'd already killed Gottlieb, and damned if he didn't try to kill me. He tried to fly away without an airplane. They had to sop him off the sidewalk with a sponge. The end."

Norman blinked. "I can't believe I'm asking this, but what happened to the Kendall girl?"

That made me smile. "Ruger got arrested for trying to pick up the bundle of money that I'd taken from Gottlieb, so he's doing fifty years for conspiracy to commit treason or something such. Heloise Kendall is living with her sourpuss old mother, who is quite pleased with how we handled things. Not bad for our first gig, huh?"

The outer door opened, and Paolo Belvedere stepped through it. He smiled his old smile. "Hello, all. Kissy, I'd like a word with you if you don't mind."

"Come into my office." I limped into my private office and sat behind my mahogany desk. "What do you want, Paolo?"

"I heard that the city issued you a P.I. license."

"Yeah, they did. So what?" I lit a cigarette. "What's it to you?"

"Kissy, this is madness! You're gonna get yourself killed. Or, you'll get those two knuckleheads out there killed!"

I plopped my feet up on my desk. "Your faith in me is touching, copper."

"This isn't a game, Kissy."

"Of course it's a game." I laughed. "That's all there is in this world, the game. For years, I cheated just so I could keep playing the game, to keep myself—and Mary—from starving. I got tired of being a grifter, Paolo. So, I gave it up. This is my newest move, and from what I can see of it so far, it's a good one. At least I'm not conning old ladies out of their pennies anymore."

"You could have been something else. Five years ago."

"Your wife? I told you then what the price of my 'I do' was. Nothing's changed my mind so far."

His eyes widened. "You'd still marry me?"

I smiled and stood up. "Thanks for the visit, copper. Come back when you have something to tell me." I showed him to the door. "And not until then."

"Kissy ..."

"Goodbye, Detective Belvedere." I shoved him out the door and shut it in his face. I took a seat next to Norman. "The nerve of that guy."

"What did he want?"

"The usual."

"Kissy, how can we afford the new apartments? This office? I thought Belvedere took Gottlieb's money away from you."

I grinned. "He did. He just didn't take *all* the money. I managed to squirrel away a few bills, in case of a rainy day. Or a rainy year." I watched Norman blink until he started to laugh.

"Kissy, I hope every case isn't like this one!"

"Me too, Norman. I hope they're more interesting."

Thank You

Writing this book took some time as writing any book does, and during the writing I wanted to talk about it. Nonstop. I subjected my friends, family, and coworkers to endless tales of Kissy Lisbon and her adventures in Cincinnati, only a few of which made it into the finished product. I don't know for certain, but I suspect that many writers have this problem, and were it not for the indulgence of our victims, we'd have a lot less to say, and far fewer people to say it to.

Big Shots and Bullet Holes began life as a short story written for the writer's group at Ohio University-Chillicothe, so I'll start there. Big thanks to Debra Nickles, Cortney Vonloh-Shirkey, and Matt Givens for the early feedback and encouragement for what eventually grew into this novel. Writing groups like the one at OUC are invaluable resources for anyone who one day hopes to become a writer, so keep up the good work.

Next are the poor coworkers that had to endure the endless stories about Kissy and the writing of the book. These long-suffering individuals not only listened, they asked questions that made me rethink scenes or even entire chapters. Were it not for their indulgence I might still be stuck on Chapter Two. Kristy Anderson, Ken Knipp, and Zach Campbell probably took the brunt of my chatter, and I thank them all profusely. Thanks for listening, guys.

I'd like to thank my father, Robert, my brother Brandon, my sister-in-law Lori, and my nephew Austin for their unending support over the years, not just for the writing of this book, but for all my literary endeavors. I'd like to offer a special thanks to my late mother, Karen, who never doubted I could do it but always wondered when I'd get around to it. Wish you were here to read it, Mom.

My friends Scott Bolderson, Aaron Booth, Mark Sowers, and Rob Thompson each supported me during the writing of this book, offing encouragement when I needed it, or the occasional nudge (with a word or with a sledgehammer) when things got tough. I know it doesn't sound like much, but just listening to the plot, or offering an opinion on human nature, really helped me pull this rabbit out of my hat. Thanks for everything, I really wouldn't have been able to do any of this if it weren't for you guys. You really are the best friends anyone could ever hope to have.

Finally, I need to thank Caitlin Keaton. She was there at the very beginning, the very first person to read the short story that blossomed into *Big Shots and Bullet Holes*. Throughout the entire writing of the book she was there: reading, encouraging, critiquing, demanding, and most of all, keeping me typing. Thank you Caitlin, for forcing me to overcome my own insecurities, and for never letting me give up on my dream. I owe you more than you'll ever know, and more than I can ever repay. If everyone had a friend like you, more people would achieve their goals. Thanks for being my friend and never giving up on me. You're the best.

About the Author

Brian David Spicer was born and raised in the Appalachian foothills of Ohio. He took to reading early, already knowing how to read by the time he entered kindergarten and developed a lifelong love of books before most kids had ever read one. While reading came naturally to him, the other subjects were a challenge. His education was always a mixed bag of excellence and mediocrity, much to the exasperation of his parents and teachers. Having just finished reading the *Chronicles of Narnia* during the fifth grade, Brian was looking for something new and exciting, but also similar to the Narnia books. What he found changed his world. He read *The Hobbit* three times that year, and has read it at least twenty times since then, and it still ranks as one of his favorite books. It was the book that made him want to be a writer.

Despite deciding to be a writer at age 11, it took many years before he tried to publish anything. Like many writers, he is a harsh critic of his own work, and most of his early writing remained unread by anyone and was eventually destroyed. After high school Brian attended Ohio University, where he obtained an Associate of Applied Business in Computer Science Technology. A few years later, after the urge to publish began to grow again, he returned to Ohio University and finished his Bachelor of Arts in English. During this time, he finally began publishing short stories: first in university publications, then in short story anthologies. He's had short stories in more than a dozen anthologies, including *Cosy Crime* from Flame Tree Press, *Out of Phase and Wicked Deeds: Witches, Warlocks, Demons & Other Evil Doers* from Sirens Call Publications, *Strangely Funny II and III and VI* from Mystery and Horror, LLC, and *Pernicious Invaders* and *From the Corner of Your Eye* from Great Old Ones Publishing. Big Shots and Bullet Holes is his first novel.

Brian, who writes under the pen name B. David Spicer because it sounds more artsy and pretentious, still lives in Ohio, not far from where he grew up. He's not particularly active on social media, but you can find him on Facebook at: http://www.facebook.com/spicerwriter/